NOBLE HOPS

A TROUBLE BREWING NOVEL

LAYLA REYNE

Noble Hops

Cover Design: Temptation Creations

First Edition Editing: Kristi Yanta, Deborah Nemeth

Second Edition Editing: Sandy Bennett, Lori Parks

Second Edition

December 2025

E-Book ISBN: 978-1-962010-54-2

Paperback ISBN: 978-1-962010-55-9

Content Warnings: Explicit sex; explicit language; violence; kidnapping; death of a parent; instances and/or discussion of homophobia.

ABOUT THIS BOOK

Trouble always finds its way home.

Assistant U.S. Attorney Dominic Price is finally on the verge of taking down the gangster who bankrupted his estranged father and now wants to settle the debt with him. Months of careful work are about to pay off, until his father's sudden, suspicious death turns the case explosive and puts everyone he loves in danger.

FBI agent Cameron Byrne has Nic's back, on and off the job. But as buried family secrets come to light, the lines between personal and professional blur, leaving Cam uncertain where he fits in Nic's world

As the danger mounts, Nic knows exactly where he wants Cam—by his side. And when the family he's only just found becomes a target, there's no one he trusts more than Cam to save them and protect the future they've fought so hard to build.

The explosive finale of the Trouble Brewing M/M romantic suspense series delivers heart, heat, and high-stakes action to the very last page.

ONE

Cam had seen Nic in all manner of dress.

And undress.

Suited was his default, the workaholic spending most of his waking hours in Assistant US Attorney mode. The gray one paired with the ice-blue tie that matched his eyes was Cam's favorite. When he switched from lawyer to brewery owner, Nic would trade the suit for worn jeans and a snug black Gravity tee. Cam liked that look a helluva lot too. Even better was when they were at home and Cam could rid him of all his clothes, strip him down, and kiss every inch of his tattooed skin.

Tonight's outfit, though, blew all the rest out of the water and confused the fuck out of Cam. He couldn't decide whether he wanted Nic to never take off his Navy dress blues or if he wanted to rip them off him this very second.

"You've got that look again," Nic murmured at his side.

"What look is that?"

Mischief sparkled in Nic's eyes, joined by the sparkle of

the red, white, and blue lights that dangled over the *USS Wisconsin's* deck. "Like you want to find the nearest empty cabin and fuck."

Cam raised a brow. "Is that an option? Because yes."

Nic threw his head back and laughed.

The sight and sound did Cam no favors in the turned-on department. "You're gonna pay for this back at the hotel room." When they weren't on a battleship in the Elizabeth River surrounded by hundreds of other current and former sailors.

"We barely got out of the hotel room as it was."

"What did you think was going to happen when you put on that uniform?"

"I might have misjudged your reaction." Sliding his arm along the rail behind him, Nic nuzzled his freshly shaven cheek. "And my reaction to you in a tux."

"You saw me in a tux at Aidan and Jamie's wedding. It had fucking tails."

"Oh, I remember," Nic whispered hotly. "And now that I can do more than just kiss you breathless in an elevator, I've got all kinds of ideas."

Biting back a groan, Cam shifted closer. "One, I kissed you breathless. Two, please tell me your ideas involve getting me out of this fucking suit." He hated formal wear and had had to wear entirely too much of it lately.

"Piece. By. Fucking. Piece." Each word was punctuated with a kiss.

Cam poked a finger through a gap in the buttons of Nic's jacket and yanked him closer. "Not fast enough."

"Captain Price."

Nic did groan then, only loud enough for Cam to hear, before he plastered on a fake grin and turned to face the interruption. His grin turned true, however, when his gaze fell on the man of the hour.

"Admiral," he said, drawing out of Cam's arms and giving the older gentleman a back-slapping hug. "You throw a good party."

The admiral returned the hug, then claimed a spot on the rail next to Nic. "Wish you would've let me throw you one when you retired."

"I didn't have a lifetime of service like you."

"Twenty years' worth, Price. Nothing to scoff at."

Nic stood a little taller, and Cam couldn't help but concur. "He's still serving as one of the best federal prosecutors in San Francisco."

"You're not biased or anything," Nic said with a smile.

He shrugged. "You make my life easier, that's for damn sure."

"You work with Nic?" the admiral asked.

Nic placed a hand on his back, ushering him slightly forward. "Admiral Bailey, let me introduce my boyfriend, Cameron Byrne, Assistant Special Agent in Charge of the FBI field office in San Francisco."

The admiral looked impressed, greeting him warmly, and Cam was doubly surprised. One, that they hadn't gotten any shit, including from the admiral, over their relationship. And two, that Nic had so fully embraced their no-more-hiding decision. He suspected the former was a testament to the respect Nic had earned as a SEAL sniper, then JAG attorney. As for the latter, they'd revealed their relationship to friends and family two months ago, officially moved in together, and Nic had filled in a 2 on the RSVP card for tonight's event for Nic's commanding JAG officer's retirement.

It had been everything Cam wanted and more, and so far, without any blowback.

On Veterans Day, Nic deserved to be honored as well. Celebrating the victories, as he'd told Nic they needed to do more of, and Cam had another celebration in mind for here at the party, before the naked celebrating they'd do in private later. He waited until the admiral moved on to other guests, then tangled his fingers with Nic's, tugging him off the rail and into the crowd.

"You need another drink?" Nic asked.

"No, I need something else."

Nic trailed close beside him, snaking his arm around his waist. "There are no stairwells open to below deck. They're all roped off. I already checked."

Good to know he wasn't the only one dealing with a case of want-to-jump-my-boyfriend. He kissed the underside of Nic's jaw, inhaling his spicy aftershave. "Want to hold you close and do something else."

The crowd parted for them at the edge of the dance floor, and Nic slammed on the brakes, shaking his head. "Nuh-uh, no way."

"What *exactly* do you have against dancing?"

"I don't do it." Nic's gaze was locked on the parquet floor, some memory giving his eyes a pained gleam. Cam had thought Nic's aversion to dancing had more to do with his inner control freak, but that look on his face indicated something else. And only encouraged Cam to press. Nic had helped him past some of his biggest fears; Cam wanted to return the favor for the man he loved.

Positioning himself between the dance floor and Nic, Cam slid his hands under the hem of Nic's jacket and flared his fingers over his hips. "That's a lie." He coasted his hands farther back, teasing the top of Nic's firm, round ass. "I've seen you at Gravity, moving to the music when you think no one's watching." Cam swayed, trying and failing to move Nic with him. "Dance with me, baby."

Torture flared in his eyes and tinged his voice. "The last time . . ."

Cam lifted a hand, cradling his cheek. "So it's not that you can't dance? Or that you don't want to?"

Nic nuzzled his palm. "There's nothing I don't want to do with you."

Heart swelling, trying to beat out of his chest, Cam followed it to Nic's lips, capturing them in a soft, gentle brush. "Don't think about the last time," he whispered. "Just think about this time here with me." He moved again, a slight shift of his feet, and Nic swayed with him.

Cam wanted to cheer. He wanted to celebrate like his seventh-grade-self had done after his first middle school dance with no injured toes. Nic's small, relieved sigh made him want to do it all the louder—on the dance floor. He wove their fingers together again and pulled Nic forward.

One shiny wingtip hit the parquet, then Nic froze.

"You can do—" Cam started.

"Call." Nic brandished his phone, the screen lit with an incoming call from Aidan—Cam's FBI partner and their friend and landlord. Cam muttered an Irish curse at the Irishman for interrupting, but if it was about work, the house, or their cat Aidan was pet sitting, they needed to know what was going on. Cam rolled his eyes with a nod, and Nic, smiling, lifted the phone to his ear. "Talley, what's up?"

A moment later, Nic's lean, muscled frame stiffened, his smile vanished, and his hand around Cam's tightened, nearly cutting off his circulation. "When?" Nic clipped, then, after an answer Cam couldn't hear, said, "We're on our way." He meant it too, hauling ass toward the exit, dragging Cam behind him.

Picking up the pace, Cam darted in front of him, needing Nic to slow down and explain what the fuck was going on because his own mind was careening along the road of worst-case scenarios they dealt in far too often. The mix of fury and unguarded pain on his lover's face made him stumble back a step. "What's happened?"

Nic's grip was bone crushing. "My father is dead."

———

Not every story got a happy ending.

Nic had resigned himself to his own unhappy ending decades ago. There wasn't a happily ever after out there for him. But over the past two years, his luck had seemed to turn. There were enough Irishmen in his life to make it so and enough signs that pointed to a proverbial pot of gold. The something special he and Cam were building—living together, working cases side by side, hanging out at the brewery—had lulled him into a false sense of security.

It was too good to be true.

Standing over a sheet-covered body in the county morgue, Nic felt his newfound life, his hope of a happy ending, burning away like the remembered desert heat.

"You ready?" Aidan asked. The FBI Special Agent in Charge stood on the other side of the table next to the coroner.

When Nic didn't reply, a hand settled on his lower back.

"Maybe we should go home," Cam said. "Get some sleep and come back in the morning."

Nic shook his head, licking his lips and forcing moisture into his parched mouth. He hadn't pulled every string in the book to catch a military lift to DC so they could make the last flight out to San Francisco to not get this over with as soon as possible. His father wasn't going to be any less dead five hours from now.

"Go ahead," he said with a nod to the coroner.

Dr. Elizabeth Jong pulled back the sheet and Nic was surprised his wasted-away father didn't vanish into dust alongside the smoldering ashes of his happy ending. The bags under Curtis's eyes were purple, his blond hair turned white was all but gone, a bruise bloomed on one side of his head, and the deep lines around his mouth made the perma-frown he wore in life even more pronounced in death. The personification of the miserable man he'd been.

"Cause of—" Nic started to ask, only to be cut off by Aidan.

"You need to make the identification first."

Nic lifted his chin and cleared his throat, making sure his voice was clear for the recorder hanging above the autopsy table. He'd seen cases go sideways before due to inaudible identifications. He wasn't about to let that happen in this one. "Assistant US Attorney Dominic Curtis Price, only son of Curtis Stanton Price, identifying the body tagged"—he looked to Jong, who rattled off the number from the toe tag, then continued—"as Curtis Stanton Price." It was a cold, clinical identification, which was all Nic could manage at the moment with his mind miles ahead of his emotions.

"Cause of death?" he asked, returning to his previous

question and gesturing at the bruising. "Blunt force trauma?"

Jong shook her head. "Preliminary exam indicates a heart attack as cause of death."

Cam sucked in a sharp breath. They'd almost lost Cam's mother to a heart attack two months ago. She'd pulled through, unlike Curtis.

"He didn't have a heart condition or risk factors," Nic said.

"Would you have known?" Aidan asked.

Fair point. Until recently, he and Curtis had been estranged for almost three decades. "I'll talk to Mary." The former housekeeper would know better than anyone if his father had had any warning signs or recently diagnosed conditions. But no matter what Mary told them, Nic had tried enough cases to know heart attacks could be induced. And Curtis, with his mountains of debt, was a prime target. He didn't think Curtis would poison himself—he was too proud for suicide—but at least one of his lenders, Duncan Vaughn, was under investigation by the FBI for a whole host of crimes, including murder. "Who found him?" Nic asked.

"Harris Kincaid." His father's executive assistant, also Vaughn's nephew-in-law who Nic had flipped months ago. "At the family office."

"Any indications of foul play?"

"None on the preliminary examination," the coroner answered.

"I want a full autopsy including a comprehensive tox screen."

"It'll delay the disposition of the estate," Aidan said.

Nic had looped him in on his father's situation this past

summer, and as a lawyer-trained-agent, Aidan recognized that administering Curtis's will, liquidating his assets, and paying off his lenders as fast as possible was in everyone's best interest. Not that there was going to be enough cash to satisfy all of them. But Nic wasn't about to let months of work building a case against the worst one go to waste. Not when he was this close to nailing Duncan Vaughn and not when he and his team had control over the evidence for a change.

"I can make it look like the disposition is proceeding," Nic said. "Meet with the family lawyer. Get it rolling. Give us time to complete the autopsy."

"Figured you'd say that, so I already filled out the paperwork." Aidan held out an arm toward the adjacent office. "You just have to sign it."

"Let's go do that, then." He turned toward the metal swinging doors, but Cam stopped him, fingers grasping his wrist.

Dark eyes swung from him to the table and back. "Don't you want—"

Whatever Cam was going to say, the answer was "No."

The only thing Nic wanted to do was get out of this cold, antiseptic-smelling room. He had a call to make. A follow-up to the one he'd made two months earlier when he'd learned Vaughn was out of the country "on business." More accurately, out of the country sheltering assets. The slow trickle of funds out of domestic accounts into foreign ones and the movement of goods via international freight were not enough to violate any laws or trigger any red flags if you weren't looking. But Nic was looking and the pattern was unmistakable. He had all the orders ready, handed down by the grand jury—asset seizure, search warrants, the full RICO and financial crimes spectrum—and no Vaughn to serve them on. Sure, he could serve them on Vaughn Investments but many of the charges were against Vaughn as an individual. More than that, Nic wanted to see his face when he did it. He wanted the gangster-fronting-as-investor to know he hadn't been intimidated.

That he would be the one to take him down.

TWO

Cam closed the front door and leaned back against it, watching Nic soldier across their living room. He'd changed out of his dress blues and into a suit before they'd left Dulles but every other part of Nic was still on-mission.

Spine straight, shoulders back, step determined as he rolled their suitcase with one hand and held the phone to his ear with the other, barking orders. After signing the autopsy paperwork, he'd immediately started making calls, not letting Cam get a word in edgewise.

He was the FBI agent, yet it was Nic on the horn, rallying the troops. First to Eddie, his former SEAL team-mate and brewery co-owner, giving him a heads-up to keep his sidearm close and put extra security on Gravity and their employees, though not telling him why. Then to Lauren Hall, their cyber agent team member, and Mel, former Special Agent in Charge and Jill of all trades, as he set up an all-hands meeting for the ass crack of dawn.

Never mind that the ungodly daybreak was only a few hours away.

Never mind that they'd been awake since the last sunrise.

Never mind that Nic's father had died.

Cam got it—his lover's reaction—mostly. When he'd gotten the call that his mother had had a heart attack, Cam had also shifted into high gear, his sole focus getting home to Boston as fast as humanly possible. Nic was doing the same sort of thing now, focusing all his energy on nailing Vaughn, who Nic no doubt suspected for Curtis's death. Cam was right there with him. But when Cam had gotten that call two months ago, Nic had held him close those first few minutes after, when his mind had been a tornado of grief, fear, and regret. Nic hadn't allowed himself that moment yet and Cam was pretty sure he'd get a Beretta in his face if he tried to force it.

He had to proceed with caution. Pushing off the door, Cam grabbed his duffel and caught up with Nic. He coasted a hand over his lower back, letting him know he was there, before nudging the suitcase out from under his hand. Nic's fingers dragged over his, lingering as he continued to talk to Lauren and Mel, and Cam internally cheered at the small breakthrough.

Ducking his chin and hiding his victory smile, Cam pushed the suitcase toward their bedroom, scaring their cat back from wherever he'd slinked out of. He turned on the light in time to see the orange ball of fluff scale the side of the bed, running from the rolling monster.

Cam parked the suitcase in the corner and stepped over to the bed, toeing off his shoes and scratching behind Bird's ears. "Not happy to see us? Did Uncle Aidan spoil you?"

Purring, the gigantic cat spread out the length of Nic's pillow and rolled on its side for more scratches. Cam indulged him another minute before venturing to the bathroom, stripping down to his boxers, and starting the shower. When the water was steaming hot, he turned to find Nic standing in the doorway.

Coat and tie gone, sleeves rolled up, he braced his elbows against the jamb, stretching. "I'm going to change and head into the office."

No, he was not. Cam closed the distance between them. "You're going to shower first."

"Unnecessary." Nic started to move back into the hallway.

Cam shot out a hand and grabbed the front of his shirt, hauling him back in. "When's the last time you showered?"

"You know that as well as I do."

He did. They'd showered together yesterday morning at the hotel in Norfolk, which seemed like a lifetime ago.

"You smell like saltwater and airplane," Cam said, and Nic wrinkled his nose. Cam chuckled. "Exactly." He tugged Nic the rest of the way into the bathroom and shifted him back against the vanity.

"You don't smell so hot yourself, Boston."

"Hence my state of undress," he said, unfastening Nic's shirt buttons.

"Hence?"

He answered Nic's raised brow with a wink. "Your fault, Counselor."

Working free the last button, Cam pushed the dress shirt open, admiring the torso that had become as familiar as his own. Muscled but not overly so, sprinkled with brown and gray hair, and covered in words, numbers, and symbols that told Nic's story, the good and the bad—emblems, sayings and teammates' names from when he was a SEAL, the rainbow frog and trident, the stark kill count. He trailed his hands up, over ridges and ink, eliciting an indrawn breath. Pushing the shirt off Nic's shoulders, Cam exposed in the mirror the part of the story he still didn't know—the giant cypress tree inked on Nic's back with the letters *GS* carved into its trunk. A mystery, a *mess* Nic had called it, and not what Cam needed to be worried about right now.

There were more immediate wounds to heal.

Tearing his eyes from the mirror, he was relieved to find Nic's closed, his head hanging slightly back. Presented the opportunity, Cam licked at the hollow of his throat and felt Nic's words rumble against his tongue.

"Thought you said I stink?"

"You're still the hottest piece of ass I've ever fucked."

Nic righted his head, smirking. "The mouth on you . . ."

That phrase, uttered when the dirty talk turned Nic on, when he wanted more, had become one of Cam's favorites, a challenge he'd never turn down. "Get in the shower and I'll put it to good use."

Nic dropped his trousers, JAG Corps tattoo flexing on his right hip as he stepped into the glassed-in shower big enough for two. "You coming?"

"Gonna get the coffee brewing, then I'm right behind you." More of that caution. Not telling Nic to go to sleep, but if it happened to be decaf Cam brewed . . .

He started the coffeemaker, grabbed Nic's phone off the dining bar, and ducked back into the bedroom, plugging Nic's device up to charge. Bending, he pulled his own out of his pants pocket and texted Mel and Lauren that they'd be in around nine.

Thank God came right back from Lauren.

Take care of him from Mel.

He grabbed the open cable on the dual charger, plugged his in next to Nic's, then headed back to the bathroom and nearly tripped over Bird, who'd made a nest in Nic's clothes.

"Fucking traitor," he mumbled.

Bird licked a paw and burrowed deeper.

Shaking his head, Cam focused on the man in the shower, head bowed under the showerhead. He stepped in behind him, making enough noise not to surprise but not so loud as to startle. "Massage?"

Nic nodded, and Cam, after a couple quick pumps of liquid soap, laid his hands on his back and began to knead the knots away, one vertebra at a time. As he worked his way up, Nic sank onto his forearms.

"See." Cam nipped his ear. "I was right, wasn't I?"

"You have to make me say it, don't you?"

"Damn straight." Cam smiled against the nape of his neck as he glided a slick hand over Nic's hip, veering for his cock.

Nic intercepted him short of his target. "I have to get into the office."

"No, you have to wind down first or you're going to be a holy fucking terror. Your cool, calm cover will be blown." He was teasing and tiptoeing around what Nic really needed—to acknowledge what he'd just been through on more than a technical case level. Cam, however, had to chip away at Nic's outer layer first, at the walls he couldn't help building. Sex worked like a charm for getting him loose in more ways than one.

And there were no guns in here.

He slipped his hand out from under Nic's, proceeding with his mission.

"I told Mel and Lauren we were headed in," Nic protested, in words only.

He didn't stop Cam from inching lower, from cupping his balls, then palming the underside of his cock, gliding an open hand down the length. Cam circled the head, stroked once, then backed off, anticipating Nic's reaction to his next words. "And I told them we'd be in by nine."

Nic whirled around to face him. "You what?"

Expecting it, Cam stepped into his space and claimed his mouth. Let the prosecutor argue that. And if Cam's tongue wasn't convincing enough, he counted on his fist wrapped around both their cocks to win the argument.

"You're not playing fair."

Cam felt the smile against his lips and grinned right back. "Never promised I would."

Diving back into the kiss, he didn't give Nic room to doubt or to think. He flooded his senses, tongue sweeping inside Nic's mouth, fist stroking their cocks, bodies grinding under the hot water. Cam didn't let up until the tension bled from Nic's shoulders, the broad muscles going pliant.

Finally.

Cam gently pushed him back, letting the shower wall hold him up as he trailed kisses over scruff and muscle, filling his own senses to brimming. Nic wove a hand through his wet hair, massaging his scalp, and Cam groaned at the soothing pressure, tightening his grip around them.

He felt more than heard Nic's answering groan. "You were right."

"What was that?"

"Need you." Nic's voice was so rough that Cam drew

back, glancing up to see what was swirling in his icy blues, but before he got a good look, Nic pulled out of his grip and turned. Bracing his hands against the wall, he shoved his ass out in invitation.

Cam couldn't—wouldn't—pass up the offer, knowing it was a surefire way to turn Nic out and lay him bare, which was what Cam was after, what Nic needed. He was getting there, the first set of walls tumbling down, but he needed a final push to make it all the way. And Cam was determined to make getting there enjoyable for both of them.

"I've got you, baby." He palmed each of Nic's firm, round ass cheeks, fingertips teasing his crack. Nic shuddered and shoved his ass out farther. Cam nestled against him, teasing, but only for a second before he dropped to his knees.

Nic's surprised "Wh—" died on another groan as Cam spread his cheeks and set about rimming him into oblivion. Cam liked nothing better than doing this for Nic, rewarding the absolute trust with absolute pleasure. For both of them. He teased around the edges, speared his tongue inside, and added a finger, then two, opening him up more. Cam grew harder with each moan Nic loosed and with each shudder that ripped through that strong, resilient body.

Shudders he wanted to feel around that part of him he'd been stroking with his free hand, his cock straining and eager.

Nic was thinking the same thing. "Up, Boston. Get inside me now."

Standing, Cam slicked up his cock and slid inside. A bigger shudder rippled through Nic, the last of the tension flowing out of him. Cam coasted his hands up his back, tracing the trunk of the cypress tree and its limbs over his shoulders, before continuing the rest of the way down Nic's long arms. Laying his hands over Nic's, Cam tangled their fingers together against the shower wall and thrust inside him, slow and long, taking him gently, until Nic begged for release.

Freeing a hand, Cam wrapped it around Nic's cock, stroking as he ordered, "Come for me."

Nic groaned out a "Yes" as he shot into Cam's hand, his elbows collapsing with his release. Cam held him up, one arm around his chest, the other hand on his bare hip, as he pounded out his release, shouting as he came inside Nic's tight, perfect ass. Feeling his own knees go weak, he leaned them against the wall, resting together, kissing and touching softly as they caught their breath.

"Am I even more right now?" Cam asked between nips of Nic's neck.

"Now you're just pushing it." Nic rotated his head, chasing after a kiss that Cam happily granted. They lazed in each other's arms until the water went lukewarm, forcing them to rinse and get out.

Dried off, towel slung low around his hips, Nic unsurprisingly followed his nose to the coffee. Cam nudged him out from in front of the pot and fixed both their mugs. He handed one to Nic, who hummed contentedly, eyes fluttering closed as he took a big gulp.

Perfectly relaxed.

Finally, the time was right.

"You want to talk about it now?" Cam asked.

Nic rested back against the half bar that separated the kitchen from the dining area, staring down into his coffee. "I don't know what to feel."

"You feel how you feel."

"You know what the dominant one is? Relief." He took another long swallow before setting the cup aside, still avoiding eye contact. "What kind of son does that make me?"

"What kind of father was he?"

Head hung, Nic covered his face with his hands, and Cam set aside his own mug. Crossing the kitchen, he wrapped his hands around Nic's wrists and gently tugged them down. "Talk to me, Dominic."

"How?" Nic's voice was ravaged, as were his eyes when he met Cam's. "You almost lost your mother two months ago, and if you had, relief would have been the furthest thing from your mind."

Cam stepped closer, holding their hands clasped between them. "If you lost me, or Aidan, or Eddie, would you feel relief?"

Gutted was the look, "God, no," the words.

"Right, because we're your family. Curtis wasn't."

Nic sagged as if it was the explanation, the permission he needed, and Cam let go of his hands to pull him into a tight embrace. Nic didn't cry; Curtis wasn't worth the tears. And Cam didn't speak; Curtis wasn't worth the words either. They just held each other, letting the tumult of other emotions run their course.

Nic was the one to pull away first, resting back against the counter and reclaiming his mug. "How am I gonna get through this mess he left behind?"

Cam grabbed his mug from the opposite counter and came back to stand beside Nic. "You do what you need to do. I'll handle the rest."

"Cam—"

He hip-checked him. "Let your family, *let me*, be here for you. You don't have to go through this alone."

Nic swooped in for a kiss. "I love you."

"Because I'm awesome," Cam said with a big smile. Mission accomplished. "We'll get through this. It'll all be over soon and then we can keep building our something without the threat of a nor'easter."

"Earthquakes, Boston. This is California."

He shook his head, then took a giant gulp of coffee. "Don't remind me. The earth shouldn't move without warning."

"Welcome to my world."

THREE

"Boston!" Nic stood by the front door, briefcase hanging off one shoulder. "We gotta go if we're gonna swing by Mary's place and still get to the Federal Building by nine."

Cam had been right. Nic felt better this morning despite the reality of his father's death sinking in. While Vaughn was still his number one priority, the gangster wasn't taking up all his headspace. He could think calmly about the rest of the to-do list, starting with telling Mary, in person, what had happened.

"I need to oil down this fucking skillet," Cam hollered from the kitchen. "And the damn cat is trying to trip me up."

"Try calling him Joe."

Cam cursed a blue streak, and Nic was still laughing when his phone vibrated, *Unknown* lighting up the screen.

The first such call in months. Coincidence? Not likely. "This is Nic Price."

Dead air.

"Hello, who's there?" Nic tried again, not expecting an answer.

Cam rounded the kitchen corner, instantly on alert. Nic turned the phone toward him, flashing the *Unknown* on-screen. Cam took one look, made a keep-the-line-open gesture, then whipped out his own phone, texting rapidly. No doubt getting Mel or Lauren up on a trace.

"You haven't called in a while."

He thought to say something about Jacksonville or to ask if it was Nicolette Sare on the other end of the line. They'd traced last spring's calls to the twenty-seven-year-old woman in North Carolina. They'd also traced the start of the calls to shortly after his father had stopped making deposits into a secret offshore account. He could ask about that instead. But all that assumed this mysterious call was connected to the previous ones, and if it wasn't, he couldn't disclose any of those facts, especially if this call was from Vaughn. As far as they could tell, neither Vaughn nor any of Curtis's other lenders knew about the offshore account or Nicolette, and Nic sure as fuck wasn't going to lead Vaughn to it either.

"I assume you're calling about my father," he said instead. If Curtis's death hadn't hit the news yet, it would soon. He wasn't disclosing any secrets with that statement. "No offer of condolences? A man is dead."

Click.

"Fuck!" Nic hung up and shoved the phone in his pocket. "Enough?" he asked Cam.

Phone to his ear, Cam raised a finger, motioning for him to wait, as he spoke to someone on the other end. "They hung up." He listened a moment longer, then his face fell and Nic had his answer. "Too short for an immediate trace,"

Cam confirmed. "Mel's already made the request for carrier records."

"Timing's not suspicious or anything."

"It could be unconnected," Cam said, approaching. Nic opened his mouth to call bullshit, but Cam beat him to it. "I agree with you, though. It's too on the nose to be coincidence. It's likely connected to your father's death at minimum."

Nic shouldered his bag again. "And maybe to Jacksonville and those deposits if someone, say Nicolette Sare, wants to make sure they get anything left in that account."

"Or it could be something more directly related to Vaughn." Cam reached past him for the doorknob. "Let's see what Mel finds." He fought with the uncooperative knob, finally getting it to turn, and swung the door open to a blast of sound that rocked Nic back a step.

"Attorney Price! Agent Byrne!" one reporter called out.

"Mr. Price, care to comment on your father's death?" asked another. And the shouted questions went on and on . . .

"How's it feel to lose your dad?"

"Will you be leaving the US Attorney's Office to take over the family business?"

"Will you be running the day-to-day operations?"

"What will happen to your father's real estate holdings?"

"How will this affect your relationship with Agent Byrne?"

Cam's hand on his back pushed him forward, out the door and off the front porch. It was the right move—ducking back inside would have looked like hiding—but for once, Nic didn't have the words, other than thinking *No* to every question that was asked and that answer wouldn't satisfy anyone.

Cam found his press feet faster. "We have no comment at this time." They pushed past the reporters, along the walkway to Nic's truck in the driveway. "Attorney Price only learned of his father's death last night. Please respect our privacy until a statement is made available."

Fuck, if only they'd cracked the blinds before opening the door or listened more closely, they would have had some clue as to the ambush, but they'd been distracted with the call.

Nic had assumed word of Curtis's death would get out and be newsworthy—he'd said as much to the caller. Curtis had been a major player in the local business scene, and he'd been an expert at covering up how far out of that scene he'd fallen. But Nic hadn't expected that many reporters or that word would spread that fast. "Who the fuck tipped them off?"

"Someone at the morgue, one of the EMTs from the scene, Harris."

Nic wanted to turn in his seat and look back to see if there was anyone suspicious at the scene, but doing so would be too obvious. Instead, he pulled down the visor and flipped open the mirror, pretending to straighten his tie while he scanned the chaos on their front lawn.

Turned out the clue he was looking for was ahead of, not behind, them. "Or it was them," Cam said with a barely perceptible nod at the chromed-out sedan parked at the corner.

Nic used his side-view mirror to get a better look as they rolled past.

Shiny silk suits and a gleaming Rolex reflected the

morning light. Vaughn's goon squad. Not the usual two henchmen who were always with him, but Silicon Valley muscle was unmistakable all the same. "You set the alarm?"

"Yeah. You think that's enough?"

"Should be. I don't know why they'd go in." Just in case, Nic opened the home monitoring app on his phone and kept his eyes glued to it until they hit the freeway. All clear, he closed the app and put a hand on Cam's thigh. "Thank you for getting us through that. If it'd just been me, I would have barked *No* at everyone."

"That's not your usual sort of press appearance."

Nic had to do them occasionally as Assistant US Attorney, but for those planned appearances he made it his business to have answers to all the questions that could possibly be lobbed at him. That was his job as a lawyer. This morning had been a surprise. For them both.

"Yours either," he said to Cam.

"Maybe not me, but I've been out to clubs and events with Jamie enough to know how to counter a press ambush." Cam's best friend, and Aidan's husband, was a former basketball star and now coach. "I learned the value of *no comment* real quick."

Nic was reminded of something else Cam had said during their mad dash to the truck. "You said *our* privacy."

Cam shot him a sweet smile and dropped a hand over his, weaving their fingers together. "Yeah, baby, because this is *our* life. I meant what I said last night. You're not going through this alone."

Nic was leaning across the console to kiss his lover's cheek when the phone in his hand vibrated, lighting up with Mary's picture. "Fuck!" He should have called her right away, before she had a chance to see the news. "Mary, I'm so sorry. I was on my way to tell—"

"Are you okay, Dominic?" Warmth filled her voice and flowed directly to Nic's chest, her concern for him palpable. She'd come to live with them when he was six, shortly after his mother's death, and she'd become a second mother to him. She'd stayed until almost the bitter end, trying to preserve something for him that wasn't worth saving, definitely not at the expense of her safety. Mel had hired her away on a part-time basis until she was ready to fully retire. "Dominic," she called again.

He swallowed around the lump in his throat. "I'm okay."

"What can I do to help?"

"Take care of you."

"If I want to take care of you too, I will. Now, what do you want for supper?" Stubborn Italian woman, always trying to feed him.

"You don't have to—"

"I'm cooking at Melissa and Daniel's tonight. You and Cameron will join us."

On second thought, that was a better idea than him leading the press to her doorstep if any were following. Or worse, Vaughn's goons. "Sounds good. But you call me before then if you notice anyone or anything off."

"I think I'll go grab groceries now, then hole up with a book until it's time for dinner."

"I think that's a good idea." They exchanged dinner details and were about to hang up when Cam whispered, "Heart condition," reminding Nic of the other reason they'd been headed to Mary's place. "Mary, wait," Nic said, catching her before she hung up. "Did my father have any concerns lately about his health, his heart in particular?"

"None that I knew of."

"Okay, thanks. We'll see you tonight."

"She okay?" Cam asked once Nic ended the call.

He nodded. "Go on to the office. We'll meet her tonight at Mel and Danny's for dinner."

Cam moved into the far-left lane, gunned the engine, and shot past the slower-moving traffic. "Safer for her too."

"I hope so."

"She's going to be fine." Cam grasped his knee. "And so are you."

Nic wasn't so sure. If Vaughn was behind this morning's surprise press attack, if he was behind his father's death, then who or what would the gangster use next to pressure Nic into giving him what was left of his father's estate? Or more? Nic needed to make his move—now—before Vaughn made a deadlier one.

———

The elevator dinged for the thirteenth floor of the Federal Building, the FBI's offices, and Nic exited after Cam, close and in step but not otherwise flaunting their relationship. Their personal one was no secret; they'd agreed no hiding. They arrived and left together each day and ate lunch together when their schedules permitted. But on the clock, they were professional. They didn't want any whiff of impropriety on the cases they worked. Their jobs and the people they protected daily depended on it.

Aside from a few respectful nods, no one bothered them on their way across the bullpen to the war room they'd set up in the conference room between Aidan's and Cam's offices. Climbing two flights of stairs multiple times a day was a small price to pay for keeping this case confined to a small, trusted circle. Which did not include Nic's boss, US Attorney Bowers, who they suspected was on Vaughn's payroll. While Bowers knew they were investigating Vaughn and had been trying to stick his nose in and block them for months, he hadn't had access to the files or their case strategy, locked behind three doors in the Bureau's domain. Seeing as Bowers did everything he could to avoid Aidan, it was the safest place in the building.

They stepped inside and Lauren's head popped up from where it had been pillowed in her arms. She gamely pretended not to have been dead to the world a second ago. "I pulled all the records you asked for. After you texted, I couldn't get back to sleep so I came in and got started." She tried and failed to pull her recently chopped hair into a ponytail, frowning. "I was planning to run downstairs and get coffee, but now you're early and I'm going to have to drink sludge."

"No, you're not," came a lightly accented voice behind them. Aidan breezed through the door, coffee tray in one hand, a venti iced monstrosity in the other.

"My Lucky Charm."

Aidan cut her a mock glare, yanking back the cup. "Do you want your coffee or not?"

Nic couldn't help but laugh, some of the tension of the past hour fading.

It faded further when Mel sashayed in on her high heels, a *Visitor* badge swinging on a lanyard around her neck. "There better not be tea in any of these cups," she playfully sniped at her brother-in-law as she tugged a cup loose. She crossed behind Nic, giving his shoulder a squeeze.

The last of the tension he'd carried in his shoulders vanished.

No one had made a big deal of the past twenty-four hours. No one acted like they should be at a wake. No one offered fake condolences or sympathy. Because these people —his family—knew him. They knew he would want to get down to work and not get mired in the guilt or lack thereof that Cam had helped him wash away last night. This morning was another day at the office, another case, and they were the best at what they did. They were here for him in the way Nic needed them most.

Nic circled the table and claimed the chair next to Lauren. "All right," he said once everyone else was seated. "I'm ready to move on Vaughn as soon as he steps back on US soil."

Lauren started to say something, but Aidan cut her off with a raised hand. "Are you sure you want to move on Vaughn before you have the autopsy results?"

"Vaughn's made his move," Nic said.

"*If* Vaughn had anything to do with Curtis's death."

"Mary said there's been no recent or past history of heart trouble."

"Your father was under a lot of stress," Mel said.

"It's possible. But so is foul play." Nic swiveled slightly, angling toward Cam at his side. "What do you think?"

"Vaughn's goons were at the house this morning. Ten to one, he tipped off the press. Meaning someone tipped him off or he already knew. This was Vaughn, one way or the other. I say make your move."

The same reasons that had led Nic to his conclusion. He

glanced across the table at Mel and Aidan. They both nodded.

"Given the deposits in federal employee and witness bank accounts that we've linked to Vaughn, his movement of assets, and the statements we've collected, I have the orders from the grand jury." Over the past months, they'd been building their case against Duncan Vaughn—bribery, leverage, tampering, not to mention suspicion of arson and attempted murder—including a wealth of information from his nephew-in-law, who Vaughn had installed as Curtis's assistant. They'd extracted all the information they could from the outside. Had enough probable cause to convince the grand jury to issue subpoenas and search warrants so Nic could get to the rest of the information he needed from the inside. He displayed his warrants on-screen. "They're ready to be served."

Cam shifted forward in his seat. "Get me the signed originals. I'll go out to HQ this afternoon."

"No," Nic said, whipping his gaze back to him. "I want to be the one to do this, and I want Vaughn there for it. No serving it on his secretary or general counsel. I want *him*."

"Nic," Cam warned.

"He's the one making this personal so I'm going to personally deliver those documents."

Cam raised his hands palms out, backing down.

Nic turned to Lauren. "Where is he?"

She and Mel had been tracking his movements these past months while Nic, with the help of the Deputy AG, had been making contacts in various consulate offices, preparing for extradition if necessary.

"On a plane back to SFO."

"What?" Nic squawked.

Cam chuckled behind him. "Way to hide the ball, Hall."

It was one of her most amusing and most infuriating habits, heavy emphasis on the latter right then.

"Nuh-uh," she said, swiping at her brown bangs. "I was going to tell you when he"—she pointed at Aidan—"interrupted me, so this one is not on me."

Cam's knee knocking against his under the table, together with Aidan's *who, me?* face, dissolved his irritation. That and the first heady whiff of the legal kill that tickled his nose—Vaughn was finally on his way back.

"ETA?" he asked.

"Flight plan shows him landing at the private terminal at noon."

Barring some forgery with his travel record, Vaughn had been abroad when Curtis died. He could have had people traveling in his place with his documentation—it was a private plane after all—but they had no evidence to support that sort of scheme. That said, even if Vaughn hadn't pulled the proverbial trigger, if Nic and his team could prove he ordered the hit, then they had him.

"We'll set up the welcoming committee," Cam said.

A knock sounded on the door, and once Nic and Lauren had shut their laptops, Aidan called, "Come in."

The door opened to the tall, massive form of Assistant Director Elton Moore. "Price," he said with a simple nod of his bald head. "Caught the news this morning. Figured I might find you all here, and since I was in town this week, that I might help." A San Francisco native who'd swiftly risen through the Bureau ranks, AD Moore was in charge of the FBI's Northern California offices.

Nic wouldn't say no to Moore's help in this instance. He was a good agent and a skilled politician, for better or worse. He would know how to navigate this PR minefield better than anyone. "Thank you for coming, El."

"Go on, please," he said, sitting on the other side of Mel.

Once the computers were open again, Harris's witness statement on-screen caught Nic's attention. "Has anyone spoken to Harris since he found Curtis's body?"

Aidan shook his head. "We took his initial statement at the scene, but he was pretty shaken up."

"Probably 'cause he knows he could be next," Lauren said.

"Speculation, Ms. Hall," Nic chided.

She hid her wince behind a sip of coffee. "Sorry, still learning." This case would be her first time testifying, and while they usually found her constant commentary endearing, the grand jury might not.

"He's supposed to be in later this afternoon," Aidan said. "Or make arrangements for us to meet him elsewhere if he thinks that's safer."

"I'd like to speak with him," Nic said.

Aidan nodded. "I'll text when the meet is finalized."

"You need to serve all the warrants simultaneously," Mel said. "Don't give Vaughn a chance to hide, run, or destroy evidence."

Nic agreed. "We have to time this exactly right."

"If you two are at SFO," Aidan said to him and Cam, "then I'll go to HQ. As soon as you give me the green light, I'll execute it there."

"I'll take the residence," Moore said. "How broad are the warrants?"

"As broad as I could get them."

"Weapons seizure included?"

Nic nodded. "We took illegal weapons off Vaughn's

associates last spring." When they'd foolishly tried to jump Nic in Gravity's parking lot.

"You collect more," Mel said, "call the serial numbers in to me. If there's at least a partial, I can track them. See where else they've been used."

"Keep your eyes open for syringes as well," Nic said, anticipating what the coroner might find upon further examination of Curtis's body.

"Is the charge sheet ready for the grand jury?" Moore asked.

"Yes, though I'd be more than happy to add to it if you bring back any surprises."

Chuckles echoed around the table until Nic leaned forward, serious again. "If you can get me what I need from these raids, I'll bring everything before the grand jury by the end of the week. We can have an arrest warrant issued before the weekend."

Cam knocked his knee again, and when Nic turned to him, he stared back with calm, confident eyes. "We'll get you what you need."

FOUR

A certain redhead was pacing anxiously outside Cam's office when he returned from walking Nic and Mel to the lobby.

"How's Nic, really?" Aidan asked, voice lowered as they stepped into his office. "Last night . . ." By the tone of voice and the concern filling his warm brown eyes, Aidan was only slightly less alarmed than him about Nic. "I haven't seen him locked down like that since before you two got together. He seemed better this morning." Aidan claimed the guest chair. "But I'm still worried."

"We talked. He feels guilty more than anything."

"About his father dying?"

Cam relaxed back in his chair, hands folded over his middle. "No, about being relieved."

Aidan shrugged. "Many people in his position would."

"It'll hit him eventually. He protects, and he'll think he failed to do so, even if his father didn't deserve it and even if he couldn't have stopped this. The only thing that'll make it better is nailing Vaughn."

"We're in motion there."

"And yet I feel like I'm ten steps behind because he kept me in the dark."

"You said it yourself, Nic protects. He was trying to protect you."

Cam raised a hand. "I know that, but I'm only just getting caught up when I need to be on top of things for the Bureau and for him." Not wanting to paint a target on both their backs, Nic had tried to keep Cam off the investigation and off Vaughn's radar. Cam hadn't given him an option once they'd committed to building something together. And yet . . . "I get the feeling I still don't know everything. Flying by the seat of my pants with this many variables is not good for me, the rules guy. I need to know where every-thing is on the board."

"And everyone," Aidan added. "Including our mole here."

Once brought in, Cam had taken point on finding the Bureau employee who'd fed Vaughn the details of their movements, including on operations. The mole had provided times and locations when Nic would be vulner-able to threats—or hits. It was an open debate between them.

"Tell me who's at the top of your list," Aidan prompted.

"Lorton and Cole."

Aidan lurched forward, eyebrows racing north. "Francis Cole? The agent Lauren's dating?"

Cam shot forward to match. "She's dating him?"

"Jamie and I saw them out at Bourbon and Branch last week."

"That's not good." And not just because it was against

the Bureau's anti-fraternization recommendation, not that he and Aidan enforced said rec.

"Tell me why you think it's Lorton or Cole."

Cam opened his laptop and shifted it so Aidan could view the screen. "This is the list of agents on each op where an attempt was made on Nic." He highlighted Lorton's and Cole's names, then popped open another document. "This is the list of agents in this office who have suspicious banking activities over the past year." He highlighted Lorton's and Cole's names again.

"Suspicious how?"

"They each had errant deposits. Not traceable to Vaughn but not traceable to anyone else either."

"Because as agents, they're smart enough to require cash."

"Likely." Cam tapped the screen. "But where does a fed get a sudden cash deposit of fifteen thousand dollars?"

"Other than family money or stock . . ."

"And we'd have records of those given that amount. Nothing. And the Bureau sure as hell didn't issue fifteen-K bonuses to junior agents."

"No, we did not." Aidan shifted back in his seat. "We'll question them."

"Not Cole."

Aidan prompted him to go on with a raised brow.

"I don't want to tip off Lauren."

The other one lifted to match. "You don't trust her?"

Cam burst out laughing. "I trust Hall with my fucking life. But I don't want to influence her actions around Cole. She could be at risk."

Aidan returned his laugh and Cam hung his head, admitting to himself how silly that sounded. "Okay, right.

She'd kick his ass." She'd been training with Mel for over a year, and even before that had been one of the best shots in the Bureau. By now, Mighty Mouse could probably take them all down. "Let me dig a little more. If he isn't guilty, I don't want to incur her wrath for scaring off a potential boyfriend."

"Now that's closer to the truth. We'll keep an eye out still." Aidan pushed to his feet, but rather than turning toward the door, he shoved his hands in his pockets. "I meant to ask earlier, how are you doing?"

Cam rose and came around the side of the desk. "Jamie told you to ask that, didn't he?"

"No, I'm asking as your friend too."

He blew out a long, slow breath. No one had asked him that over the past twelve hours, and truth be told, he didn't feel like he had the right to answer it even now. This was Nic's family, his life, on the brink, but tied as he was to Nic, more and more each day, it was his life now too.

"I'm worried," he admitted. "Things were going so well for us. We were getting settled. Hell, I even got him to dance a little last night."

"No shit? He wouldn't even dance with my niece at the wedding."

"No shit." His voice sounded as forlorn as his smile felt. "Vaughn was always hanging over our heads, but we were investigating quietly and orderly. Without threats or loss of life. Now Nic's father is dead, it's anything but quiet, and the timeline's been accelerated." He scrubbed both hands over his face before letting them fall to his sides, helpless. "I don't know if we're ready for this."

Aidan moved to stand in front of him. "You love him?"

Cam didn't have to think twice about his answer, and it

made him grin, despite the unsettling conversation. "Yes, more than I thought possible."

Aidan squeezed his arm, returning the smile. "Then you're ready."

Bowers was waiting for Nic when he returned to his office —in his chair behind his desk like he owned the place in addition to his shiny corner office on the other side of the floor. He didn't bother to stand or wipe the scowl off his face when Nic entered.

"Saw the news," he said. "I'm surprised you're here."

Gritting his teeth, Nic shut the door and slid into one of his visitor chairs. *Of course I'm here* was on the tip of his tongue, but then the contradiction of Bowers's statement cut through the red haze of irritation. "If you're so surprised, then why were you waiting for me in my office?"

How had he known when Nic had left Cam's office? Were the two moles communicating? Nic was convinced Bowers was Vaughn's inside man in the US Attorney's Office. The coincidences stacked up such that they couldn't be coincidences—a sniper aiming for Nic on one mission, thrown over the hood of a car on another, then a shootout at his brewery after he'd left the office one night. Bowers knew his twenty in all those cases and he'd consistently tried to stonewall their investigation into Vaughn. When that hadn't worked, he'd wanted to know everything about their actions, their plans, their strategy. No doubt so he could run and tell his puppet master.

But unlike the other government employees Vaughn

paid, Bowers had no financial records tying them together. At least none that they'd found yet.

Smart enough to require cash, which made nailing him harder and finding the leverage Vaughn had over him more difficult.

"What are you doing about your father?" Bowers asked, predictably dodging Nic's question.

"Why does it matter to you?" he bit back. He should be more respectful—Bowers was his boss—but after this morning's hassles, Nic's patience was wearing thin. He owed none of the minuscule remainder to Bowers.

Bowers hesitated, face scrunched, as if debating how best to rip into Nic.

A more obvious threat or a litany of admin complaints? He went with the latter—safer and more annoying—ticking items off with his fingers. "Caseload, scheduling, more PTO."

"What's that supposed to mean?"

"Between San Diego, Boston, and Virginia, you've barely been here this year. Seems you're off all the time."

Nic held up a single digit. "One week."

"One week what?" Bowers sneered.

"That's how much time I've taken off this year." He was also an attorney; he could tick things off with his fingers too. "San Diego, for work. Boston, for work." Bowers opened his mouth, ready to protest, but Nic silenced him before he got a word out. "Yes, a few days at the end of the Boston trip were PTO for my partner's sister's memorial. And a few days to move when I got back, then one day to travel to Virginia for my Navy admiral's retirement, where, as it happened, I spoke to several other federal prosecutors, so really let's not count that as PTO either. And all of that was August or later. I wasn't gone at all the first part of the year."

"Your partner, who works for the FBI." Stymied, Bowers had changed directions. "Don't you think that's a conflict?"

Nic wouldn't be baited. He'd been ready for this line of attack for some time. "Quite the opposite, actually."

Bowers rested his forearms on Nic's desk, staring him down. "Think the Deputy AG will say the same?"

"Considering Jack met me and Cam for lunch in Norfolk and commended our work on cases together, I'm pretty sure he would."

Bowers's face fell and his skin blanched. Nic bit back a smug grin. "The fact remains," Bowers griped, "I need to know when you'll be out of the office to schedule cases. You'll need time off for the funeral and to administer your father's estate."

Now they were getting to the information Bowers was really after. "I schedule my own coverage and run my own calendar," Nic said. "Always have." He didn't trust Bowers to not crater him. Just like he didn't trust Bowers asking questions, in a roundabout way, as to how fast his father's estate would be administered. He did, however, trust that, whatever his answer, it would get back to Vaughn. Nic wanted to test how fast. "As for dealing with my father's estate, it's on hold while we await an autopsy." Let him run with that crumb.

"An autopsy?" Bowers's beady eyes narrowed. "The news report said he died of a heart attack."

"He did."

"Then why—"

"Covering all my bases."

The older man stood, coming around the side of the

desk, glare imperious. "Seems like a waste of taxpayer money to me."

No, Vaughn was just impatient to get paid. And maybe also Bowers, if Nic's compliance was a condition.

"I've worked for the government in one form or another for almost thirty years. Longer than you." Pushing to his feet, Nic circled around the opposite side of the desk, coming to stand behind it. "I think the taxpayers will spot me this one."

"I thought you were estranged from your father. Why do you care how he died?"

"Because I do serve this country. I am a retired military officer and an officer of the court. It's my job, my duty to uphold the law." *Where does your loyalty lie?* His question was unspoken but clearly hung between them. Bowers didn't answer, scrunching up his face instead. His usual pissed-off look.

The standoff lasted another couple of seconds until Nic's desk phone blared into the silence. He glanced down and recognized the number. "I need to take that."

Bowers moved to button his suit coat and missed the hole the first time. Nic fought his smug smile again until Bowers's next words wiped it clean. "Be careful, Price. You don't want to do something that'll cost you that job you love so much. Or someone else's." Challenge—threat —made.

"I know what I'm doing." And accepted.

"We'll see," Bowers muttered on his way out the door.

Fuming, Nic picked up the phone. "Dennis, one second, please." He tossed the receiver on his desk, crossed his office to close the door, then returned to his chair and picked the phone back up. "You were next on my call list. I assume you've heard the news."

"I'm sorry for—"

"Save it. You know better than anyone it's utter horseshit."

Laughter echoed on the other end of the line. In an ironic twist of fate, his father's personal attorney had become a mentor of sorts to him. Dennis Selby had been the first to greet Nic at the local bar association when Nic had landed back in San Francisco at the USAO, and he'd been a wealth of information ever since—local politics, confidential informants, and he could get a reservation at any restaurant in the city.

"I was going to say I'm sorry for the headache."

Nic groaned, closing his eyes and sinking back into his chair.

"I'm afraid that's the sum of it. Curtis named you executor."

As Nic expected. He'd already assumed as much—one last *fuck you* from his father—and he wanted to be the one to administer the estate, to make sure his father's messes were cleaned up, no longer a threat to Nic's family. But hearing Dennis say the words, it felt like a noose tightening around his neck.

"At least there's not much of an estate to manage," Dennis added.

"Curtis was so far underwater he drowned, just say it."

Dennis inhaled sharply. "He didn't really, did he? Because that—"

"Heart attack," Nic clarified, righting his head and opening his eyes. "Though I've ordered an autopsy."

"That'll delay the disposition."

"I'm aware. Pull together what you have on the remaining assets and let's meet on Wednesday. I can check it against my own records. As soon as the autopsy is wrapped, we'll proceed accordingly."

"Look, Nic, there's something—"

"Wednesday, Dennis." He ran a hand over his jaw, realizing he hadn't shaved. "I've got enough on my plate until then."

"Wednesday," Dennis confirmed, then added, "I am sorry that you're having to go through this."

"We've been estranged—"

"I mean the hassle, dealing with the estate of a man who didn't respect you. He missed out. You're one of the best attorneys I've had the privilege of knowing."

"Thank you," Nic said. "It means more from you than it ever would from him."

"We'll get through this, Dominic."

Just getting through today would be a good start.

FIVE

Cam was more than a little disappointed.

The press had wanted a show this morning and now that he and Nic were ready to give them one, Vaughn was arriving at SFO's private terminal. Sure, Cam could have leaked what was about to happen—like someone had leaked the news of Curtis's death—but their friends also frequently used this terminal. Privacy was part of what they and others paid for here. He didn't want to violate that expectation for their sake.

Without a crowd of press, the line of suited federal agents with him and Nic standing in front was unmistakable. Which was probably why Vaughn was taking his sweet-ass time disembarking. Cam had offered to storm the plane with his agents but Nic wanted to wait. That, however, was twenty minutes ago and Nic's shoulders were inching higher. Cam wanted to lay a hand on his arm or back to ease him, but with the agents behind them, he settled for stepping closer and putting their heads together like they were having a tactical discussion.

"He wants to provoke you," Cam whispered low. "You need to bring back the mask. Be the magician."

Nic glanced sideways, taking his eyes off the G5. "The magician?"

"That's what Aidan calls you." Cam chuckled at Nic's eye roll, glad for the break in the tension. "I know it's a mask, but it's still remarkable how you pull it up on command and keep your cool no matter the situation."

"That's not being a magician. That's being a SEAL."

"Then that's who you need to be." Nic had given him this lecture more than once over the past year, and it had saved him time and again. Kept him in the Agent Byrne mindset when Cameron Byrne, brother and son and former thief had been scratching beneath the badge's surface. "You need to be Captain and Assistant US Attorney Dominic Price right now, not Dominic Price, son of Curtis Price."

Nic's shoulders lowered another notch. "Thank you for coming with me."

"No place else I'd rather be." Cam shot him a grin, then stepped back into position as the jet door opened.

Duncan Vaughn appeared at the top of the unfolding stairs. Cam had seen pictures of him—in the press, in their case files, in Mel's surveillance videos—but they didn't do the man justice. Headful of coiffed blond hair, a trim, tight body encased in tailored designer threads, and, as he descended the stairs, a bright white smile, the lines at the corners of which were the only indication of his age.

He sauntered over, whiskey-brown eyes locked on Nic. "Dom, so good to see you." He gave Cam a passing glance, then returned his rapt attention to Nic. "And you've brought backup. I thought you didn't need it."

"Duncan Vaughn, Assistant Special Agent in Charge Cameron Byrne."

He checked out Nic instead, in a way that made Cam's skin crawl. "Have you come to accept my offer, Dom?"

What fucking offer? Cam didn't voice the sentiment, not in front of a suspect, but that feeling of being ten steps behind became twenty.

"I told you then that I was never going to work for you." Nic, to his credit, didn't flinch. The magician back at work. Not that Cam liked his words one bit. Or Vaughn's that followed.

"And I told you that's not exactly what I had in mind." Cam's stomach roiled. Make that thirty fucking steps.

"Well, you can put both out of your mind for now," Nic said.

"Of course." Vaughn reached out, laying a hand on Nic's arm. Cam locked his hands behind his back to keep from shoving Vaughn off. "I'm sorry for your loss," Vaughn went on. "You must be busy dealing with your father's estate."

"That's on hold for the moment."

Vaughn lifted his manicured hand, waving it in the air. "Something about an autopsy."

Cam's personal irritation subsided, professional instincts roaring to the fore. "That information's not been released to the public." Meaning either they had a leak inside the morgue or Bowers had failed Nic's test. Cam bet the latter.

Vaughn, for his part, wasn't the least bit fazed, giving Cam a wink. "Offer's open to you too, Agent Byrne."

Fucker.

Cam winked back at him. "Conflict of interest."

"I imagine so." His gaze slid back to Nic. "All right then, Prosecutor. Let's get this over with." He held out a hand. "You have some papers for me."

Very well informed. Cam was likewise convinced Bowers was on the take. Or on Vaughn's blackmail list at minimum.

Unbuttoning his jacket, Nic withdrew two folded papers from his inside pocket. "Duncan Vaughn, you are officially under investigation by the FBI and US Attorney's Office for suspicion of bank fraud, financial crimes, witness tampering, and various RICO violations."

"Tell me something I didn't know." Typical Vaughn. Brazen about the fact he pulled all the strings but good luck following those strings to the puppet master.

"Along with arson and murder."

Vaughn's eyes widened, just a smidgen, but Cam saw it. So did Nic, a smug smile gracing his handsome face. Apparently, those were not sins Vaughn thought they'd be able to connect. Well, surprise, surprise. He'd picked the wrong family to fuck with.

Nic handed him the first sheet of paper. "In connection with our investigation, search warrants are being executed on your corporate headquarters and personal residence. Agent Byrne will be leading his team through a search of your aircraft." He passed Vaughn the second folded sheet. "Your presence is also requested for an interview at the Bureau this week. If you fail to appear, a grand jury subpoena will be issued. If you ignore the grand jury, an arrest warrant will be issued."

To Vaughn's cold-blooded credit, he didn't react further. No visible increase in his pulse, no tightening of his lips or eyes. Just a disinterested scan of the documents before he tucked them inside his jacket. "That won't be necessary. You've been busy, Dom."

"His name is Nic," Cam ground out, hating it more each time Vaughn used *Dom*, sensing the nickname was part of the story he was missing, and that Nic hated it as much as he did. Rotating, he signaled his agents into action. "Search every inch of this overpriced flying heap of metal."

"Do you need me here for this?" Vaughn's voice dripped with boredom. "It seems I need to speak with my lawyer."

"As long as your flight crew has keys to any locked compartments," Cam said, "then no, we don't need you here."

Vaughn nodded, perfect hair fluttering as the breeze caught it. He smiled, politely at Cam, then leeringly at Nic. "Have a good day, gentlemen."

He swaggered to the idling town car as agents swarmed the plane. Cam waited until they'd all ascended the stairs before he rounded on Nic, every ounce of pent-up frustration pouring out.

"What fucking offer is he talking about?"

"We should go—"

"What haven't you told me?"

Nic ran a hand over his stubbled jaw, clearly reluctant, and Cam did reach out then, grasping his elbow and yanking it down. "Tell me."

"Vaughn came by Gravity one night when you were in Boston."

"He *what*?"

"He made his usual threats, but he also offered me certain access."

"Certain access?" What the ever-loving fuck?

Nic shoved his hands in his pockets, blue gaze averted. "He intimated he would be open to a sexual relationship."

"Jesus fucking Christ." Cam plowed his fingers through his hair, tugging at the ends as he began to pace, feeling like he needed to run a mile to catch up now. "That's not in his file."

"Because he's paid people to keep quiet."

"You know this?"

"Mel has a list."

Cam stormed back in front of his lover, nose to nose. "Which you haven't shared with me. Dammit, Dominic." Fuck, if they weren't out on the tarmac where agents could see them, he'd either shove him in the chest or plant a kiss on him so hard he wouldn't forget to keep him in the loop ever again. He settled for letting his eyes and words convey both. "You can't keep me in the dark on this case anymore, professionally or personally."

Message received, judging by Nic's raised hands and rocking step back. "Full disclosure, here on out."

Cam took a step back as well, reining in his temper. He also needed to be Agent Byrne right now. Not Cameron Byrne, Dominic Price's boyfriend. Problem was, they argued so well as both it was an addiction Cam couldn't turn off in either form. "You didn't take him up on his offer?"

"Of course not."

"Did you consider it?"

"I wouldn't have slept with him."

Because that was so much better. Goddamn SEAL, thinking he could do it all himself. "But you would have flirted to get an inside track."

Nic's blue eyes flashed. "How's that any different from your undercover work?"

"Because I'm a trained agent," Cam said, voice louder again.

"It doesn't matter. Aidan and Mel talked me out of it."

"Thank fuck."

Nic talked right over him. "Then we went to Boston and when we got back, Vaughn was out of the country." He patted his suit jacket pocket where copies of each of the documents they'd served on Vaughn were tucked. "And I decided to go about things the way I knew how to handle them best."

Cam was still simmering, but Nic had made the right decision. For now. He should trust that he'd stay on that path but . . . "Is there anything else you're not telling me?"

"Nothing else."

Cam stepped closer, lowering his voice. Doing his damnedest to retract the anger and project that this was about more than just the case. This was about them too. "If I'm going to have your back at home and at work, you have to tell me everything."

Nic brushed a hand down the inside of his arm, fingers tangling briefly between them. "Understood, Boston. Now, can we go join the inspection of the overpriced flying heap of metal?"

It was a fight to hide his smirk, and judging by Nic's answering one, Cam had failed. "Lead the way, Counselor."

Following Nic across the tarmac, noticing the determined set of his back and shoulders, Cam couldn't help but think about the tattoo underneath the layers of fabric. About the initials he still didn't know the story behind.

Cam suspected he was still missing the most important information of all.

———

Cam had reined in his temper at the airport, but once back at the Bureau, one look across the bullpen to his friend and partner in the conference room and simmering ratcheted back up to boiling. With the conference room crawling with agents processing evidence under Lauren's direction, with Agent Cole snooping around the edges of the activity, and with Aidan standing next to AD Moore, Cam couldn't explode in there either. The mental daggers he was glaring must have been powerful enough, though, causing Aidan to glance up and catch his stare. Cam flashed him two digits and a nod toward the interrogation rooms, and Aidan was out the door seconds later. Rather than speak in the bullpen, Cam headed for Holding Room Two, trusting Aidan would follow.

The door shut and Aidan started to ask, "How'd the service—"

Cam cut him off, the last of his restraint vanishing. "Why didn't you tell me Vaughn propositioned Nic when I was in Boston?"

Aidan crossed his arms and leaned back against the wall. "We talked Nic out of pursuing it."

"Well, Vaughn's not done pursuing him."

"As a means to get to Curtis's money."

Maybe, but the way Vaughn had checked Nic out, Cam didn't think that was all Vaughn wanted with his boyfriend. Even if it was, it didn't make Cam feel any better.

"Do you not trust Nic?" Aidan asked with a raised brow.

"Of course I trust Nic."

"But?"

Cam circled the interrogation table, debating whether to get into this with Aidan, but he had to get into it with someone. Needed to get it out. They were all supposed to have each other's backs. "The SEAL side of him makes him want to do more."

"It also keeps him calm."

"On the outside." He shrugged out of his suit coat, tossed it at the chair, and loosened his tie, trying and failing to open the collar button. "Do you know how many times we've argued about him staying in the surveillance van on ops?"

Aidan chuckled. "Jamie told me about the one in Boston."

"And that wasn't even the worst time."

"Cam—" Aidan started, pushing off the wall.

Cam paced the opposite direction. "I feel like I'm constantly playing catch-up because no one, including you, looped me in on this until I got back from Boston. And apparently, I haven't been looped in all the way."

Aidan grabbed his bundled-up jacket, shook it out, and draped it over the back of a chair. "You told Nic this?"

"Yes, and now I'm telling you again." He stopped right in front of Aidan, needing his partner's—his friend's—reassurance. "Is there anything else I don't know?"

"You know what I know."

Cam hung his head. "Fucking lawyers."

"Hear, hear," Lauren quipped, voice echoing over the speakers.

Cam didn't bother lifting his gaze. "Eavesdropper."

"That's what you pay me for."

He extended his arm toward the observation window, raising his middle finger, as did Aidan, and Lauren's applause rang through the speakers. "A-plus for coordination. Now, can I bring in Agent Lorton?"

Aidan glared at the window. "You're starting to sound like Mel."

"Learned from the best. I'll bring Rick in. Comm units are in the corner console." She made a racket leaving the adjoining room, much noisier than when she'd apparently entered. *Why was she working for the FBI and not the CIA?* Cam wondered daily. And daily thanked whatever had led her to them as the tension in the interrogation room eased.

"Is this settled?" Aidan asked, retrieving the earbuds.

"As long as I'm kept in the loop."

"You have my word." He offered Cam one of the comm devices, then after tucking in his, pulled out chairs for both of them. "Now, how are we going to play this? Lauren briefed you on the money?"

Cam unbuttoned his sleeves, rolling them up to the elbows. He usually didn't get to this point until later in the afternoon but fuck if this hadn't been the longest day in recent memory. "She did. I'm still aiming to eliminate him as a suspect."

Aidan lowered into the chair next to him. "You think it's Cole?"

Cam nodded. "The way he's been hovering . . ."

"All right, then. That's how we'll play it."

Lauren opened the door, handed Cam a file, then ushered in Agent Rick Lorton. She ducked back out and into the observation room where she'd be reading Lorton's biometrics during the interview, the perks of interviewing suspects and witnesses in this room.

Cam was ninety-five percent certain Lorton was neither a suspect nor a witness, but he needed to be one hundred percent. In his late twenties, the junior agent was the epitome of boy next door with his fresh face, thick blond hair, and big green eyes. "Agents, you wanted to see me?" And he had the Midwest accent to go along with his looks.

"Have a seat, Rick," Cam said, starting out friendly.

The agent folded all his corn-fed muscles into the chair across from them. "Is there a reason we're meeting in here and not one of your offices?"

Because of the aforementioned biometrics reading. "Because evidence exploded everywhere," Cam said instead.

"From the search this morning? Duncan Vaughn, if I heard right?"

If he heard? Or if he knew?

"That's right," Aidan said. "But we're actually doing some follow-up on the Kristić case, and we wanted to ask you some questions."

"Oh, sure, whatever I can help answer," the big kid said, relaxing in his chair.

"You asked to be put on that case?"

"I did."

"Why was that?"

"I thought I could be useful, and I wanted to work with Agent Byrne."

First Cam had heard of it, but with everything that'd been going on the past year, he hadn't had a chance to get to know all the agents yet. "Why's that?" he asked.

"I want to do kidnap and rescue," Lorton answered

without hesitation, then averting his gaze, picked at the fuzz on his sweater. "I lost a friend when I was younger. They never found her."

It was a story Cam knew well, but in his case, it had been his sister, whose body they'd found twenty years later. "That why you joined the FBI?"

Lorton nodded. "Certainly wasn't the money, living in this town."

Cam could commiserate. If you weren't born and raised in the Bay Area, the sticker shock never wore off. At least being from Boston, he was used to somewhat higher prices. But a kid from Oklahoma . . . that had to be even worse.

Aidan opened the folder and pulled out a bank record. He pushed it across the table toward Lorton. "Bet this fifteen-thousand-dollar deposit helped."

Cam whistled low. "I'm the ASAC, and I didn't get that big a bonus."

All the big guy's ease disappeared. "I'd rather not talk about that."

"We need to know who the money came from, Rick."

"Why's that?"

Aidan rested his forearms on the table, looming even while seated. "Because when my agents receive mysterious deposits after they've specifically requested on to a case, one where agents' lives were in jeopardy, I want to know why."

"I'd never—"

"He's just doing his duty as SAC." Playing the good cop, Cam tried to project ease in a room where the tension was ratcheting up.

Lorton bounced on the end of his chair, earnest and

nervous. "It's nothing that would put our cases or other agents in jeopardy."

"Then why won't you tell us?" Cam asked.

"It's not strictly allowed."

"Because it's illegal," Aidan said.

Wide green eyes shot to Aidan as Lorton waved his spread hands. "No, no, no, it's legal."

"Rick, you're gonna have to tell us," Cam coaxed.

He sighed, shoulders rolling forward. "I model."

Not surprising. He was a good-looking kid if you liked the corn-fed sort.

Too pretty for Cam, but as a model, yeah, Cam bet he sold some photos. But fifteen-K worth?

Lorton clasped his hands in front of him. "Mostly naked."

So much for wholesome. "Porn?"

Lorton did the jazz hands thing again. "No, stock footage for ads, book covers, and the like."

Aidan closed the file. "Which someone could identify you by. You're trained for undercover work, Lorton. That's why we don't allow it."

"Look . . ." He yanked out his phone, tapped at the screen, then handed it across the table. "I never show my face, and I have no distinguishing marks."

Cam smirked. "Just a sick set of abs."

Lorton shrugged, gaze averted again. "If it pays the bills . . ."

"He's clear," Lauren reported through the comm. "He's telling the truth."

"Dude, my mom read romance novels to me as a kid," Cam said, taking the tension down again. "Nothing to be embarrassed about."

"I'm not," Lorton said. "That extra income—which is a year's worth, by the way, so really, it's not that much—is the only reason I'm getting by out here. But I know it's technically not allowed."

"If all of them are like that"—Aidan nodded at the phone—"if you can't be identified, then it's technically not a violation."

Lorton slumped in relief, letting out a big breath. "If at some point it does become an issue, I'll stop."

"Hopefully it won't. That'll be all, Agent Lorton."

Standing, Lorton retrieved his phone and turned toward the door.

"Hey, Rick," Cam called, stopping him before he opened the door. "Get me a signed one with you on the cover, and I'll send it to my mom."

He nodded, flashing a model-worthy smile. "Sure, man."

"And you're on the next K&R case that comes in the door."

His smile grew wider, into a genuine one. "Thank you." He opened the door, and Lauren met him outside, the two of them strolling across the bullpen together.

Cam popped out his earbud.

Aidan did the same. "Well, that was the last thing I expected."

"But he's eliminated."

"Which leaves Cole. Bring him in for questioning?"

Cam's first instinct was to answer yes. He wanted to nail the traitor's ass as much as Aidan, especially if he'd been manipulating all of them, worming his way on to their cases and flirting with Lauren. But then his learned instincts kicked in. Maybe they could use Cole's efforts to their advantage.

"No," he told Aidan, a plan coming together in his head. "We might be able to use him."

SIX

"Who the hell authorized warrants against Duncan Vaughn?" Bowers slammed Nic's office door shut, rattling the walls.

Nic didn't startle or jump. He was honestly surprised it had taken Bowers this long to charge in. Probably because the US Attorney had had to come all the way from his club, the wrinkled golf polo and waft of cigar smoke giving away where he'd been.

He did find Bowers's word choice—*against*—interesting. Nic set aside his pen and laced his fingers together on his desk blotter. "I don't need authorization to ask the grand jury for warrants on the target of an ongoing investigation." Bowers opened his mouth to protest; Nic talked over him. "But I did get it from them and the Deputy AG."

Bowers's round face flamed red. "You and Jack Hayward are awfully cozy."

"What exactly are you implying?"

Bowers was seriously grasping at straws to even suggest

there was anything more than professional between him and the happily married Deputy AG.

He seemed to realize that too, backpedaling and trying another argument. "I'm your boss," he said, jutting a thumb at his chest.

"And Jack is yours." Nic crossed one leg over the other, hands resting in his lap. "As for Vaughn, you've known about this case for months. You know I've been working it with the FBI and grand jury."

"But I didn't know you were going to serve warrants today."

"Vaughn was back in the country. It was time to move." Nic shrugged one shoulder. "Why does it matter if I told you about a routine service of process?"

"Routine?" Bowers scoffed. Nic admittedly had been pushing it there on purpose, and Bowers predictably took the bait. "This is far from routine. Duncan Vaughn is a high-profile local business figure. This is a high-profile case for us. We can't afford a misstep."

"I don't misstep."

Bowers didn't argue that one. "Maybe I wanted the press there."

That Nic would believe, though he thought it more likely an excuse. A cover-up. He played along anyhow like he would with a witness or suspect on the stand, leading them down Nic's chosen path. "A photo op? That's what you're upset about? That I didn't include you?"

"It's a win for our office."

"Not yet. I haven't officially brought charges."

"Is that your next move?" That was the very direction Nic had anticipated. Had led. Back to Bowers fishing for information.

"Depends on what we find in the evidence collected." It was a hedge and the truth. He couldn't tell Bowers everything, and they were still processing evidence, but it was enough to set Bowers on edge, rocking on his feet, exactly as Nic had intended. He'd be more likely to make a misstep, off balance as he was, and then Nic would catch him too.

Bowers froze, as if he realized his tell. "When's Vaughn coming in for questioning?"

"Tomorrow."

"I want to be there for it."

Of course he did. Which put their biometrics reading in jeopardy if it was too crowded in the room or if Bowers was there to eavesdrop.

"Give me a thirty-minute heads-up." On that directive, Bowers spun on his heel, yanked open the door, and stormed out, charging across the bullpen toward the elevators. Back to his club. So much for actually working.

Shaking his head, Nic picked up his pen, ready to get back to revising orders for another case, but before he put ink to paper, his phone rang. "Nic Price," he answered.

"This is Coroner Jong." She sounded as tired as he felt. He glanced at his watch. She'd just come on shift when Curtis had been brought in. It would be nearing the end of her twelve hours now. "I don't have the tox screen results yet," she said, answering Nic's first question before he even asked. "But I did fully examine the body."

"And?" If she was calling instead of emailing, she must have found something out of the ordinary.

"There were puncture marks we didn't see before."

"Where?"

"Inside his mouth. Soft tissue of his right jaw."

Nic winced. He'd seen that before in cases where the killer was trying to hide a murder behind apparent suicide. It usually took a bit for the bruising to appear and that was assuming the coroner even knew to look for it. It wasn't as easy as spotting bruising on the limbs, torso or . . . "The bruise on the side of his head?" There'd been an angry welt rising there under Curtis's thinning white hair.

"Where they knocked him unconscious. It wasn't what killed him."

Nic tapped his pen on the blotter, a timeline of events coming together in his head. "Whatever they injected him with did when he was unconscious."

"Looks like it. With something that induced a heart attack."

At least there was no pain then, beyond the initial blow. Unless . . . "Did he know? Did he feel his heart give out?"

"I can't say for certain but very likely not."

Nic blew out a held breath, dropping his pen and slouching in his chair. No matter the shit his father had put him through, he hadn't wanted him to suffer in death. He'd seen enough of that in the desert, in war. He didn't wish that on anyone, even Curtis Price. Knowing he'd been taken by surprise, a hit to the head, then likely died while unconscious, was a relief to his mind and soul. A little of the guilt that lingered fell away.

"Call me as soon as you know what he was injected with," Nic said. "And if you find anything else." He made sure Jong had all his numbers, Cam's too, before hanging up and heading for the stairs, needing to update Cam and the team. He had a hand on the stairwell door when his phone vibrated. He glanced at the screen and cursed.

He ducked into the stairwell, bringing the phone to his

ear. "Hey, Eddie, I'm sorry again for the early morning phone call. And that I didn't call back sooner for an update."

"Don't apologize," Eddie clipped, his SEAL voice seeping through before he took it down a notch, closer to his laid-back, flirtatious off-duty self who brewed beer. "Saw the news. Guessing that's what the wake-up call was about?"

Nic rested against the cement wall, closing his eyes and enjoying the chill of the stone, letting it cool the desert heat beneath his skin. He had enough to do already—juggling two jobs—without the complications of the past twelve hours. Monday was supposed to be his catch-up night at Gravity—payroll, paperwork, and the like—of which there would be a ton as he'd been gone all weekend. That stack was only going to get bigger. "Yeah," he said. "And I don't think I'm going to make it into the brewery tonight."

"No shit, buddy. Looks like your life went tits up."

"Thought we were done with that when we left the desert."

"Speak for yourself." Eddie chuckled. "At least a third of my other job is dealing with people's tits-up situations." Search and rescue was one of the primary tasks of the local Coast Guard unit Eddie had transferred into from the SEALs. "Now it's your turn. What do you need me to do?"

Like the rest of his friends, Eddie knew him well. And he knew the SEAL side of him better than anyone. No sympathy or coddling. Just an accurate assessment of the situation and detailing a mission to tackle it. Forever his teammate.

"Keep Gravity running for me."

"I can do that."

"And keep the heightened security up." Nic had been jumped and shot at on brewery grounds, and Vaughn had visited once too, the night he'd made the overture Cam had been stewing about earlier. Vaughn had wanted to make it clear that Nic was vulnerable anywhere, and that he'd use Gravity as leverage if there was no other means of collecting on Curtis's debts. Not a dime of his family's money had gone into the brewery—all of it was funded by Nic and Eddie themselves—but Vaughn didn't care about that.

No matter how tangentially connected to Curtis, it was a valuable asset Vaughn intended to force Nic to liquefy. Or liquefy himself by fire or other means to get the insurance proceeds if Nic didn't cooperate. "Round the clock, Vasquez."

"I got a couple Coast Guard buddies who wouldn't mind helping out for some extra cash."

"Do it," Nic said. It had been a better-than-average year, saleswise. They could afford it, especially to safeguard their future. "You scheduled to be out anytime soon?"

"Team's on routine exercises for the next month unless they need extra hands on an emergency, but it would only be local."

Good. While Nic was happy with their assistant manager hires, he still wanted either himself or Eddie there or at least near. This was their venture, dreamed up on a blistering hot day, hiding in a sandy trench.

"Thanks, Eddie, for everything."

"Anything else, you let me know. And when the dust settles or if you just need a break, get by here and taste your special brew."

Nic pushed off the wall, rubbing a hand over his left

hip. One of the few places left on him to ink that would still be covered by his suit, and he had a good idea of what he wanted there, a version of what would be on the label of the new brew. "How's it looking?"

"Might be our best yet," Eddie said, smile audible in his voice.

"Logo back from the designer yet?"

"Just came in. Let me email it to you. It's sweet as fuck."

Nic switched the phone to speaker, then opened his email, waiting eagerly for the message to load. He opened the attachment and gasped, putting a hand on the wall to steady himself.

The clover. The apricot. The name—Fighting Boston Irish—and emphasized initials—FBI Stout—their double meaning clear.

Finally, something had gone right today. Something he wanted to do desperately for the man he loved. "It's perfect."

———

The FBI conference room was a virtual maze. Agents scurried about, boxes of files and evidence were stacked against the walls, and more plastic bags covered the table, waiting to be tagged. They'd made a decent dent over the past few hours but there was still a mountain's worth of paper, objects, and data to process. Cam straightened from where he'd put a lid on another full box and froze at the sight of Nic standing in the doorway.

"Clear the room, please," Nic ordered gruffly. His shoulders, however, weren't raised to match and one corner of his mouth was hitched up, fighting a smirk.

"Except you four," he added, eyes lighting on him, Aidan, Lauren, and Moore. Eyes that were determined, maybe even a little excited. Cam recognized that look. It was the same sexy-as-hell confidence Nic got just before stepping into a courtroom. Just before shredding a suspect on the stand.

He had something.

Lorton was the last one out the door, first checking with Lauren if she needed anything. Cam noticed a difference in the way she responded to him versus Cole. Less obvious, more genuine, the quirky, overcaffeinated motormouth they were all used to. Cam mentally reaffirmed his decision not to question Cole yet. He didn't want to upset the trap he suspected Lauren was setting.

"You have news," Aidan said, drawing Cam's attention back to Nic.

"Two pieces." Nic closed the door and moved to the head of the table. "Any syringes found in the searches?"

"None at the house," Moore said from the opposite end of the long oval table.

"None at HQ either," Aidan said.

"And none on the plane," Cam added. "The coroner found an injection site?"

"Puncture marks inside Curtis's mouth." Nic yanked his jaw aside, indicating the inside of his right cheek. He let it go and wiped his hand on his shirtsleeve.

"Knock out or poison killed him?" Moore asked.

"The latter. It was a heart attack brought on by whatever he was injected with. Toxicology is still processing."

"Do we need to go back and search the sites again?" Lauren asked. "Now that we know what we're looking for."

Cam shook his head. "Vaughn wasn't the one who did it. He was on a plane."

"We need warrants on his associates," Aidan said.

"Next on my to-do list. We have more complete bank records now?" Nic asked Lauren.

"Vaughn's hard drives are still decrypting." She slid into her chair behind her computer. "But I assume so, as soon as they're up."

"Let's see what lines up with recent payoffs and purchases. Segment anyone with connections to pharmaceuticals. Doctors, nurses, vets, users, dealers, law enforcement."

Her blue eyes widened. "Law enforcement?"

"Access to evidence," Cam surmised, reminded of their case in Boston where a leveraged cop was asked to destroy evidence for a local crime boss. "Once the coroner confirms the drugs, we can narrow the segments further."

"On it." Her glittery purple nails flew across her keyboard.

Cam shifted his focus back to Nic. "You said two pieces of news."

Nic's gaze shot to Moore at the other end of the table. "El, you might want to step out for this."

The AD rolled up his shirtsleeves, the pristine white a sharp contrast against his dark skin. "I'm in the shit now. I want to know all of it."

Cam could commiserate. "We all need to be fully up to speed."

Nic's gaze bounced back to him, a silent apology in his icy blues. Cam tilted his head in thanks, and Nic straightened, addressing the room. "I'm fairly certain Bowers is Vaughn's mole in my office."

"That's a serious accusation, Price." Moore braced both hands on the table edge. "How certain is *fairly*?"

"Ninety-nine percent if I had to put a number on it." He rested his forearms against the back of the nearest chair, thumbs drumming an idle rhythm in the air.

Glancing down, Cam realized he was doing the same and shoved his hands in his pockets.

"I ran a test this morning," Nic said. "Told Bowers about my father's autopsy. Vaughn mentioned it as soon as he stepped off the plane."

"You think he radioed ahead?" Moore asked.

"It could have been someone at the morgue," Aidan suggested.

"Hence the one percent doubt," Nic replied. "But I trust Jong, and just now Bowers was all over me about the raids today."

"Wanting details?" Cam asked, unsurprised.

"Yes, and claiming he wanted to be there for the press op."

"Or to be there as Vaughn's eyes and ears."

"He wanted to interfere. One way or the other." Aidan paced the narrow strip of space between the table and boxes, absently twirling a pen. "I'm tired of this shit. *His* shit."

"Talley," Moore cautioned.

"Oh, come on, El." Aidan chucked his pen at the table, clearly frustrated. "He's been up our asses for years now. You have the complaints to prove it."

Cam tried not to show his surprise, Lauren's gasp loud enough for the both of them. "You filed formal complaints?" she asked.

"Why didn't I know about this?" Nic interjected.

"Because he's your boss." Moore's raised voice brooked no argument. He was the highest-ranking LEO in the room, even if he wasn't always there to flex his considerable muscle, physical and political. "I've been conducting that investigation, and I've got enough for professional misconduct. But if you can give me enough for criminal charges . . ."

Aidan was vibrating with anticipation, a lion ready to roar, while the spark in Nic's eyes grew brighter. Cam was surprised the two didn't high-five right there. They could scent the kill.

"He's insisting he be present at Vaughn's questioning," Nic said.

"Let him," Aidan replied. "Won't affect our strategy."

Nic looked down the table to him. "Anything else from the raids?" Cam gestured at the boxes, then at the mess covering the table. "There's a metric ton of shit here, Boston. Give me the high points."

"Box ten," Lauren said without looking up from her screen.

Cam shifted over to the boxes, uncovering the one with the ten sticker on the end. He lifted the lid and pulled out two evidence bags. He placed the bags on the table in front of Nic, the heavy metal inside making a loud *thunk* as they hit the wood.

"Desert Eagles," Cam said, as Nic picked up one, then the other, running his thumb over the scuffed serial numbers. "Weapon of choice for Vaughn's goons."

"Same as the ones I lifted off them earlier this year." Nic laid each bag back on the table. "Was there enough for Mel to run?"

"She's trying," Lauren answered. "Box five for the mortgages."

"Mortgages?" Nic said, tensing.

This was the part Cam had been dreading. It was good evidence—would help Nic's case—but it would not help his peace of mind.

Box five was on Aidan's side of the table, and he came up with a thick bucket folder, handing it to Nic. "Unrecorded deeds of trust."

"He files them when he needs the extra leverage," Cam added as Nic riffled through the documents.

He got toward the back, forehead creasing, and Cam held his breath. "There are reconveyances in here too, dated last week, and another deed of trust for . . ." His eyes fluttered shut and he dropped the folder on the table.

Cam stepped toward him—no need to keep up appearances for the others here—but Nic held up a hand, keeping him at bay. Two deep breaths and he opened his eyes, looking at Lauren, who'd stopped her manic typing. "Have you confirmed the other lenders have all been paid off?"

"Last payment cleared Friday," she answered quietly.

The whole room went quiet, the implications impossible to ignore, especially to a group of trained investigators.

Nic pulled out the chair closest to him and collapsed. "So, two days after Vaughn pays off all his other lenders, my father signs over everything to him, then dies." His voice dropped into an octave Cam had never heard before. "Is murdered."

Cam sank into the chair beside him, laying a hand on his arm. "We'll get him, Dominic. This helps your case, doesn't it?"

"Yes, but . . ."

"We'll get extra security up everywhere."

Elbows on the table, Nic put his face in his hands, scrubbing up into his hair, tired and frustrated, ten times worse than Cam probably felt. Cam wanted to pull him into his arms, chase the day and awfulness away at least for the span of an embrace, but that would be too much, even for those in the know here.

He wouldn't have gotten a chance anyway, Nic suddenly dropping his arms. "Did Harris know about this? Did he prepare these?"

"That's on my list of questions," Aidan said. "If he shows up."

Nic glanced at his watch. "He missed his appointment, didn't he?"

Aidan nodded. "We sent agents after him."

"Maybe he's passed out drunk somewhere," Lauren offered, then quelled when Nic shot her an icy glare. "Sorry, sorry." She turned back to the computer. "I'll go back to decryption."

"How much longer?" Aidan asked.

"Where's your husband?" she shot back. "I'm working as fast as I can, but it would go faster with another me."

Cam bit back a laugh.

Aidan, not so much, snickered aloud. "He'll be back from Washington tomorrow." Jamie was up there for a game, then a couple days of scouting.

"Vaughn wants it to go faster," Nic spoke up. "The press this morning, the new loans, murdering my father. We need to be moving faster."

Moore pushed aside a stack of bags, exposing a lockbox. "Maybe something in here will help." He pushed it toward the center of the table. "We found it at the residence." He looked to Nic. "This is skirting the warrant. I'm willing to open it, but you need to be onboard too."

"It's a gun case, isn't it?" Nic said. "We have evidence of illegal weapons. There may be more in there." He turned to Aidan. "You want to do the honors?"

Aidan smirked, withdrawing a slim leather pouch from his inside coat pocket. Lockpick tools. Nic could have asked Cam to do it or Cam could have offered—he'd be faster at it than Aidan—but Nic wouldn't put him in that situation again. And Cam wouldn't offer unless it was necessary. They were already toeing enough lines.

As it was, Aidan, a better-than-average lockpick, a skill shared by the Talley brothers, had it open in minutes. "It's not guns." He narrowed his eyes as he turned the box around.

Cam and Nic both stood, leaning over to get a better look inside.

At pictures.

Polaroids, snapshots, negatives. All of the same woman.

She was beautiful and not in Duncan Vaughn's typical arm-candy model sort of way. Strawberry blond hair, hazel eyes, and an easy, natural smile.

And by Duncan's appearance in the ones he shared with her, they were around the same age. Some of the photos had to be decades old, faded and curling at the corners. Cam moved to pick one up, and Nic grabbed his wrist, holding him back.

Cam turned and gasped. He'd never seen Nic look so pale, so surprised. He wouldn't have thought that level of shock possible on the former SEAL.

"Who is she?" Cam whispered.

Nic loosened his grip and reached forward, snagging

one of the woman. He stared down at the Polaroid and Cam realized it wasn't only shock in his eyes. There was sadness and longing there too. It was like he'd seen a ghost, one he missed very much.

"You know her, Price?" Moore asked.

"Victoria Scott." He laid the photo down reverently, then looked up, not hiding his pain from anyone. "She was almost my stepmother."

SEVEN

Cam pulled the truck to a stop outside Mel and Danny's condo, on the curb of the neighborhood park that anchored South Park, and Nic couldn't help but shiver. Earlier this year, they'd had a mission go sideways here, Bowers throwing a wrench into their sting and Nic getting thrown over the hood of a car as a result.

"Think it'd be too much to ask them to move?" Cam mumbled.

Nic glanced at the mind reader in the driver's seat—surprised and not. They were so in sync, had both lived through that night, that Nic wasn't shocked Cam's thoughts had mirrored his own. What was surprising was how fast they'd gotten here. In what felt like no time at all, he'd gone from meeting and knowing Cam as Jamie's best friend to needing him like he was the other half of his soul.

Only one other time had he fallen so quickly and so completely.

Memories of Garrett flooded his mind as he stared out

the window, eyes lighting on the perfectly arranged trees around the park, fall colors glowing in the halos of the streetlamps. Garrett's mother, Victoria, an arborist and landscape artist, had been brought in to save the cypress trees on the family property. She'd been a quiet, unassuming presence, unfailingly kind, and a breath of fresh air after loud and brash wife number two who hadn't lasted a year. Even his father's mood was improved by Victoria at first. When he was gone on business trips, when he wasn't there to look down on his son for doing "yard work," Victoria would encourage Nic to help, would teach him about plants and bringing things to life. Each day was a new discovery, a new ounce of self-confidence, Victoria having a positive effect on him and on the environment around him. Then one day at the start of the summer, she'd brought her son and discovery was too simple a word for the ways Nic's life had changed forever.

For the better, no matter how it had ended.

Where he was a lanky and awkward teen, Garrett kept his compact, slot receiver's frame in constant motion, barely restrained energy always crackling beneath the surface and flashing in his stunning hazel eyes. Add in the easy smile and headful of chestnut hair that flamed red in the sun, and Nic had thought Garrett Scott was the most beautiful boy he'd ever seen. And there was no way such a beautiful boy would have anything to do with him, especially after he'd watched Garrett fuck a gorgeous waiter at a party one night. Wishing the whole time with every cell in his teenage body that he could be that waiter, that they could swap places.

But that wasn't all Nic had wanted, and somehow, miraculously, he'd gotten what he wanted for a change.

Garrett never looked down on him, had made it his mission to make Nic laugh, drawing him out day by day, whether in the cypress grove with his mother, in the kitchen with Mary, or just the two of them tossing around a football. Or watching movies curled up on the couch, closer and closer each night. Nic hadn't and still didn't warm up to people easily, but Garrett had been like a magnet, irresistible. Nic had been in love with him before that first summer was over, and his love for the beautiful boy had only grown by leaps and bounds during the years that had followed. Their relationship had been illicit and dangerous, right under Curtis's nose, and until recently, those had been the best years of Nic's life. He'd loved and been loved for who he was, happy for the first time since his mother's death.

He'd taken something for himself, that happiness, and drawn Garrett and Victoria closer, loving them with all his might, and in doing so, plunged them into an uncertain future. He'd cost Garrett the dream he'd had since he'd first picked up a football, Victoria her job. Hell, for all he knew, he had well and truly destroyed their lives.

A hand came gently down on his thigh, bringing him back to the present and to the other man who'd stolen his heart almost as quickly. "Sorry," Nic apologized, covering Cam's hand with his own. "Spaced out there for a minute."

"After the day you've had, it's allowed." Cam wove their fingers together. "Are you sure you're up for this tonight? We could go ho—"

"I need to talk to Mary."

"About what was in Vaughn's lockbox?" Cam shifted in his seat toward him. "Do you want to talk about it? You didn't say much this afternoon."

"I'm sorry. I had a status conference on another case."

True, but he'd also used that as an excuse to duck out before anyone asked the hard questions. Questions and truths he didn't want to talk about ever again, but more and more of his life—his past—kept getting drawn into this case. And he was going to have to ask Mary some hard questions tonight. Aside from asking Vaughn directly, she was the next best person to help tie together these latest revelations.

Cam's thumb swept across the back of his hand, redirecting his wandering mind again with a whispered "Baby."

Nic shook off the cobwebs and focused on the man in the truck with him.

He wasn't sure how much of this story would come out by the time this case was over, but Cam deserved to know it. Should be the first to know it. "I have no idea why he had pictures of Victoria."

Cam's fingers tightened around his. "I meant do you want to talk *about* Victoria. One look at those pictures and it was like you'd seen a ghost."

"Because I had. I haven't seen Victoria since high school graduation."

Cam inhaled sharply and drew down his brows, the investigator putting it together in a second. "You took the punch for *her*?"

Hand still in his, Nic gazed out the window again as the picture reel of that awful day played through his mind. "She told him she was leaving, that she'd packed my bags too, and he went ballistic. I stepped in the middle."

She'd had all their bags in the foyer, packed and ready to leave. After two weeks of utter hell, he'd felt as light and bright as a hot-air balloon, ready to take off into the future with the mother he never thought he'd have again and the boy he never wanted to be without. And then his father had charged in, demanding to know what the hell was going on. He'd accused Victoria and Garrett of trying to steal his son, of tainting the Price name, of milking him for a place to live in the lap of luxury. Never mind that they weren't married yet. Never mind that the so-called luxury had begun to dim the day after he'd put an engagement ring on Victoria's finger, first with emotional abuse, the sort Nic was all too familiar with, and then with the more physical manifestations of power, thinking he owned everything and everyone under his roof. Never mind the nightmare of the two weeks after he'd caught Nic and Garrett together under the cypress trees Victoria had brought back to life. Never mind that nothing and no one would have changed the fact that Nic was gay. Curtis was never going to have the heir he'd wanted; Victoria and Garrett Scott were just convenient punching bags.

"I'm guessing her trying to take you only enraged him more."

"I suspect he wished he'd let me go once I screamed in his face that I was gay and that he didn't have the power to change that."

"Then why didn't you?" Cam asked, drawing his gaze back with a tug on his hand. "Why didn't you go with Victoria instead of to the Navy?"

"I wanted to get them out safely. I didn't want him to follow me. Turned out he was happy to get rid of all of us."

Cam's brows snapped together again. "Them? All of us?"

Shit, that'd been more of the story than Nic had intended to tell tonight.

And Cam, goddamn brilliant investigator that he was, kept putting the pieces together. "Wait, is GS related—"

For once, Aidan's obnoxiously loud car was right on time. The gleaming black Aston Martin roared past them and into a spot two cars ahead. Nic withdrew his hand. "Aidan and Lauren are here."

Cam reached for him with a "Nic, wait," but Nic beat him to the door and out of the truck, Cam's muttered "Damn it" echoing behind him. Cam caught up with him before he made it to Aidan's car, drawing him around with a hand at his elbow. "This isn't over."

Nic chuckled, Cam's persistence a comfort as much as it was a menace. "I didn't figure it was, Boston."

Cam wasn't laughing. He stepped closer, into Nic's space. "Remember what you promised earlier?"

"Not to keep things on the case from you."

"And now this may be related."

Nic smirked. "Nice argument, Agent."

Cam's serious agent face broke, a smirk to match. "I do question witnesses for a living."

"You're also good at knowing when to let up, when to play good cop."

Cam's smirk grew into a smile, dark eyes warm as he rested a hand on his chest. "No, that's just me being a good boyfriend."

"Add cocky to the list."

Cam waggled his brows and Nic pushed him back playfully, but not so far he couldn't grab his boyfriend's hand, walking together to meet Aidan and Lauren.

Lauren reached into her purse and pulled out a bottle of Maker's. "Is it one of these sorts of dinners?"

"Three Irishmen present," Cam quipped. "Yes."

"I watched *The Wire* too, but I wasn't sure if that whole Irish wake thing was real."

"It's real," Aidan confirmed, accent thicker for effect before he reined it back in. "Though we're not going that far. We have a full day tomorrow."

Lauren swiped at her bangs and pouted dramatically. "You're a terrible Irishman. Where do I report this?"

"I'll be sure to give you the number of the home office."

They all laughed as they crossed the street.

"But first, food." Aidan glanced up at the open loft windows. "I can smell it from here."

"Chicken marsala," Nic said, the aromas of red wine, mushrooms, and seared chicken taking him back to his childhood. It had always been one of his favorite dishes, second only to Mary's cioppino.

"Oh God, the marsala we used to get in North End," Cam said, practically moaning, his accent more pronounced, something that had faded since they'd returned from Boston. Nic realized how much he'd missed it and how much that trip had changed them for the better.

Using the hand in his, Nic yanked Cam to a halt. Other hand around his neck, Nic hauled him in, stealing a quick, hard kiss. "You are a good boyfriend," he whispered against his lips. "I wouldn't want to go through this with anyone else, or alone." That's what the old Nic would have wanted, but the one holding Cameron Byrne's hand, the one who knew he had someone to call, someone to tell his story to, someone to go home to after a no-good horrible day, wanted this man with him, always.

Cam's dark, heated eyes stared back at him. "I'm with you, baby."

As was his family.

And Nic wanted to be with them tonight too, more than he even wanted sleep. Hand in hand with Cam, walking into Mel and Danny's condo to the smell of marsala, to Danny flirting with Mary by the stove, to Mel scowling at the bottle of whiskey Lauren offered, Nic relaxed for the first time since they'd left the house that morning.

Cam closed the door behind them, and Mary eyed them over her shoulder. "Cameron, kitchen now."

Cam's eyes twinkled. "The chef calls." He loosened his fingers, gave Nic a smacking kiss on the cheek, then hurried into the kitchen like a kid at Christmas.

Mel appeared at Nic's side, two glasses of whiskey in hand. "He took to Mary quickly," she observed, offering him a glass.

Nic took a sip, smiling as two dark-haired, six-foot-plus Irishmen took orders from a five-foot-nothing slip of an Italian woman. "She's actually a lot like Cam's mom. And she cooks."

Mel laughed. "Same reason Danny has taken to her."

He glanced to the side, a streak of worry running through him. "Not you?" He was the one who'd encouraged this arrangement. He'd hate to hear it wasn't working out for Mel too.

"Oh, I've taken to her. That woman has made my life a million times easier. I owe you."

"Glad to hear it." He tilted his glass for a clink, the toast capped by a "We're ready" from Cam in the kitchen. Nic threw back the rest of his drink, set the glass aside, and followed Mel to the kitchen.

Mary wrapped him in a big hug. "Eat first," she said. "We'll talk after about arrangements and anything else."

Arrangements, *fuck*. Nic had skipped right over that in

favor of the case and the estate disposition. Something else to add to the list. For after. After was good. Otherwise, he wasn't sure how much he'd actually eat, and he didn't want to miss out on the food or this bright moment with his family.

Dinner was a loud affair once everyone got past their first mouthwatering bites. Danny baited Cam into an East Coast-West Coast football debate, Mel and Aidan entering the fray to plead the Miami Dolphins' case, while Lauren ignored that debate completely, discussing with Mary TV shows she'd marathon-watched. At some point, Aidan began pitching Mary on coming to work for him, drawing a death glare from his brother.

"Why the hell do you need help?" Danny argued. "Jamie's practically a chef."

"Yes, but he's also the messiest person alive."

"Let me answer this now," Mel interjected. "No."

Laughter erupted, and the conversation moved on to Q&A with Mel about the latest bounty she'd chased through Alaska. The woman could write a book with the stories she was collecting.

Nic took the opportunity to lean closer to Mary, asking, "What happened to retirement?"

She smiled serenely. "This I don't mind." She gestured with a hand at the group around the table. "I'm getting to know your family. And it's only two days a week. I come in, straighten up, and cook enough to feed them all week. They're easy to please and always appreciative."

"I'm glad it worked out." His smile dimmed a little as he pushed around the last bite on his plate. "I should have thought of it sooner."

She bumped his shoulder. "Everything happens when

it's supposed to, Dominic." Nic looked up, right across the table at Cam, their eyes catching, and Mary laughed softly. "And yes, I mean him too."

Cam continued to check in with him throughout the meal, a glance here, a kick under the table there, and given the look Mel shot him as they were clearing the table, they hadn't been fooling anyone. For a while now. Mary had the same look on her face as she came out of the kitchen. "Give him a kiss, then let's go up to the roof. We'll sort things out."

Cam stuck his head out of the kitchen, cheek lifted. "You good?"

"All good." Nic stole a kiss from his lips instead, then followed Mary upstairs and claimed the lounger next to the one she'd stretched out on.

Her gaze drifted out over China Basin, their chairs arranged to see south toward the ballpark and the water. On a clear night like tonight, no rain, no fog, no bright stadium lights, it was just the stars above and the moon rippling on the dark water. "I come up here every time before I leave," Mary said. "Reminds me why I love it here so much."

Nic understood that feeling. As much as he'd enjoyed the work in San Diego, it had never felt like home, not like this. The city that had grown up with him, the ballparks he couldn't stay away from, the water on either side that didn't make him feel trapped so much as free. The Bay Area was home, always would be, and he didn't regret his decision to pass up the job in San Diego, especially not since Cam decided to stay and make this his home too. Now, they had to protect it.

Mary shifted on the lounger, curling on her side and

covering up with the blanket. Her relaxed, casual posture made it easier to stomach her words. "Let's start with the easy stuff. Funeral arrangements?"

Easy.

His father wasn't the first person he'd lost—his mother when he was six, other soldiers killed in combat—but it was the first time he was directly responsible for the after. He wasn't religious, neither was Curtis, so in a way, arrangements were easy. No church service, just cremation and a scattering of the ashes at the house. There was no need for more; he wasn't about to entertain a public service. And if anyone wanted to send flowers or condolences, they could do so in the form of a donation to a charity Nic would designate. He and Mary had it sorted in less than ten minutes.

Yet there was something unsettling about being the last Price, the last of his immediate family. Not exactly grief, but a vague sense of emptiness, of being untethered like when they'd been out to sea with no other ships or land in sight. He rubbed his hip, reminding himself of his strongest tether to the here and now, to the reality and future he wanted, one where he wasn't alone. But still that uneasiness lingered. Perhaps also because Nic couldn't avoid the hard stuff any longer.

"I need to ask you some things related to the case, but I can't go into all the details."

"I work for a bounty hunter, Dominic. I'm used to half stories."

He swung his legs around, facing her with his feet on the ground, elbows resting on his knees. "Did you know Victoria before she came to work for Dad?"

Mary shook her head. "She came by recommendation

from the landscaper your father used for the commercial properties."

"Do you know if she was seeing anyone romantically? Garrett's father was out of the picture by then, but was there anyone else?"

"Not that I know of."

"Did she know Duncan Vaughn?"

Mary's relaxed posture evaporated. "I figured that's where this was headed," she said, resignation in her voice. She straightened in her chair, pulled her knees up to her chest, and wrapped the blankets around her folded body like a shield. "They grew up together. Duncan was her best friend, and he was in love with her."

That fit with all the pictures in the lockbox, a collection of memories of the woman Duncan had loved, though none of the pictures had seemed romantic. They were just shots of Victoria or of the two of them as friends. No hugs, no kisses, nothing remotely date-like, and no pictures of Garrett. What else had Mary seen that wasn't in those photos? "What makes you say that?"

"He came to the house a few times once your father had started courting her. She'd been seen around town with him and Duncan was upset."

"He was trying to talk her out of getting involved with Dad?"

She nodded, gaze drifting back out over the Bay. "When word got out they were engaged, he waited until your father left for a business trip, then visited one afternoon. They had a shouting match in the garden."

"I don't remember . . ."

"You and Garrett had gone to a ballgame."

That made sense. With his dad out of town, Nic would

frequently use the club level tickets that hadn't been given to clients and sneak off with Garrett for an afternoon at the ballpark. They made it to their seats only half the time, often diverting to a shadowed corner of the concourse to make out. They'd never appeared as more than friends in the seats, afraid some of the regulars around them might say something to Curtis. Which sounded like what Duncan had been doing too, only showing up to confront Victoria when Curtis was out.

"What happened?" Nic asked.

"He tried again to convince her to leave. Confessed he'd always been in love with her and proposed."

Nic gasped. Until today, he'd never suspected that Victoria was at the center of the animosity between Duncan and Curtis.

"But he wasn't the same Duncan Vaughn then," Mary continued. "And she had Garrett to worry about. He was her whole world." And he'd become Nic's too. "She could take a chance on Duncan, who barely had a cent to his name, or she could provide a future for them with your father, who up until then had been nothing but good to her."

"Was she in love with Duncan?"

"She was so upset after their fight that I thought maybe. I talked to her afterward and she swore she wasn't. But he was her best friend; she didn't have the heart to tell him that."

"So he still thinks Dad stole her."

All the pieces clicked into place. Everything was starting to make sense now.

Everything.

What Duncan had once told him Curtis had stolen.

What Duncan had taken from Curtis. He'd set out to destroy Curtis the way he perceived Curtis had destroyed his life by cratering his chances with the woman he'd always loved.

"He's the one your father was in debt to?"

"I can't answer that." Though he figured he'd done as much by his words.

"After Victoria disappeared," Mary said, "Duncan confronted your father, demanding to know where she'd gone. He told Curtis one day he would pay for hurting her, for stealing her away from him."

With his fortune, and now it looked like his life. Had he made Victoria and Garrett pay too? And if not then, would he now, thinking that removing Curtis would somehow impress her?

"Do you have any idea where Victoria and Garrett went? Did you ever hear from them?"

"Not a word."

He needed to talk to Mel. Find and warn them. He'd never intended to contact Victoria and Garrett again, afraid he'd only bring them more pain than he already had. He didn't want to disrupt their lives a second time. But he'd never forgive himself if he let any harm come to them because of Vaughn's vendetta.

Mary covered his hand where it had fisted on his knee. "He's a dangerous man now, Dominic. Everyone here knows that. Vengeance has fueled him for thirty years."

Had it fueled the murder of his father too? Almost certainly.

"Dominic!" Cam's shout rang up the stairs. In his agent voice, this late at night, it couldn't be good news.

By Mary's wide-eyed look, she sensed it too.

He patted her hand, then stood and crossed to the stairs. Cam was at the bottom, hands braced on the rails.

"What's going on?" Nic asked.

"Moore just called. We know why Harris Kincaid missed his meeting this afternoon. He's dead."

EIGHT

In an eerie repeat of the morning, Cam navigated Nic's truck down another winding, tree-lined street, dodging parked cars and emergency response vehicles. No press vans yet, but it was only a matter of time. As soon as they connected Harris Kincaid to Curtis Price, reporters were bound to start asking questions. Cam wanted answers before that happened.

Aidan's Vanquish helped clear a path for them, the roar of the engine scattering cars and people. Cam pulled into a spot next to the coroner's van and let the truck idle, staring at the spooky sight ahead. One town over from Cam and Nic's place, Harris's house looked about the same size and style but not nearly as well kept. The front lawn was overgrown, the box hedges dying, and in the harsh glare of headlights and emergency vehicle strobes, the peeling paint and rotting wood were apparent. Together with the crime scene spotlights inside, backlighting the huge front windows over which were hung lingering Halloween decorations, the place looked almost haunted.

"This is what put Harris underwater?" Cam muttered disbelievingly.

Beside him, Nic pointed to the young woman sitting on the front porch, rocking a small child in her lap. "That's why," he said. "Better schools and higher property values."

Were better schools worth being indebted to your gangster uncle-in-law? Worth losing your life? Cam doubted Harris's kid would grow up to think so.

"Versus our place," Nic carried on, "this one's probably worth half a million more, at least."

Cam's low whistle covered his delight at hearing Nic refer to the rental as *our place*. He felt the same, more each day, and on this day, when their world had been turned upside down, it meant everything.

"He's taken a personal interest in this case," Nic said, drawing Cam's attention back to the scene. Cam followed Nic's gaze to Moore, who'd come out of the house to speak with Harris's wife.

"You're not doubting him again, are you?" It had taken serious work to get Nic to bring the AD in on this case. It'd been worth it, Moore providing critical information and political juice when they'd needed it.

"No, it was the right call to involve him, but I am still debating how much our interests truly align. Ultimately, he's a political climber."

Cam lolled his head against the headrest, side-eyeing Nic. "Says the man climbing the DOJ ladder."

"Says the FBI ASAC," Nic fired back.

They both smirked until Cam returned his attention to Moore, standing tall and in charge on the porch. Nic was right to a degree. "I don't know why he's climbing it. But he's on our side with this one. It somehow benefits him."

"But if we step out of line, do something that doesn't benefit him . . ." Then they'd lose his favor and the leverage he provided, if not their jobs.

Cam nodded. "Proceed with caution."

They met Aidan and Lauren in front of the truck, and Moore intercepted them halfway up the front walk. "What've we got?" Aidan asked. "You wouldn't say on the phone."

Moore eyed the gathering crowd of neighbors across the street. "Let's move this someplace more private."

They dodged the exiting crime scene techs and huddled in the garage, which, like most Silicon Valley cottages, wasn't big enough for today's cars and served as storage and a mudroom instead.

"It looks like a suicide," Moore said.

"Looks like?" Cam asked.

"Hung himself from his bolted-in chin-up bar."

Cam winced while Aidan scoffed, repeating, "Looks like?"

"It looked like Price's father had a heart attack," Moore said with a significant glance at Nic, who seemed a million miles away.

Cam moved a step closer. "But Harris could be a suicide. Between the debt, the pressure Vaughn was putting on him, the pressure we were putting on him, and the pressure he no doubt put on himself. Then after finding Curtis . . ."

"It could be," Moore agreed. "Sixty-forty shot here."

"That's more of a shot than most suicide cases."

"I'll see what else I can find on his computer," Lauren said.

"That's the other reason I give it a sixty-forty shot," Moore said. "Toward looks like."

"You found something?" Aidan said.

"The opposite. Harris's computer is gone."

"Maybe he left it at the office."

"Not according to the wife. He never went anywhere without it."

Which left two possibilities as far as Cam could discern. It was taken or it was hidden. "There a safe it could be in?"

"The wife says not usually, but yes, there is one, and yes, it could be in there."

"She didn't check?" Aidan asked.

"She can't get into it." Moore's dark gaze shifted back to Cam. "I understand you're the man to talk to about cracking it."

Cam hesitated, and Nic, who'd been quiet until then, came to life, laying a hand on his shoulder. "We can wait—"

Cam shook his head; this was necessary. "We don't have time."

"Okay, then," Moore said. "Talley, let's go talk with the wife. Get us clearance."

"I'm gonna coordinate with the techs," Lauren said. "If his laptop is here, we'll get them to process it on the scene so I can get right to work."

They headed out of the garage, leaving Cam behind with Nic, whose hand was still on his shoulder. Cam covered it with his, squeezing. "Thank you."

"Of course," Nic said. "We can let Aidan give it a go first."

Cam shook his head. "I'll be fine with you here." He slid his hand off. "Though should you be?"

Nic's brow furrowed, eyes thankfully sparking again at the challenge. "Meaning?"

"This is your dead father's dead executive assistant."

"He's also my star witness in the case against my dead father's loan shark, who's also his uncle."

Cam lifted a brow, Nic having made his point for him. "Conflict of interest much?"

"My only interest here is justice. And not dying." He stepped back, hands on his hips. "I don't see a conflict."

Not yet.

But it was plain as day. And growing by the day if not by the minute. Cam didn't voice the concern, though, the both of them distracted by a commotion on the other side of the crime scene tape at the end of the drive.

As they approached, Vaughn's blond head was easy to spot.

"Civilians are not permitted on the scene, sir," one of the officers said to him.

Vaughn pointed at Harris's wife, who'd stood upon seeing him. "That's my niece," he said, calm as could be, a hint of impatience in his voice but no anger. He was confident he'd get through eventually. "Beth Kincaid."

"He means you aren't permitted on the scene," Cam said, coming to stand next to the officer.

"I beg to differ, Agent Byrne." He flashed him a smile, absurdly inappropriate given the context, then flashed Nic an even brighter one. "I have a right to be with my family."

Cam was not at all amused. He ducked under the tape, coming up in front of Vaughn. "Not if you're a suspect."

"Beth called me in tears. She said Harris committed suicide."

Cam stepped closer, getting in Vaughn's face. "Cause of death has not officially been determined."

"Let him through," Nic said behind him, likewise eerily calm.

Cam glared over his shoulder. Nic's eyes were anything but calm, stormy icy blue instead, and the set of his shoulders, his spine . . . Cam knew that look.

Determined, Nic had a plan and needed Cam to trust him.

Glancing back at Vaughn, Cam lifted the tape and Vaughn scooted under it, stopping in front of Nic.

"Thank you, Dom."

Nic answered him in the same cool tone. "Don't thank me yet."

Vaughn smiled wider, then headed up the walkway to his niece.

Ducking back under the tape, Cam followed Nic to the opening of the garage. "What was that about?" he asked when Nic turned around.

"That was me pulling up that mask you mentioned earlier. And also . . ." He pointed at the eaves overhanging the garage.

Eyes widening, Cam spotted the small home security camera there. "Ten to one," Nic said, lowering his voice, "there's one of those on the patio too, right by the front door."

Right where Vaughn and Beth were sitting. "You want to see what he says," Cam said.

"I also want to know if this is the first time tonight he's been here." Cam looked back at him. "You think the computer's in the safe?"

"If I saw my gangster relation on the front porch the day after I'd discovered a body and papers were served on him, I'd be hiding evidence too."

"Sounds like I've got a safe to crack."

"Only if you can." Nic skimmed a hand over his lower

back, out of sight of the swarming officers but exactly the grounding Cam needed.

"You're here. I'm tethered. I can do it."

———

Cam entered the conference room with a pink, brown, and orange box in each hand, skirting past Nic who held the door open for him. "We come bearing doughnuts."

Despite his vow in Boston to never eat Dunkin' again, once Cam had learned there was a new one on their way from the house to the office, all bets were off. His colleagues had reaped the rewards ever since, as Lauren did today, looking up from her computer with a tired smile.

"My heroes." She took one of the boxes from Cam and dug right in. "You're lucky he didn't eat them all on the way here," Nic said as Cam slid the other box onto the table.

With his free hand, Cam shot Nic the bird. "Well, if someone hadn't kept me up all night."

Lauren clapped her hands over her ears. "Earmuffs!"

Cam laughed around a bite of blueberry-glazed doughnut.

"It was nothing that fun," Nic said, headed for the coffeemaker. "He pretended to be Vaughn, and I grilled him for hours."

"Waste of a night. You're ready." Cam reached for a second doughnut, and Nic shoved a cup of coffee in his hand instead.

"That's four already, and as for last night, I want to be prepared."

"I think I can help with that," Lauren said, losing the

battle with a powdered one, her navy blazer from yesterday taking a sugar beating.

"You cracked Harris's computer?" Cam asked.

The slim MacBook had been locked away in a wall safe, hidden behind the framed alphabet poster in the nursery. When Lauren had carried it out last night, Vaughn's eyes had flashed with what looked like fear, the first crack Cam had seen in his shiny, too-cool veneer.

"I did," she said.

"Then what am I here for?" came a familiar voice behind them, the drawl unmistakably Southern.

Cam twisted to see his best friend entering the conference room ahead of Aidan. He was half out of his chair when Jamie pulled him the rest of the way up and into a back-slapping hug. "Brother," Cam said, feeling like the missing piece of the team, of his support system was back where it belonged.

Jamie drew Nic into a hug next. "Whatever you need."

"Thank you," Nic replied.

They'd gotten close while working the case with Cam in Boston, and Cam was relieved the two most important men in his life were now friends.

"Yes, thank you," Lauren said. "And there is something you can help with." She spun out the chair beside her, beckoning Jamie over.

"You're official?" Cam asked Jamie as he sank into the offered chair.

"As official as he can be," Aidan said. "And I've brought him up to speed."

"Excellent." Lauren pushed one of the laptops toward him. "I got pulled off decrypting Vaughn's work computer before I could finish."

"I'm on it." Jamie pulled the computer toward him with thinly concealed glee, the hacker gleam bright in his too-blue eyes. His fingers hit the keyboard, and he was lost to the rest of the world.

Returning his focus to Lauren, Cam asked, "What did you find on Harris's computer?"

She reached for the wires in the middle of the table, plugged them into Harris's laptop, and his desktop display appeared on the in-wall monitor, a picture of his wife and baby. Cam had the strong suspicion they were the reason Harris did everything. They disappeared as Lauren opened the applications folder and double-clicked the icon for the same whole-home security system Cam had on the rental.

"You were right about the security system," Lauren said. "And about Vaughn visiting earlier in the day."

"I'm sensing a but."

"But . . ." she drew it out. "I think wrong about the cause of death. I think he may have actually committed suicide."

She hit Play, and a view of Harris's front porch appeared, Vaughn and his muscle waiting impatiently at the door.

Nic tensed beside him, shoulders up, hands clenched. Tightly coiled, observing, determining how and when to strike. A far cry from the man who'd debated over the doughnut order less than an hour ago. He was no longer Dominic Price, boyfriend, but Dominic Price, attorney, and the SEAL who was scratching just beneath the surface. Ready to explode. Cam knocked a knee against his under the table, letting him know he was there. Nic's shoulders ticked down a hair. With the day ahead, Cam counted that tempering of the fuse a win.

"Time?" Aidan asked.

Lauren popped up the time stamp on-screen, then fast-forwarded five minutes until Harris answered the door.

"He was stashing the computer," Cam said.

"Probably," Aidan replied.

When the door finally opened, Harris tried to prevent them from entering, arguing with Vaughn that now wasn't a good time, that he had a conference call to attend to, but the goons cleared a path for their boss, easily shoving rail-thin Harris aside.

And then nothing.

"We have anything from inside?"

"No, unfortunately, but there's this." She fast-forwarded twenty minutes to the front door opening again, Harris looking noticeably paler as he saw Vaughn and his men out.

"You made the right decision, Harris," Vaughn said, clapping his shoulder. "I'm sure you'll keep making them." And then he left, down the front porch steps, bodyguards on his six.

For his part, Harris appeared dazed and devastated, holding himself up by the door.

"He was still alive when they left," Aidan observed.

Lauren nodded. "There's no evidence they came back on any of the cameras, which were inactive later in the evening."

"Whatever Vaughn said to him inside," Cam said, "it was enough to push him to—"

"It doesn't make sense," Aidan interrupted. "He loses everything if he commits suicide. No life insurance payout, restrictions on his retirement, he leaves his family with nothing."

"If there was anything left there to even give," Cam added.

"Not everything." Nic finally spoke up. "Did you scan in the real estate documents from the folder you gave me yesterday?" he asked Lauren.

She nodded, and they appeared on-screen a second later.

"In Harris's package, there was a reconveyance. Unsigned and undated, so I didn't think anything of it then."

Lauren scrolled through the documents, pulling up the document in question, and Cam cursed.

"Holy shit," Aidan echoed across the table.

Nic was out of his seat, next to the projection, pointing at the address line. "It's for their house." Then he pointed to the Lender/Grantor and Borrower/Grantee lines.

"Duncan was going to release the loan and reconvey the house," Cam said. "Free and clear but only back to Beth Kincaid."

"That," Nic said, "is what Harris had to offer."

NINE

Biometric readings were a no-go for Vaughn's interview. Too many people in and out of the interrogation room. Nic had worried that might be the case. Inside, he and Cam sat across from Vaughn and his attorney, Carl Patton. Contrary to his insistence yesterday, Bowers decided to stand on the other side of the glass in the observation room with Aidan, Jamie, Lauren, and El. Nic suspected his boss had remembered the capabilities of this room or had been reminded of such by someone—Vaughn's FBI mole—and wanted to overhear the analysis. Nic wouldn't have that, nor would he further remind Bowers of the full capabilities of Holding Room Two, in case Bowers might be in here for questioning one day soon.

"Dom," Vaughn started once they were all situated. "You look refreshed for having had such a late night. Your partner is good for you."

He cast a significant glance toward Cam, making it clear he knew they were more than colleagues. That Cam was important to him. They hadn't hidden it, and after stepping out of the house together and being captured on the morning news, everyone knew it. Right then, Nic couldn't help but wonder whether they should have kept things hidden until this was over, whether he should have taken that job in San Diego, whether he should have gotten involved with Cam at all. It wasn't fair to put him at risk.

But then Cam shifted next to him, fire in his eyes and a not-so-subtle threat in his voice. "And it'd be good for you if you'd refer to the AUSA as Attorney Price."

Vaughn backed off. "Of course, Agent Byrne."

Cameron Byrne could take care of himself just fine. And he was the partner Nic needed, personally and professionally.

Back on steady ground, Nic relaxed back in his chair, unbuttoning his suit coat. "We have some questions for you."

Vaughn spread his hands in invitation. "I'm an open book."

Hardly.

With so many closed doors, Nic had a hard time choosing which one to knock on first. He and Cam had gone over several scenarios last night. Nic decided to go right for the one at the end of the hall, to the heart of what he suspected this was all about. And because he wanted to start by knocking Vaughn off balance.

"What was your relationship with Victoria Scott?"

Vaughn's eyes flared before they narrowed and the corners of his mouth tightened, like he was holding back a curse or a gasp.

Bingo.

When he didn't speak, his attorney did for him. "What

does this have to do with the warrant executed on Mr. Vaughn?"

From the evidence box on the floor between them, Cam withdrew a handful of the pictures from the lockbox they'd seized and spread them out on the table. "These were found at Mr. Vaughn's residence."

"She was a childhood friend," Vaughn said, voice measured, flat.

"Whom you kept pictures of until she was in her thirties?"

"She was my best friend."

No inflection but by the twitch of his fingers, the start of the motion to curl them into a fist, aborted as soon as he realized what he was doing, Nic was more sure than ever that Victoria was the reason they were all here.

He pushed the door open some more. "I heard tell you wanted more."

Patton cleared his throat. "Again, I ask, what does this have to do with the investigation into my client?"

"Establishing motive."

"Motive for what?"

Nic answered but kept his eyes locked on Vaughn, watching for any reaction, any other tells that escaped Vaughn's control. "The murder of Curtis Price."

Vaughn spread his hand on the desk, fighting that fist. "Your father died of a heart attack."

"Did he?"

Patton jumped in again. "Your warrants also state Mr. Vaughn is under suspicion for an overly broad list of financial crimes."

"Curtis Price was also a victim of those," Cam replied.

Vaughn spoke directly to Nic. "Your father was a terrible businessman."

"Duncan," Patton warned.

"The deeds of trust are on record, Patton." He waved his other hand in the air like he was swatting at a gnat. He probably did view his attorneys that way, convinced they were a necessary evil. "Yes, I made a loan to him."

"And when he didn't pay," Cam said, "you made threats against him and Attorney Price to collect."

"His word against my client's," Patton argued. Then to Nic, "And you should be recused. You stand to benefit if your father's debts to Mr. Vaughn are excused."

This was one of the scenarios Cam had thrown at him last night. As a result, Nic was prepared, and Cam knew it too, shifting back in his chair, smiling at the trap Patton had stepped into. Nic bit back his own, barely, as he pulled a folded paper out of his jacket pocket. "A pledge." He set the unfolded sheet on top of the photos. "Any money I receive from my father's estate will go to pay his debts that are deemed legal. If any money is left over, I'll donate it to the Trevor Project and to RAINN."

Patton snatched up the document while Vaughn tilted his head, considering him with assessing eyes.

"So you know the kind of man your father was?"

"The fact I thought the Navy during Don't Ask Don't Tell was a better place for my gay eighteen-year-old self than my own home should answer that question." He leaned forward, forearms on the table. "I've told you before and I'll tell you again, with your attorney present, I don't want a cent of Curtis's money. There's no conflict of interest."

Picking up the serve Nic had lobbed, Cam got them

back on track, likewise homing in on Vaughn's motives. "Did you loan money to Mr. Price with a plan to ruin him for stealing Victoria Scott from you?"

Vaughn couldn't stop the fist from forming this time. "She wasn't mine to steal."

"Answer the question," Cam pressed.

"I did not," Vaughn snapped. "We're in the same business—real estate investment. I made him several loans, one businessman to another."

"Even though you didn't think highly of him as a businessman?"

"He needed a bailout," Vaughn said. "I could provide it."

It was a weak comeback and not a refutation of the argument. Patton knew it. Point for Cam as pride swelled in Nic.

And the agent had another teed up to go too. Reaching into the box again, Cam righted himself with two evidence bags, the pistols thumping on the table as they landed. "Do you provide guns too, Mr. Vaughn?"

"All of my client's firearms are licensed," Patton replied.

Cam tucked the bag tight around the weapon, the plastic stretched over the barrels. "Even these with the scratched-out serial numbers?" He pushed the bags farther across the table.

"Those are not Mr. Vaughn's weapons."

"I'll admit that your client's fingerprints are not on them," Cam said. "They're wiped clean. But they were collected from his office."

Patton angled toward Vaughn. "How many other people are in your office each day?"

"At least a half dozen."

"We'll need their names."

"We can provide that," Vaughn replied.

"Who among them would be likely to use illegal weapons with their serial numbers scratched out?" Cam asked.

Vaughn shrugged. "I can't control the weapon of choice of everyone who walks into my office."

"You sure?" Cam said. "Desert Eagles seem to be popular."

"I can't imagine who you're talking about, but I can assure you, whoever used or owned those guns"—he nodded toward the table—"they're not on my payroll."

"Let's talk about that," Nic said, reentering the fray. "We have money running from accounts that trace to you or your companies to at least seven different municipal employees."

"Investors." Vaughn sat back, crossing one leg over the other, looking intrigued. Or maybe relieved that Nic had chosen another door to open.

"Try again," Nic said, determined to make him second-guess that relief. "There are no registered investments to these people."

Everyone startled as a commotion erupted on the other side of the glass.

Just as Nic had intended. This line of questioning, this door, wasn't only meant for Vaughn's ears. The noise quieted and Nic prompted Vaughn for a response again. "Do you have an explanation?"

"Not every investment has to be registered, Attorney Price," Patton replied. "I'm sure you know that. And dividends pay out regularly."

"That's correct," Vaughn said.

"Lump sum payments, though, other than on a sale or IPO, that's less common, wouldn't you both agree?"

The door opened behind them. "Attorney Price," Bowers barked. "A word, please."

Vaughn didn't bother hiding his smirk. "Problem, Dom?"

Nic pushed to his feet, with an "Excuse me" to Vaughn and Patton and a look at Cam, which the agent correctly read.

"I'll stay." Neither of them wanted to leave Vaughn and Patton alone in the room to confer. Granted, they had the right to ask for that, but if they weren't asking, Nic didn't want to give them the opportunity.

Nic barely left the room before Bowers jumped down his throat. "What the hell are you doing?" he demanded, loud enough for the whole bullpen to hear.

And loud enough to draw Aidan out of the observation room. Good, another attorney, another witness. "Let's go to my office."

Neither he nor Aidan gave Bowers the opportunity to object, heading in the direction of Aidan's office and assuming Bowers would follow. Aidan closed the door and Bowers started right back in on where he'd left off. "Do you actually have anything, Price?"

"Enough that I got a warrant."

"Who do the accounts trace to?"

"Not you, if that's what you're worried about." He probably should have held that for another time, played the card when the timing was exactly right, but after twenty minutes of cat and mouse with Vaughn, his exhausted patience and Bowers's righteousness got the better of him.

Bowers's beady black eyes looked like they would pop out of his head. "What did you just say?"

"Oh, you heard me."

He chose not to respond, deflecting the blame and accusations back on Nic. "You're leading a witch hunt out of my office."

"The witches were innocent, sir," Aidan said with a smirk. "Duncan Vaughn is not. Are you?"

Aidan's utter smugness, his going along with Nic's play, tamped down Nic's own frustration. Two against one, and they had Bowers and this case in hand.

"As I mentioned before," Nic said, "the Deputy AG reviewed all of this and signed off on the warrants."

"As did AD Moore," Aidan added. "The FBI has been building this case for some time."

"Well, I sure hope you have more than what you've put on display today. It might have been enough to convince our bosses and get warrants out of the grand jury, but indictments?" Bowers scoffed, hands on his hips. "There's no smoking gun. You can't win without."

Nic straightened and stepped forward, towering over Bowers. "I've won plenty of cases with less."

"But do you want to lose this one?"

Fair question. But before he could give Bowers credit, the US Attorney began digging his grave again, fishing for himself and for the man who was truly his boss. "What else do you have?"

"We're still processing the evidence collected in yesterday's seizures and at Harris Kincaid's house last night."

Bowers blanched. "What did you collect from Kincaid? I want to see it, right this minute."

Nic took a step back, buttoning his coat again.

"Respectfully, sir, I have my target in Agent Talley's interrogation room. The evidence has been vetted. Now I'm going to go ask the man it's concerning what it's about. If you have a problem with that, take it up with the Deputy AG."

Aidan opened the door, making it clear this conversation was over, and Bowers charged out, to the elevators instead of the observation room.

Probably to call the Deputy AG. That call wasn't going to go the way he planned at all.

On their way back across the bullpen, Aidan voiced what they both had deduced from that showdown. "He was fishing."

"And he caught a shark that's going to take his line."

Crinkles formed at the corners of Aidan's warm brown eyes dancing with amusement. "Would that be you or Duncan?"

Nic returned the sly smile, barely tucking it away before Aidan opened the interrogation room door for him. "As you were, Attorney Price."

Nic slid back into his seat, begging the room's pardon.

"Everything okay, Dom?"

"Better than okay, Duncan."

Patton interrupted their stare-down. "Do you have proof those deposits actually trace to Mr. Vaughn?"

"Enough that the grand jury granted us warrants."

"If that's all—"

Nic reached into the box, claiming the stack of deeds, and placed all but one of them on the table in the spot Cam had cleared for him. "Curious that you also have unrecorded mortgages from at least three of those investors."

"Were you going to record them," Cam asked, "if they got behind on their payments?"

"Don't answer that," Patton said.

Nic laid down the last sheet of paper. "Even more curious, this reconveyance to Beth Kincaid was drafted before her husband's death. It would wipe out the debt on their house completely. Have you ever forgiven a family member's loan before?"

Vaughn remained silent, no longer happy with the line of questioning behind this particular door.

"Or is this what you used to convince Harris Kincaid to kill himself?"

"Okay, that's enough." Patton rocketed to his feet. "We're done here."

Vaughn, however, remained seated. "He killed himself. You just said that. I didn't have anything to do with that."

Nic leaned forward, adding a thumb drive to the stack. "On the contrary." He tapped the drive. "You visited Harris hours before his suicide. You showed him that reconveyance and made him a bargain he couldn't refuse. He killed himself because you didn't give him another choice."

TEN

Cam pushed through the doors of the county morgue, not especially happy to be here again. Even with the promise of evidence, the morgue wasn't the sort of place one looked forward to visiting—the smell, the artificial lights, the specter of death that hid in the dark corners. But he'd fought the early rush hour traffic to get here before Jong went off shift, her phone call making it clear she'd only give the evidence to him in person.

Nic's orders.

After that interrogation today, after Bowers interrupted exactly when he did and showed almost all his cards, they were more convinced than ever that the US Attorney was dirty. They had to find the moles ASAP and tighten the information circles in the meantime.

So he was here to receive information, possible evidence on Nic's father's death, without Nic by his side. Bowers had seen to it this afternoon that Nic was punished and distracted. They'd been on a solid trail, tying evidence to motives for both Vaughn and Bowers when Nic had been yanked off it for an emergency motion—to do Bowers's job for him. Cam felt sorry for whoever was on the other side of that case and for the judge. It was Nic being sidelined in the van all over again, except this time it was Bowers Nic was pissed at instead of him. Small blessings, though waiting at the morgue counter for an attendant was starting to feel like a curse.

Finally, Coroner Jong herself appeared through the swinging steel doors, snapped off her gloves, and extended her hand. "Agent Byrne, I'm sorry for the wait. I went ahead and let everyone go for the day."

Cam barely hid his shiver at her cold hand slipping into his. "Cam, please."

"Elizabeth, then." She smiled, tired yet friendly, then nodded toward the back. "Please, this way."

"Nic sends his apologies for not making it," Cam said as they walked down the hallway. "He's stuck in court."

"That's what his text said." Instead of entering the examination room, she walked another ten or so feet and turned into an office. Cam let out a relieved sigh, then sucked it back in at seeing two syringes on her desk. "Nic said to only give you this in person."

"Give me what?"

She pulled out her desk chair and Cam moved his hand over his sidearm, ready to draw. He dropped it as she righted herself with two folders in hand, covering his motion with an adjustment of his jacket.

"What've you found?"

"This is the file on Harris Kincaid." She held the top one out to him. "I rushed the toxicology."

"Okay, what am I looking—" Cam paused at the third drug listed after the acid reflux OTC and allergy meds. It was a drug he recognized from kidnap and sexual assault cases. Cases where a victim went "willingly" with their attacker. Or so it appeared.

Scopolamine.

Legal when prescribed by a physician. On the street, when not, it was known as Devil's Breath. A powerful, dangerous drug that could open a person to suggestions. Victims were often described as walking zombies. In too high a dose, it was deadly.

He studied the tox results again. "He didn't technically die from the scopolamine, did he?"

"No, he died of strangulation. No question, he hung himself."

"Because someone planted that suggestion in his head."

"And with that drug in his system, it wouldn't take much."

Add in the other bargaining chip Vaughn had been holding over Harris—the house, lien free, to Beth—it had no doubt been plenty.

Jong tapped the other folder against her hand. "These are the toxicology results on Curtis Price."

He traded with Jong and flipped open Curtis's file, looking for scopolamine and finding calcium gluconate and potassium phosphate instead. "I'm not familiar with these."

"Individually, in small doses, neither is deadly. Calcium gluconate is used to counteract too much potassium in a body and regulate heart arrhythmias."

"But together in what does not look like small doses?" He'd read enough tox screens, seen enough syringes to know the one that had injected Curtis must have been full to the brim.

"Together, they mimic the symptoms of a heart attack.

Severe hypertension and heart failure. The potassium phosphate speeds up the effects of the calcium gluconate."

So why was the killer in a hurry? A question for him to consider for Nic.

He had another one for Jong. "Were they injected together?"

"No, they actually can't be mixed. Let me show you." She grabbed a petri dish off the counter behind them, set it on her desk, and picked up the syringes.

Cam took a step back, still not over every horror movie he'd seen as a kid nor the creepy vibe of the place. But when Jong added the second liquid, he peered over her shoulder, intrigued by the reaction that was happening on the plate. Unlike oil and vinegar, these two liquids combined to form a solid. "That's what happens in the body?"

She set the syringes aside. "In the heart. We found one twice that size in Curtis's."

Cam whistled. No wonder it looked like a damn heart attack. "So that's why there were multiple puncture marks?"

She nodded. "Side-by-side, in the mouth."

Cam rested back against the counter, as he worked out what Vaughn and his henchmen must have been thinking. Normally he'd do that with Nic, but without him here . . . "Did they think these drugs, either in Curtis or Harris, wouldn't be detected?"

"We wouldn't have found the drugs in Curtis without the autopsy and full tox screen that Attorney Price ordered."

"But you would have found the scopolamine in Harris's system?"

"Not necessarily. That was clearly a suicide. If the FBI hadn't already been looking at him in connection with another matter, we probably wouldn't have run a tox screen."

So had Vaughn known by then that Harris was working for them? Or not yet? By the sound of it, the latter. Or maybe Vaughn just didn't care? Or didn't think the drugs could be traced? Vaughn didn't shy away from threats, and he was good enough to cover his tracks. Was Cam's team better? He knew two hackers who could find anything.

"Can I get copies of those files?" Cam asked.

"These are yours." Jong slapped both in his palm again.

"Thank you. And you'll let us know if you find anything else."

"Of course. I'll ring you both."

Jong walked him back out to the lobby. "Please tell Attorney Price his father's body will be released by the end of the week."

That took the excitement out of the leads a bit. "I'll do that."

Outside, he stopped next to Nic's truck and took a picture of each tox readout. Faster than fighting with auto-correct over the spelling of drug names. That done, he opened the secure call app Jamie had loaded on all their phones and dialed Lauren.

She answered on the first ring. "We're probably going to be late getting to Gravity." They'd planned a meetup there tonight. Out from under the watchful eyes of Vaughn's spies and with the added benefit of beer. Thank fuck.

And Cam would need it to soften the blow he was about to level on Lauren. "I'm about to make you later." She groaned, and Cam could picture her falling dramatically back in her chair. He laughed, then asked, "Jamie in there with you?"

"Yup."

A click, the blast of background noise, fingers striking keys, then a "Hey, brother."

"Coroner found drugs in both Harris's and Curtis's systems. Sending you tox screen results now."

Cam lowered the phone, inserted the pictures in a new text to them both, and hit Send. Twin *dings* sounded on the other end of the line as he brought the phone back to his ear. "We're looking particularly at the scopolamine, the calcium thing, and the phosphate thing."

"Real precise there, buddy," Jamie said.

Lauren was already ahead of them both. "Vaughn's not stupid enough to purchase them himself. He'd have paid or leveraged someone. We'll run it against the segmented lists Nic had us create. This will narrow them."

"Start with whether they were in evidence lockup, and if so, who had access and when. Focus on FBI and USAO."

"On it," Lauren confirmed.

"You think it's Bowers, don't you?" Jamie asked.

Cam fucking hated to think it—that Nic's own boss had had a hand in his father's death—but it would explain the intense reactions, the increasing desperation, and his single-minded focus to crater this case. "I think Vaughn has him by the balls, and I want to know why."

———

Cam fished the last glass out of the dishwasher, set it on the bar towels with the others, then lifted the bar flip for Eddie to roll through a keg. "Whatcha got there?"

Eddie grinned, smile bright in his light brown face. "Your favorite, as I hear tell it." He shuffled the keg under the taps, moved the hand truck out, then crouched, pompadour of jet-black hair just missing the back bar lip as he reached back to hook up the keg.

"Imperial?" Cam asked.

Eddie straightened, wiping his hands off on his Coast Guard tee. Another stain added to the streaks across his six-pack visible through the skintight cotton. "Finish drying those"—he nodded at the upside-down pints collecting condensation—"and I'll give you a taste."

"Fuck yeah."

"One for me too," Lauren called from the other side of the bar where she and Aidan were pushing tables together.

"Me three," Aidan added, with Mel chiming in, "Make that four." Jamie asked for water, and Cam filled him a glass from the sink while Eddie filled pints. On the last glass, Cam's, Eddie paused. Palm resting atop the tap handle, his dark eyes sparkled with mischief. "There's something else I should get you a taste of, but Nic'll kill me."

"My boss first, you second," came a voice behind them, sharp enough to cut glass. Nic stormed in, jacket bunched in one hand, yanking his tie loose with the other.

Eddie had a pint of the pilsner ready for him by the time he reached the bar. "Drink."

Nic grabbed it and chugged, the beer snob guzzling his precious liquid gold. That good a day, then.

"It's like I don't even know you." Eddie shook his head with exaggerated disgust.

Cam laughed. "You win your motion?"

"Of course I did." Nic lowered the half-empty glass. "You got something to nail Bowers?"

"Of course I do," Lauren chirped from where she sat at the table.

"Good, because if his ass isn't nailed to the wall by the time this is all said and done, I'm going to—"

Eddie slapped a hand on the bar. "Wait! Let me get out of the room before something you say becomes not privileged."

"You taught him well," Aidan said.

"No," Nic replied. "He just slept with half my law class."

"And a few of those prosecutors too. What can I say, men in suits are my crack." Consistent with the man who seemed to have condoms stashed everywhere. Stretching over the bar, Eddie yanked Nic's tie the rest of the way off, laughing, then shoved it into Cam's palm. "But don't you worry, yours is one suit I never touched." He shook his ass as he shimmied out from behind the bar to raucous laughter.

Even at his expense, Cam appreciated that Eddie's joke had loosened the stubbled jaw on his favorite suit.

But it wasn't enough to turn all of Nic's anxiety off. "We set on extra security?" he asked Eddie before the brewmaster escaped.

"Yep. Team members are going to chip in this week and weekend. And those three"—Eddie waggled a finger at Mel, Jamie, and Lauren—"double-checked and updated the security system. We're set." He held out a fist for a bump. "Taste your brew and leave me notes."

"Thanks, buddy," Nic said, bumping back.

Eddie disappeared down the hallway and Cam came around the other side of the bar, glass in hand.

"Your brew? Or my brew?" At home, between the pages of a romance novel he'd snagged from his mom in Boston, Cam had preserved the airplane napkin Nic had given him there, on it a drawing of the logo for Gravity's Fighting Boston Irish Stout. A new imperial brew formulated with Cam in mind.

The mention of it now dissolved more of Nic's tension and drew him closer, an affectionate, sexy smile sneaking out. "Wouldn't you like to know?"

"Okay, lovebirds." Lauren strode past on the way behind the bar for a top off.

"Was that you and Agent Cole I saw taking a coffee break together this afternoon?" Nic asked.

"Maybe it was." She held a pinky to the corner of her mouth, waggling her brows, oblivious to the foam on her top lip, which destroyed any semblance of evil mastermind.

Nic wasn't buying it either, looking like he might object, and Cam, realizing he hadn't brought him up to speed, laid a hand on his back. "She chose those words deliberately. Let the woman work."

Nic raised a brow. "She's playing him?"

Cam directed him toward the tables. "I think so despite the whole failing at Dr. Evil thing."

"Where's Moore?" Nic asked, as they claimed their chairs.

"Dinner with the mayor and DEA's deputy admin," Aidan answered.

"Do we know what that's about?"

Cam had a speculative answer, but then he lost it, whatever he was going to say flitting away as Nic stretched an arm across the back of his chair. It wasn't anything new, but it was something normal after forty-eight hours full of abnormal. Until that moment, Cam hadn't realized how badly he'd needed that too. He'd been so worried about Nic, so focused on doing whatever he could to keep Nic grounded and to move the case along, that he'd barely taken the time to breathe himself. They'd been so deep into Attorney Price and Agent Byrne mode that Nic and Cam felt too far away. So if he lost his thought, took an extra moment to lean back into the warm comfort of Nic's arm and pretend everything was normal, Nic and the rest of the team would have to forgive him.

Nic, watching out for him, tapped his outer shoulder, bringing him back to the convo just as Aidan was saying they'd catch Moore up in the morning.

"All right," Nic said. "So what'd I miss between the interrogation and now? You got something on Bowers?"

"Let me start with toxicology." Cam grabbed the two folders from the center of the table. "We got results back from Jong. She rushed Harris's."

Another smile. "Finally, a break."

"More than that." Cam handed him Harris's folder first. "Harris was given a drug that made him prone to sugges-tion." He handed over the second folder. "And your father was injected with two different drugs that when combined made his heart blow up, literally."

Nic flipped open each folder, scanning the reports, before he tossed them back on the table. "They trace back to Vaughn?"

Mel shoved another file across the table, SFPD's crest printed on the front cover. "Last year one of Vaughn's thugs was accused of date-raping a woman he picked up in a club. Scopolamine was found in her system."

Nic's eyes flared icy hot. "And the asshole is still a free man?"

"The charges were dropped. Erased, in fact." Mel nodded at the folder. "That file isn't supposed to exist."

And yet here it was, which was why Mel was the best at what she did on and off the books.

"The arresting officer received sizable but not triggering wire transfers from an offshore account." Lauren slapped a bank record down on top of the files, and Nic drew the stack closer, riffling through the documents.

"Do we know where he got the drugs?"

"Probably a dealer on the club circuit," Mel said.

"You got enough for warrants?" Cam asked.

Nic closed the file, tucking the bank records inside. "Yes, on the goon and probably on Vaughn too, especially taken together with the reconveyance to Beth."

"He recorded it, today after the interrogation," Aidan said. "Over the counter to make sure it hit the record by close of business."

"Wow," Nic scoffed. "He's just flaunting it now."

"Is he?" Cam turned slightly toward him. "If he says he's just helping out his niece, what looks worse, to hold it now or record it?"

"Fair point," Nic conceded. "He's only doing what he told us he would."

"But you were also right in the interrogation," Cam said. "We need to prove it's not his normal course of business."

"I'll cycle back through Vaughn's laptop," Lauren said. "Look for others."

"Ghosts, too," Jamie said. "And I'll also run a search through land and corporate."

As they techno-babbled back and forth, Nic shifted in his chair, knees bumping Cam's. "Why did you want to start with the tox results? And I'm still waiting for the nail in Bowers's coffin."

"Sheldon and Amy over there"—he jutted a thumb at Jamie and Lauren, got two middle fingers in return—"were also segmenting lists like you suggested for those with any pharmaceuticals connection."

"You found a connection to the drugs Curtis was injected with?"

Cam looked to Mel, who slid another SFPD file across the table. "The new SFPD chief is much more helpful than that old guy."

"Thank fuck," Aidan huffed.

Nic opened the folder, then tilted his head a moment later, brows drawn as he scanned the charge sheet. "This is a manslaughter case. Wrong drugs administered by a health care professional."

Cam understood his confusion; he hadn't immediately seen the connection either. "A manslaughter case your boss yanked from SFPD last week."

"Chief's likewise none too fond of Lou Bowers," Mel said.

Nic rapidly flipped pages, the crease between his brows deepening. "But this case isn't on our docket. It wasn't even discussed in our weekly status meeting."

Cam held his hand out to Aidan, who put a stack of photos in them. Cam spread them out in front of Nic. "Those nails you requested. Plural," he said with a wink. "Bowers wasn't after the case. He was after the evidence."

The pictures showed Bowers at the evidence locker downstairs after hours, carrying out the box of evidence SFPD had sent over, including an insulated cold container on top.

"The log still shows the box and vials as there," Cam said. "Bowers never intended to bring a case. No one would go looking for it."

"Did he think we wouldn't see this?"

"He tried to wipe the video," Jamie said. "I found it."

"It's on a flash drive in the safe in your office," Cam said.

Nic stacked the photos slowly and set them atop the folders on the table.

Then he sat back in his chair, thumbs tumbling, mind no doubt racing through all the scenarios that had run through Cam's head earlier when he'd seen the video. Had Bowers actually been the one to kill Curtis? At least that was where his investigator's brain had gone.

But Nic's had zeroed in on the question he needed answered most. "What does Vaughn have on Bowers? Because this"—he gestured at the stack—"is almost the complete story. Someone give me the fucking hammer."

"Witness tampering," Mel said.

"What?" Nic exclaimed. Only Cam's hand on his knee kept him seated.

"He was an up-and-coming AUSA. Needed to win a big case to seal his promotion. There was a witness for the defense that cast doubt on his case, on the charging officer. The witness changed their tune."

Lauren placed a balance sheet on the table. "Right about the time Bowers made a significant outlay of cash."

Nic recognized the entity name from the deeds they'd seized. "To Vaughn."

Cam nodded. "That's why we didn't find a deposit in Bowers's account. It was a withdrawal."

"Vaughn's had him by the balls ever since." Nic propped his elbows on the table, face in his hands. Cam barely heard Nic's curse, but Nic's misery when he dropped his hands was impossible to miss. "I have to take this to DOJ." Nic was nothing if not a loyal officer of the court, of justice. This was the highest betrayal.

And Aidan was asking him to wait. "Not yet, Price."

"Talley," he growled.

"Aidan's right," Cam said, and Nic's angry gaze whipped to him. "You've all but proven Bowers is a carrier pigeon for Vaughn. Let's use him to feed Vaughn the info we want him to have and also use him to confirm who the moles are in our offices. That witness tampering isn't going to go away. You can spring it anytime—at the right time— when we need it."

"But he could tamper with other cases in the meantime."

"I checked the docket," Aidan said. "Nothing of any interest to Vaughn that could be affected. And Bowers is too busy playing politics or covering his ass to even try cases right now."

"He's on the board," Cam said. "But he's our pawn now. We determine how and where to move him."

Nic finally cracked a grin. "Didn't know you liked chess, Boston."

"I fucking hate it," he admitted. "But 'we determine where to bury the casket' seemed a little too on the nose."

Nic's laugh was music to his ears as were the words that

followed. "Okay, the pawn is ours. Let's use him. But there's still another piece on the board we can't forget. Maybe even the queen."

"Who's that?" Cam asked.

"Rebecca Wright."

Cam startled at first, surprised at hearing her name come up again.

"From the case last April?" Aidan said, likewise surprised.

But Cam had shaken his off, catching on to where Nic was headed.

Rebecca had been the leader of the heist crew Cam had gone undercover to infiltrate on the Kristić case, and there had been a series of tests he'd had to pass to prove his skill and loyalty, including . . . "The flash drives I stole from AD Moore's condo. It was a job for Vaughn."

"Knowing how Vaughn operates," Nic said, "he would have had someone else contact her. Deliver the order. What if it was Bowers?"

ELEVEN

Nic held the door open for the departing crowd, Cam carrying a case out for Lauren while Eddie, Aidan, and Jamie talked basketball. Nic expected Mel to be on their heels but only heard the echo of her stilettos from afar. He followed the *click-clack* back into the tasting area, finding Mel behind the bar, pulling a pint of Belmont Red Ale for herself. A pint of Alto Pils was already waiting for him.

He climbed onto a stool, a rare chance to sit a spell on this side of the bar. "Thank you again for your help on this."

She took a long draw of the ale, humming pleasantly.

"You should have said that one was your favorite."

She peered over the rim of the glass. "And you should have expected I would help. I need to see this one to its conclusion."

"Because you started it while you were at the Bureau?"

"Vaughn's been skirting the law for too long, compromising federal employees and cases, manipulating people down on their luck. Working for an honest company now, for an honest family who had to claw their way back from nothing, only makes me want to shut him down more. And that asshole boss of yours."

"No arguments there." Nic held his glass out for a clink.

She tapped back and took a sip. "Got some more information on our other mystery too."

"Nicolette Sare?"

"It took some digging. She's not on any social media, and while she's got a college transcript, there are no associated pictures." Mel sat down her glass, withdrew her phone, and after a couple taps, slid it across the bar, under Nic's nose. "Aside from her North Carolina driver's license photo, this is the only other picture of her I could find." She pointed with her French-tipped nail to the figure in the background. "That's her."

It was a picture of a martial arts studio in a promo article about an upcoming tournament. The picture's focus was on the studio owner and tournament chair in the foreground, the students practicing in the background blurry. The only female in the group, Nicolette stood taller than at least half the men and something about her was familiar, though without a clear picture of her face, he couldn't place her or what had made him think that. What he did clearly see, even in the blurry picture, was the color of her belt.

"She's a black belt?"

"Expert rank," Mel confirmed. "Though I can't say which level just from the picture."

"Still sounds impressive." Turning back to the picture, he spread his fingers to enlarge the image. And only made it blurrier. "Is she blond in this picture? She was a brunette in the DMV photo."

"And five-foot-four, which that woman most definitely is not."

"Her documents are fake," Nic surmised. "Witness protection?"

"Or deep cover, or military intelligence if she's in Jacksonville."

"Any of those are a possibility. Or she could be hiding from someone."

Mel drained her glass, waited for Nic to do the same, then carried them over to the sink. "I've got a voicemail in to the studio owner, but he hasn't returned my call. Put a call into the Marshals as well."

"I'll check again with naval intelligence." He drummed his thumbs on the bar, turning over the questions this latest news prompted. "If this person is hiding, why the hell is she calling me?"

"When was the last one?"

"Yesterday morning."

Mel's gaze shot to him, brow raised. "They started again?"

"Right as news of Curtis's death broke. Nothing suspicious there."

Rounding the bar, Mel propped a heel on the bottom rung of the stool next to Nic's, bouncing her foot as she contemplated. "Do you think this person across the country works for Vaughn?"

"Aside from the timing, that seems like a stretch, especially if she has a life there in Jacksonville. But it also seems like too much of a coincidence. They're connected somehow."

"Through your father and that offshore account."

"I agree. We just have to figure out how."

"Figure out what?" Cam said, strolling back into the tasting area.

"Who those *Unknown* calls are originating from," Nic replied, arm out for Cam to slide in next to him. "And how they're connected."

Cam sidled up next to him, fitting perfectly to his side. "A threat?"

"I hope not. We have enough of those already."

Conversation paused with the vibrating of Mel's phone on the bar top.

She picked it up, tapped the screen, and a sly smile tipped up the corners of her mouth. "Speaking of threats"— she dropped the phone in her pocket—"my husband wants me home."

"He that stupid?" Cam asked.

Nic couldn't agree more. Mel was the last person on earth he'd threaten. He liked his balls, thank you very much.

Mel's sly smile morphed into a full-on smirk. "Oh, he's not stupid at all."

"Aidan rule!" Nic mock-protested, while Cam pretended to be Lauren, hands covering his ears. "Don't want to know."

She sashayed toward the exit, laughing, and once they heard the entry door click shut, the keypad's red light glowing down the hallway, Nic nudged Cam around to his front and between his knees.

"You sure piped down from when you first came in here." Cam looped both arms around his neck. "Thought you were going to tear the bar apart."

"That's about how I felt then." He grasped Cam's bare forearms—warm, muscled, and solid, the dark hairs prickling his fingertips. He never wanted to let go. "Closer now."

"Closer?" Cam's voice dropped an octave.

Nic felt that kind of closer too. They hadn't had much time for foreplay lately. He missed it, wanted to draw this out a little longer. And to celebrate a small victory here at the end of a day full of ups and downs. "Closer to nailing Vaughn and Bowers. To ending this." He tightened his hold. "This could work, Cam. I've been playing at confident, bluffing, but I believe it now. We've got leads on all fronts. I just need the evidence, then I can put charge sheets in front of the grand jury. I can taste the indictments."

Cam inched closer, elbows dipping. "If I get you the evidence, and we end this, then what happens?"

Nic coasted his hands up, over the rolled cuffs of Cam's sleeves, over his shoulders, to his neck, fingers teasing the ends of his hair. "We move on with the rest of our lives."

Cam likewise wove his hands into Nic's hair, playing along with a sexy smile. "And what life is that?"

Wanting to play, to keep drawing this out, Nic waited until he was an inch from Cam's lips, the agent drawing him in, then slipped off the barstool and ducked under Cam's arm. Grinning, arms spread, he was far too proud of his far too simple maneuver, but he felt lighter than he had in days. He was going to enjoy this while he could.

Cam laughed even as he cursed. "Fucking SEAL."

Rushing back into his arms, Nic ate up Cam's infectious laughter, swallowing it in a kiss and letting it fill his insides with warmth and love. Tasting victory. Maybe, just maybe, happily ever after was within reach despite it seeming so far away forty-eight hours ago.

Cam had unfastened half his shirt buttons by the time

Nic came back to his senses, remembering the future he wanted to show his boyfriend. He slipped his hold again, drawing a frustrated growl from Cam. "Worth it, I promise." He grabbed Cam's hand and tugged him toward the distillery. "Come with me."

They wove through the first room of big silver tanks and into the second cooler one, to the back where he and Eddie had made extra room between the stout tanks.

"You making wine now?" Untangling their hands, Cam circled the four-stack of barrels that were racked in the middle of the aisle over the drainage grate that ran the length of the distillery. He crouched on the far side, running a hand over a barrel head. "Or better yet, whiskey?" He glanced up at Nic. "These are whiskey barrels from Ireland."

"Nah, someone else has that whiskey covered." He winked, and Cam groaned, tapping his head against the steel hoop on the end.

"You just had to go there, didn't you?"

"Of course I did." He pointed at the metal workbench and wall-mounted shelves behind Cam. "Hand me the thief?"

Standing, Cam looked back and forth between him and the workbench. "The what now?"

"The big metal baster thing."

"Why the fuck didn't you just say that?"

Nic rolled his eyes. "A glass too, please," he said, then went to work, slowly twisting out the bung. He wanted to do this carefully so as not to waste any. When Cam appeared at his side, thief and glass in hand, Nic held him back with a hip. "It could bubble out, so stay back a little." Cam's hand on his ass didn't help his concentration, but it fell away once Nic got the barrel open and a small bit of foamy head bubbled out, filling the air with yeasty, hoppy aromas.

"It's beer," Cam said, voice full of wonder.

Taking the glass and thief, Nic sucked up a sample big enough for two and deposited it in the glass. He balanced the thief on the adjacent barrel, then lifted the glass, examining. It was dark in color, smooth and thick in texture, and by its rich aroma, only a few months from where he wanted it. He took a sip. Full-bodied, roasted hops, a hint of Kona coffee, a dash of wood smoke, char, and malt, the brew was still a little sharp, but it was well on its way to mellowing out into something smooth and unique. Yes, not too long now.

He held the glass out to Cam. "Tell me what you think."

"Am I supposed to swirl it like wine?"

"Only if you want to look like a hipster fool."

Cam did stick his nose in the glass and take a giant sniff, which anyone who loved beer as much as he did would. "Smells fucking amazing." Readjusting, he took a small sip at first, then face lighting up, a longer draught. Eyes closed, head tilted, he swallowed slowly, savoring it.

It was all Nic could do not to run his tongue up the side of his neck and over his bobbing Adam's apple.

Cam righted his head and opened his eyes, the darkness swirling with unconcealed appreciation and pleasure. "Nic, this is the best fucking stout I've ever tasted." That meant a lot coming from an Irishman. Cam took another longer gulp before handing the glass back to Nic. "The whiskey barrels give it a wicked taste."

"Finish," Nic said with a wink. He'd teach Cam the proper terminology eventually. In that future he was starting to believe in. The one where he closed the case against Vaughn, bottled his special brew, and inked his left hip.

A hand waved in his face. "Finish what? When?"

Nić shook his head, chuckling, as he mentally tallied the years terminology lessons would seemingly take. Years he'd be happy to spend with this man. "It's not done yet." He pointed to the barrels, saving the lesson for later. "It still has a little aging to go in the barrels, then in the bottles. I'm hoping to have it ready for St. Patrick's Day."

"Which stout is this? It doesn't taste like the Gravity ones I know."

"Because it's yours. Fighting Boston Irish Stout." When Cam didn't say anything, Nic filled the silence with more words, carrying on as he returned the glass and thief to the workbench. "Danny had the barrels brought over from the Jameson distillery. I thought it appropriate. It's your stout, an imperial, but also our family's, a little of all of us in a way. We all had a—"

Hand on his shoulder, Cam spun him around, cutting off his words with a thief of a kiss—stealing his breath, his heart, his whole world. He could take it all as long as Nic got to spend the rest of his life tasting his beer on Cam's lips. He'd never tire of the taste, especially this one. His best beer.

Their beer.

"You like?" Nic mumbled between snatched breaths.

"Yes, I fucking like." Mouth drifting over his jaw, down his neck, Cam forced his head back, exposing his throat to tongue and teeth while his fingers worked open the rest of Nic's shirt buttons. "And I'm going to show you how much right now." Nic groaned as warm hands glided up his torso, chasing away the chill of the cool distillery. Cam pushed the shirt off his shoulders, pressed a thigh against his erection, and skirted his lips over the shell of his ear. "I love it so much I'm going to bend you over those barrels and fuck you."

Knees weak, Nic flailed for the workbench behind him. Cam held him up instead by his ass cheeks, hauling him in and grinding their cocks together. "You like?"

"Yes, I fucking like," Nic moaned, mirroring Cam's earlier words, though with a truckload more desperation that he wasn't the least bit embarrassed about. He was, however, going to be embarrassed if he came in his pants like a teenager, and at the rate they were going, snatching kisses and touches amid the rough rocking of their hips, that embarrassing conclusion was fast approaching. He needed to get Cam moving faster. One surefire way to do that. "You gonna talk or act?" he challenged, purposely picking an argument.

Sure enough, Cam stepped back, dark eyes blazing with lust and competition. "Says the man who talks for a living."

Nic pushed off the workbench, closing the distance between them again. "Not seeing the man of action."

Cam grabbed him by the belt. "I'll show you action."

The race to shed each other's clothes was on. By the time they were done, naked, heaving, and hard, Nic was braced over a barrel, hands wrapped around either end, legs spread wide, ass inviting. He grinned over his shoulder as Cam ripped into two packets of lube. "And you were prepared."

"Snagged them from your office before you got here." He emptied the packets into his hand, rubbed his palms together, warming the lube, then took himself in hand, stroking as he stalked back over. He slid his other slick hand down Nic's crack, stretching and teasing his hole.

Nic's grin died on a groan. "Oh fuck."

Cam leaned over him, warm body and hot breath all around. "In a minute, baby, I promise." He continued to tease, to open him up, in time with his other hand shuttling up and down his cock.

Nic rocked his hips with the rhythm, riding back on Cam's hand and fighting to keep the tension in his arms. He had to. Otherwise, he'd tip this end barrel and the others would go rolling off their racks as well. Dominos. Like the senses connecting his body to his heart, falling at the smell of them wafting together with the beer, the hot heat of bodies and sweat against the cool air, the sound of Cam getting him ready, the feel of his fingers inside him, the expectation of more. "Please, Cameron."

"Yeah, baby, you're ready."

Cam's hand disappeared, replaced by something infinitely better, cock stretching him wider and filling him full. Pain gave way to pleasure and Nic hung his head, groaning in satisfaction. Cam's echo of the same boomed behind him. A slick hand landed on Nic's left hip where it belonged, as Cam guided him, picked their rhythm back up, then played it faster, going harder. This wasn't one of those fucks where they nipped and kissed and savored the connection. This was action, just like Nic had wanted tonight.

In control of their actions, their world, together. The both of them racing ahead after two days of clearing roadblocks, work and otherwise.

"Why haven't we done this before?" Cam asked between grunts.

"Done what?"

"Fucked back here in the distillery."

"Didn't have the barrels before."

Cam reached around, grabbing Nic's dick with his warm, slick hand. "Then I'm even more excited about my beer." He bit his shoulder and Nic had to fight again not to collapse. "Hope it's a regular feature."

Nic laid a hand over Cam's other one on his hip, their fingers tangling. "I plan for it to be, for a long time. If you'd like that."

He wasn't just talking about the beer.

Cam followed, judging by his sharp inhale and the pounding in Nic's ass that ratcheted up in intensity. Cam's hand under his slid around his torso and up, until it softly circled his neck, angling his head around.

Dark, hooded eyes bored into his. Yeah, he got it. Cam's answer was in his eyes, in his kiss, in the taste of love mixed with stout, and in the "Yes, I like," he whispered in Nic's ear as they came together.

TWELVE

The next morning, Nic left Cam with a kiss on the sidewalk in front of the Federal Building. Cam had offered to accompany him to Dennis's office but dealing with his father's estate was a purely legal exercise. An exercise that hinged on the outcome of their case against Vaughn. Nic had asked Cam to spend his morning on the latter instead. That's where Nic needed him most right now.

Hailing a cab, he slid in, gave the driver the intersection nearest Dennis's office, then spent the drive down to Financial typing an email to Eddie, giving him notes on the FBI Stout while editing out the NSFW bits from last night. He squirmed in his seat, ass still sore and dick perking back up at the memory of how it got that way. Nic couldn't wait for all this mess to be over, for the FBI Stout to be released, for more nights like last night. Years of them, he hoped, making love with Cam and making plans for their future.

A phantom tingling on his left hip reminded him of another plan he needed to make. He jotted off another quick email to his local tattoo artist, asking to schedule some sessions. It would be a nice surprise for Cam. He hit Send just as the cab reached its destination.

While most of the big law firms filled multiple floors in the downtown skyscrapers, the more specialized practices—defense, family, immigration, estate, the ones that had been in the city for decades—had long ago claimed the older, smaller buildings dotted among the metal giants. Holdouts mostly, owned by the law firm itself, local real estate companies, or by wealthy Bay Area families who'd invested in properties in San Francisco before it had become one of the most expensive places in the States.

Truth be told, Nic preferred the older buildings. They were architecturally distinct, inside and out. Old San Francisco at its finest, or at least those that had survived the earthquakes and fires. He entered a two-story building with brownish-red masonry work, hand-carved crenellations, and an arched doorway trimmed in patina brass. Bypassing the older-than-time elevator, Nic scaled the stairs to the second floor of office suites.

Dennis's had the best view, away from the street and overlooking the green space between buildings in the back.

The receptionist greeted him kindly and gestured for him to take a seat in one of the waiting room chairs. Through the glass wall, Nic spotted Dennis at the head of the conference room table, speaking with a woman whose back was to Nic. She had silvery white hair, thick and beautiful, and beside her was a younger woman with blond hair who he guessed was her daughter. On the other side of the daughter, back ramrod straight, sat a Marine. An officer. The black-and-blue uniform was a dead give-away as was the man's high and tight crew cut and the black-and-white cover on the table, its gold insignia ornament and gold-and-red rope visible above the brim. The woman's son, he presumed, and the cup across the table probably belonged to their other parent, up from the table to use the restroom maybe. A family here to get their estate in order.

"Dominic."

Nic startled at Mary's voice, not expecting her here. She appeared out of the hallway that led to the restrooms, drying her hands. The cup on the table was Mary's? But those weren't her—

He looked back to the conference room at the same time the officer—the major, a gold leaf shining on his shoulder—rotated in his chair. Nic glanced from his shoulder to his face, and if he hadn't been seated, his ass would have hit the floor, the crumbling foundation of his world that had only recently been shored up blown to bits.

The major stood, headed for the conference room door. He looked and moved like a distilled version of the boy Nic had fallen in love with decades ago.

Gone was the slot receiver with crackling energy and shaggy chestnut hair. In his place stood a compact fighting machine. There was no other way to describe this man. Bearing rigid, movements efficient, a hard, combat-honed body the uniform did nothing to hide—solid arms and broad shoulders, a cut torso that led to a trim waist, and muscled legs that strained the seams of his navy dress pants.

But those eyes. While his body had filled out and changed, Garrett Scott's eyes had not. Framed in long dark lashes, catching the morning sun reflecting off the glass, the every-color hazel shimmered and Nic was as captivated now as he had been as a teen.

"Dominic," Mary said from lower at his side, a few steps back.

The fact that he'd stood and moved toward the conference room snapped him out of his daze. Dennis was also up now, rushing past Garrett and over to him.

"What's he doing here?" Nic asked low.

"I think you better come into the conference room," Dennis said.

He said something else too, but his words were drowned out by the blood rushing in Nic's ears.

The two women had turned around.

The older one was Victoria, which made sense as Garrett was here. Her strawberry blond hair had gone white, but her face was as kind as ever, if a bit more wrinkled. She smiled wide, like she couldn't be happier to see him. The younger woman, taller than Victoria, shared her mother's features, but her smile was cautious, guarded, not quite reaching her eyes.

Her eyes.

Not the same warm, sparkling hazel as her mother's and brother's.

Blue, like ice.

Like his.

Everything fell into place.

The *Unknown* calls from Camp Lejeune, home to the US Marine Corps, in which her brother was a major.

The *Unknown* calls that had started when the money Nic's father had been depositing into an offshore account had stopped, the calls resuming again when news of Curtis's death broke.

Victoria and Garrett disappearing completely off the

map twenty-seven years ago. The age of this young woman, if Nic had to guess.

Vanished because Victoria had been protecting her unborn daughter.

From her abusive father. From Nic's father, who'd died. And now they were here, showing themselves to him. Victoria and Garrett, ghosts back from the abyss, and the sister Nic never knew he had.

"Dominic," Mary urged, shaking his arm. "Maybe you should sit back down."

The world snapped into a flurry of motion. Garrett turning to his mother and sister, herding them back into the conference room. Dennis hurrying his receptionist out and closing the doors behind her. Mary grabbing a bottle of water off the reception desk and shoving it in Nic's hands.

Dennis appeared back in front of them. "Nic, if you'll join us in the conference room, I'll explain everything."

Nic saw red, fire prickling the underside of his skin, a sandstorm tearing apart his insides, but his mouth was too dry to utter more than a seething, "You knew."

"I'm your father's attorney, Nic. Not yours."

Shaking off Mary's hand, he guzzled back half the water, then threw the bottle aside. While the water had quenched his parched mouth, it did nothing to douse the betrayal, hot and bitter, coursing through his veins.

This man was supposed to be his mentor. Someone he considered a trusted colleague and friend. He took a step closer, getting in Dennis's face. "You knew I had a sister and you didn't tell me!"

"Nic—"

"We've been in the local bar together for years."

"I urged Curtis to tell you, but he thought they'd be safer if no one knew, including you."

Safer.

Fuck!

There was another Price heir now. Another point of leverage for Vaughn to press, either directly or against Nic.

Nic stepped back, turned, and covered his face with his hands, hiding a moment from this new, upside-down reality. He wished like hell Cam was with him, because fuck if he wasn't coming untethered, the past unmooring him from the present, from the reality they'd been building. Their future had seemed right there for the taking last night and now it was hurtling away at warp speed.

A hand landed on his back; it wasn't the one he wanted.

"Dominic, where's Cameron?" Mary asked, as if reading his thoughts. "Do you want me to call him?"

"No, he's at the office." Nic dropped his hands. "Did you know?"

Her eyes could have shot daggers. "How dare you ask me that?"

She was right; how dare he. It was completely inconsistent with their conversation Monday night, with every conversation and shared tear since the day Victoria and Garrett had left. He wrapped an arm around her shoulders and drew her into a hug. "I'm sorry," he mumbled into her hair.

She held him tighter. "If I'd known, I would have told you. You'd keep them safe like you did me."

But they weren't safe. Not since he'd gone after Vaughn, hastening the inevitable confrontation. He hadn't thought there was anyone but trained professionals in the line of fire, and hell, he'd tried to keep them out of it for over a year. Now, though, his sister, Victoria, and Garrett were all targets. All because of his goddamn pursuit of justice.

Fuck, he should've just tapped into his retirement and paid Vaughn off.

Made the problem go away before the gangster ever got wind of this. Maybe he still could. The logical part of his brain knew sharks like Vaughn never truly stayed gone. He'd have paid off a criminal, and whenever Vaughn wanted something—a case swung his way, a charge dropped, an opponent taken legally out—he'd dangle that fact over Nic's head and make him dance. Just like he controlled Bowers. But the protector part of Nic was scrambling, any and all scenarios back on the table. In any event, he couldn't keep them safe as long as they were here, right under Vaughn's nose. He had to get them into hiding.

"Nic." Victoria's soft voice trembled and Nic glanced her direction again. Standing in the conference room doorway, her eyes were shiny with unshed tears. "You look good. Filled out"—her chuckle was watery as she looked him up and down—"but good."

He unwound from Mary, smiling. "So do you, V."

She rushed him the next instant, slamming into his middle and wrapping her arms around him tight. He couldn't help but return the hug. Couldn't help but bury his nose in her hair and inhale the smell that was uniquely hers, the same after all these years.

Three women had raised him, each with a distinct smell stamped into his brain. His mother, until he was six, the fragrance of Shalimar perfume—woody, vanilla, with a hint of floral—so that whenever he smelled Earl Grey tea, the bergamot would trigger a rush of memories, some he was still just becoming aware of. Mary, who he couldn't pin one fragrance on but who would forever be associated in his mind with the aromas of the kitchen, her love poured into every dish she'd ever prepared him. And Victoria, then and now, still smelled like the earth and the sun—comforting warmth personified. She'd only been in his life for three years, but in that time, she'd given him courage, acceptance, and love.

"God, I missed you," she mumbled against his shirt, which was growing damp from the tears she'd let loose. "I thought about you every day."

"We had to stop her going after you multiple times," Garrett said, his voice deeper, richer, than it had been at eighteen. "Especially when you visited the base." His sister, almost as tall as Garrett's five-ten, stood next to him, clutching his hand. They'd protected her that long, even when he'd been so close. Now they'd shown themselves, thinking it safe, when it was more dangerous than ever. "She almost made it on a flight to your commissioning in San Diego."

Victoria drew back, glaring over her shoulder at her son. "I wanted to give him his present in person." She was wiping tears from her eyes when she turned back to Nic. "I wanted you to know someone was proud of you. You'd kept me—*us*—safe, so I wanted to give you something to keep your medals and ribbons safe."

"The travel case?" The zippered leather pouch with the US Navy crest on the front had arrived anonymously and he'd carried it throughout his service. Well used and well loved, it now lived in his safe at Gravity, with all his service medals and ribbons safely inside.

Nodding, she hugged him again. "I'm sorry I wasn't able to be there."

"You were." Holding her tight, he met and held Garrett's gaze over her head. "You always were."

They stayed like that, Victoria in his arms, Garrett in his sights, until the other family member present cleared her throat. Garrett looked affectionately over at his sister. "Had to stop this one a time or two as well. She's wanted to meet you for a very long while now."

Taking him by the hand, Victoria led him over. "You saved more than my and Garrett's lives that day. Nic, this is your sister, Lette."

"Mom tells me I'm named after you." The young woman held out her hand. "Nicolette Sare."

Nic slid his hand into hers, impressed by her strong, sure grip. "Or Nicolette Scott."

She smirked, the same one he frequently saw in the mirror. "Or Nicolette Price, if we want to get biological."

Icy fear flooded his veins.

This was his flesh and blood, the sibling he never knew he had, and a fresh target for the man gunning for his family.

————

Out of an abundance of caution, Nic was having the Sares escorted back to their hotel separately. Garrett had left with Mary twenty-five minutes ago, Mel had departed ten minutes after with Victoria, and now Nic was waiting for Eddie to arrive to escort Nicolette. He'd see her to the hotel, then ferry Garrett back to the Federal Building to meet with Cam and fill him in on the latest developments.

Or clusterfuck, more accurately.

How had everything in the dark of last night seemed so

hopeful, so promising, and in the light of morning, utterly dark? And what about the darkness the woman sitting in the conference room had just stepped into? She had no idea the jeopardy her future was now in.

"You should go talk to her."

Nic's eyes remained on Lette as he spoke to Dennis. "Has anyone else seen that will?"

Dennis had read aloud Curtis's will a short time ago, and it had included bequests to both him and Lette—the house and any remaining funds in the offshore account, among other things.

"Only the six of us around that table today, plus Curtis. And I won't file it with probate until you give the go-ahead."

"If Dad's lenders had found out about her, about the offshore account you set up . . ."

"Everything was being monitored. There's no evidence anyone connected knows about her."

Did that include Vaughn? The worst and only one of his father's lenders left, who'd killed Curtis. "My father is dead, I have a sister, the lo—" Nic cut himself off. He was sure that what he was about to say, what Garrett used to be to him, was no longer true.

"Her father is dead too," Dennis said quietly. He stepped closer, clasping Nic's shoulder. "I'm sorry, but I was keeping her safe as best as I could within the bounds of legal ethics."

The rational part of him, sidelined by his earlier anger, understood that. Hell, that same part of him might have done the same. Had done the same in not telling Cam the whole story at first—for his safety. And Cam didn't even need protection. "I'm sorry for snapping earlier. You did what you thought was right. What you could do."

Dennis squeezed his arm. "Thank you for saying so, even if you're still coming to terms with it." They laughed lightly before Dennis grew serious again. "I'll deliver updated probate documents to you by the end of the week."

He disappeared toward his office, and Nic hesitated with his hand on the conference room door. He was eager to talk to Lette, to get to know his sister, but he felt like his awkward teen self all over again, not knowing where to begin. Not wanting to scare her with his intensity or the truth of the situation they were in. He could approach her like a witness—he was good at handling those—but she wasn't a witness. Lette was his sibling. All his life he'd been an only child and now he wasn't. What did he know about being a brother? He absently ran a hand over his hip, the left one, and a frame of reference clicked into place.

Cam.

He'd been around Cam and his brothers in Boston. Witnessed the love and devotion they had for each other and their family, even when they weren't always on the same page. They came together and held each other up when it counted. Cam could pick up a phone, say he needed them here, and Nic had no doubt they'd get on a plane as soon as possible.

But Cam wasn't his only frame of reference. Others clicked into place.

Aidan and Danny, together with their sisters and nieces and nephews, the Talley clan tighter than any he'd known.

Jamie with his sister and utterly devoted to his nieces.

The lengths Mel had gone to for her deceased brother.

Eddie and his other SEAL-team brothers who'd kept Nic alive, who'd hauled his injured ass out of the field and back to safety.

He already was a brother, but now he was a brother by blood too. He could make this work. What all those examples had in common was trust. Which was what he needed to start building with Lette, especially if he was going to keep her safe.

Taking a deep breath, he pushed open the conference room door. Lette jumped a little, twisting in her seat to look over her shoulder. Her blue eyes were still a bit wide, as they had been when he'd vaguely warned of the danger that required the extra security, but they were also determined, bravely holding his gaze. So much like his own.

"Just me," he said, one hand raised as he gently closed the door.

"I'm not usually this jumpy."

He took the seat next to her. "Garrett still jumpy enough for the both of you?"

"My brother cannot sit still to save his life. I don't know how—" She cut herself off, brow furrowed. "I mean, my other brother."

"It's fine, Lette."

"No, it's not, because I did know about you." She reached beneath her shirt collar and lifted out a chain, and on the end of it was something he never expected to see again. "I've always known I had two brothers." She handed him his high school class ring.

He turned it over in his palm, thumb running over the bearcat on each side and the ruby on the top, remembering how he'd shoved it into Garrett's hand the day they'd fled. He felt Lette's gaze on him and he let her look her fill, eyes still locked on the ring as he tried to wrap his brain around the fact he had a sister and she was sitting next to him. "They always said I looked like you—all limbs, blue eyes, same smirk, especially when I was arguing."

He glanced up, smiling. "I'm almost afraid to ask what else they told you about me."

"All good, Nic. And any time we got news of you, through the military grapevine or when you'd give a press conference about a case you won, we'd celebrate for you."

He'd had this whole family, one member of which he didn't even know about, all of whom celebrated for him. Yet without him.

"And your celebrations?" he asked hoarsely, wanting to know about the others he'd missed.

"Garrett's graduation from East Carolina, though I was only five, so I don't remember much."

"Did he play?" Nic couldn't help asking.

She didn't have to ask what he was referring to. "Club level."

Of course Garrett wouldn't have played varsity. He'd been good enough to make almost any team, certainly ECU's, but he would have drawn too much attention.

A delicate hand closed over his forearm. "He wanted to be around more, to help Mom with me. His club team won, all four years."

Nic swallowed hard and looked up, finding nothing but warmth in Lette's blue eyes. No judgment or anger on her other brother's behalf for the dream that had been wrecked. "We had big parties for his commission, Mom's retirement, and when I got into, then graduated from School of the Arts."

"School of the Arts?"

He twirled his class ring around his pinkie, the only finger it fit now, as he listened, fascinated, to Lette telling him about the North Carolina School of the Arts. She'd earned an undergraduate degree in production design and visual effects and a graduate degree in film production. She spoke with such enthusiasm about the school, filmmaking, the technical aspects she'd specialized in, and the job she was interviewing for—the original reason they were out here—that he was sure she was talented beyond what he could understand.

He felt profound sadness that he hadn't been there for each new discovery she'd made, for each decision along the way. Each victory. "I'm sorry I wasn't there for your celebrations."

Her hands, which had been gesturing wildly with excitement, landed back on his arm. "It's not your fault. Mom and Garrett made a choice. When I was old enough, I agreed with it. We're the ones who're sorry."

"I am the last person to question those reasons. I left too, just in a different direction. To sea."

She laughed. "Now that we don't have in common. I get seasick as hell, even on a fucking ferry."

He laughed too at the irony—two brothers, one in the Navy, the other a Marine—and their sister couldn't handle the water. He'd have to introduce her to Jamie. They could sit on shore together while the rest of them took boats out, assuming she wanted to meet his family here and be a part of his life beyond this visit.

"I think it'd be worse," she said, "if we'd known you'd stayed. Or if you left and we had stayed, don't you?"

Fuck yes. No question. "Our father was not a good man."

"But he was our father."

Was.

Curtis Price was really gone. Intellectually, Nic knew that. He'd spent the past few days dealing with the fallout. Some emotional part of him knew it too, had even felt it that night he and Cam had returned home, and again in the conversation with Mary the night before last. But sitting here, with the morning light bright in this conference room, reflecting off his newfound sister's blond hair and blue eyes, the same exact coloring as Curtis's, the truth of the matter sank in completely. It wasn't the lonely truth he'd expected; he wasn't the last Price after all.

"It's sort of a relief," Lette whispered. Nic's gaze whipped back to hers. "Shit, I'm sorry."

"Don't be." This time he reached out but waited with his hand over hers until she nodded, only then lowering it and putting the class ring back in hers. "I feel the same."

"Something else we have in common," she said with a small smirk.

His wasn't nearly so restrained. "Does that make us terrible?"

"No," she said, smirk stretching into a warm smile like her mother's. "It makes us survivors."

Two of them, four counting Victoria and Garrett. The family he'd thought he lost. He wouldn't let that happen again.

———

Nic's text came an hour later than Cam expected it. Nic had estimated ninety minutes, tops, for the meeting with his father's attorney. There'd be the reading of the will, Nic would have to fill out some paperwork as executor, and then it would all be tucked away in a folder at the attorney's office until they received the final autopsy report on Curtis and resolved Vaughn's case. When Nic's terse **Down here now** text finally came through, Cam figured he knew how that meeting had gone.

Not according to plan.

Cam made his way to the lobby elevators. Doors sliding open right away, he counted it a win until Agent Cole called out, "Agent Byrne!" He backed out of the cab, and Cole's hand came down on his shoulder. "Do you have a minute?"

"What can I do for you?" he asked casually.

"I was wondering if there's anything I can do to help on the Vaughn matter." He was too eager to be on this case, just like his suspected boss was no doubt eager for information.

"Keep Agent Hall in caffeine. That's probably the most valuable thing you can do right now."

The junior agent looked crestfallen at first, then he rallied. "Have matters escalated?"

Randomly fishing or did he know something Cam didn't? At the rate at which things were moving on this case, the latter was possible, but Cole of all people shouldn't be in the know before him. Unless it was news Lauren had planted. "Why do you ask?"

"I came up in the elevator with AUSA Price and a Marine."

"A Marine?"

"Yeah, full uniform and everything."

Wariness crept up Cam's spine, some instinct warning him this was not good. Outwardly, he played it cool for

Cole. "AUSA Price was a SEAL. The Marine was probably an old Special Forces buddy."

"Odd timing, don't you think?"

"Big city, don't you think?"

Cole chuckled, playing chastened well. "Guess you're right."

"Sit tight." Cam stepped around him toward the stairwell door. "We'll let you know if you're needed."

Not giving Cole a chance to reply, Cam exited through the stairwell door and hoofed it down to Nic's floor. Striding across the USAO's floor, he said good morning to the staff and attorneys he passed and only hesitated a moment outside Nic's closed door. He'd texted him to come right down, after all.

He pushed it open. And greetings, questions, words, all died on his lips.

Nic stood next to the window talking to a shorter man, the Marine. Cam recognized the uniform from his younger brother's closet, but Keith was nowhere near as highly ranked and decorated as this man. A major. Who was standing closer to Nic than an old Special Forces buddy probably would. Hand on his arm, he gazed up at Nic like they were the only two people in the world.

Jealousy snaked through Cam, and on its heels, the sharp claws of fear and doubt. The shared intimacy between the two was obvious, making Cam feel like an intruder.

"I'm sorry," he said, making his presence known. "I should've—"

Nic's gaze shot to his, and he backed away from the other man. "I told you to come down here, didn't I?" His voice was as terse as his text.

"Yes, but—"

"Close the door, Boston."

Still terse, but Cam read the use of his nickname as a good sign. He'd take all those he could get right now amid the weird tension. He closed the door and stepped farther into the room, intending to introduce himself.

Nic, however, spoke first. "There's been a development."

"On one of our cases?" he asked obliquely, not sure how to proceed with the other man in the room. Nic was speaking like he was somehow involved, yet . . . who was he, exactly? Did he have clearance? He trusted Nic not to compromise the case, but what the ever-loving fuck was going on?

"In a manner of speaking," Nic said.

Not a fucking answer. "Don't lawyer me."

The major huffed a laugh. "He spoke like that as a kid too."

Nic glowered at him. "I did not."

"You so did. Not to your father but to everyone else." A childhood friend, then. "Mom would catch him doing something he wasn't supposed to, and he would dodge and swerve, making any argument he could as to why he shouldn't be in hot water."

"I was developing a skill."

"I hope you're better at that skill than dancing."

The verbal roundhouse to his gut, combined with a lightning strike of clarity to his brain, forced Cam to grab the back of the closest chair.

The last time Nic had danced . . . *Them* . . .

The Marine stepped forward, hand outstretched. "Since Nic's lost all his manners, I'm Major Garrett Sare."

"GS," Cam mumbled.

"I'm sorry?"

Cam glanced at Nic for confirmation and caught just a glimpse of Nic's pained expression before he directed his gaze out the window. He'd take that as a yes, then. One answer, a million more questions.

Cam cleared his throat and shook Garrett's hand. "Special Agent Cameron Byrne."

"You work with Nic?"

"I do."

"We live together too," Nic added.

Garrett's hazel gaze whipped back and forth between them. "You're together?"

Nic stepped away from the window and leaned a hip against his desk. "We are, which is why I called him down here. He needs to be brought up to speed, professionally and personally."

Cam was both comforted and annoyed. "*He* is still in the room," he sniped, then added more civilly, "but thank you." Nic nodded, and Cam returned his attention to Garrett. "You're here about Curtis?"

Garrett looked to Nic for guidance. "Everything?"

"Yes, everything."

"All right, then." There was a Southern twang to his voice. Not like Jamie's drawl—Cam would bet Garrett wasn't raised in the South—but he'd lived there long enough to pick up some of the accent. "I'm here about Curtis and my and Nic's sister."

All thoughts of accents vanished. "Your *sister*?"

"My mother, Victoria, was pregnant when she left Curtis."

So that's why Victoria had finally had enough and

packed their bags to leave that day. She'd had another life to protect.

"On Nic's graduation day," Cam said.

"He's told you?"

"Some of it." Crossing his arms, Cam moved next to Nic, worry of a different sort filtering through his investigator's mind. "So you're here now to collect?"

"Cam," Nic admonished.

"I'm here about *you*." Cam wanted both men to be clear who his priority was in this scenario.

"My father was providing a stipend for my sister."

"The offshore account?"

Nic nodded. "And Nicolette is also provided for in the will."

"I'm not here to collect," Garrett said. "We don't need Curtis's money anymore. Mom never wanted it in the first place."

"But you took it?"

"I did." Not even Cam could deny the heavy regret in Garrett's voice. "To pay for her college and to buy an extra life insurance policy that would pay out if I was killed in combat. I was recruited into MARSOC. That's—"

"Marine Corps Special Operations Command," Cam said. "My brother's a sergeant."

"Then you understand how dangerous it is."

"To a degree."

"I had a risky deployment coming up, and Nicolette had just been accepted into a prestigious arts academy. Mom and I had scraped together all our money to pay for it, but we were still short. If anything happened to me, then it would have been a massive shortfall. I didn't want Nicolette's dream to die. So I paid for and insured it the best I could."

"With money from Curtis?"

"He owed Victoria the child support," Nic argued. "Years of it."

"She didn't want to ask for it," Garrett said. "Money never comes without strings. We didn't want to owe him or be connected to him. After the way he reacted when Mom tried to take you, we didn't want him to have some claim on Lette. That's why we never asked until it was necessary. If we could have found any other way, we would have."

"How'd you get Curtis to pay?" Cam asked, still trying to piece together the past. "I can't imagine he did so willingly. You'd been gone almost twenty years then."

"I had pictures of what my mother looked like after he beat her."

"Not to mention an illegitimate child."

"I'm not proud of what I did, but I'm proud of my sister. It was worth it."

"You should have told me," Nic said.

Garrett shook his head vehemently. "I wasn't risking your future either. You'd already sacrificed enough for us."

"You're risking her future now by being here."

"So tell me what the fuck is going on," Garrett demanded. "You're acting like we're in more danger now than when we left."

"You are!"

"Where's your sister now?" Cam asked.

"Back at the hotel with Mom."

"Mel's on them," Nic said, answering his next question. "I told them to stay inside."

"You freaked them out is what you did."

Nic straightened, voice booming. "I'm trying to keep them alive!"

Cam drew closer, laying a hand on his back, calming as much as claiming. "If you're not here to collect," he said to Garrett, "then why are you here?"

"We were here in the area—Nicolette had a job interview—and we saw the news about Curtis. We got the call from Dennis that same afternoon. We gave Nicolette the choice, and she's always wanted to meet her other brother. We thought the coast was clear, that it was safe with Curtis out of the picture."

"Well, it's not," Nic grumbled, practically vibrating.

"I'm gathering that. So tell me why."

"Curtis was in debt," Cam explained. "To some very dangerous people, one in particular who's made threats against Nic."

"And now you've just handed him another Price heir," Nic said. "Another point of leverage he can go after directly or use against me."

"He doesn't necessarily know about Lette yet," Garrett said.

"He'll know as soon as we file the will with probate."

"Which is delayed because of the autopsy." Cam found himself in the unlikely role of peacemaker. De-escalation seemed in order all around. "If we can quickly wrap our case, then no one will be the wiser about your sister until our target is indicted." He turned his attention to Garrett. "When's your flight home?"

"Sunday."

"Okay, we'll keep you and your family safe until then."

Garrett gestured at his uniform. "We're not helpless."

"I can see that, but Nic deeply regrets the way things went down last time." Cam moved closer still to his lover, arms brushing, fingers tangling between them. "I won't let him go through that again."

THIRTEEN

Cam ditched his coat and tie in his office, rolled up his shirtsleeves, and was leaning against the far corner of the room when Nic returned from seeing Garrett out. Cam had a million questions, all battling to get out, but seeing his normally stoic, perfectly put-together boyfriend shut the door and fall back against it like it had been the longest day of his life and it was only noon, the third such day in a row, Cam bit his tongue. He crossed the room and took Nic in his arms. Just as Nic grounded him, Cam wanted to do the same for him, which he did, judging by the way Nic's body sagged against his, arms tightening around him like Cam was the only thing holding him up.

"I've got you," Cam murmured, and dropped a kiss on his temple.

"Just when I thought things were turning our way . . ."

Nic dropped his head on Cam's shoulder, and Cam was sure Nic could feel his heart about to beat out of his chest, equal parts worry at the dejection in Nic's voice, so foreign for him, and adoration, because he let Cam see that, not hiding anything from him, for better or worse.

"One setback." Cam carded his fingers through Nic's hair, more of the sexy gray showing every day.

"Three, if we're counting."

"Stop counting," he playfully chided with a swat to Nic's ass. "Unless it's your breaths, in which case, take a few extra to settle."

Nic took the recommended inhales, plus a few more, then rested their foreheads together. "Thank you."

Cam waited for his eyes to open. "I love you."

"I love you too." Finally, a smile, if an exhausted one, right before Nic brushed his lips over Cam's. It was a slow, gentle kiss, probably the only thing that would be in this already rough-and-tumble day, and Cam let Nic take all that he needed. Cam needed it too—this reminder of their connection, the threads of the rope being reinforced. Cam would hold Nic to his word. Nic hadn't let the rope go for him when Cam had needed him to hold tight, and Cam wouldn't let go now either, nor would he let Nic, or anyone else for that matter, cut through it with a KA-BAR.

Giving him a quick peck, Cam stepped back and nudged Nic toward the table. "Sit and catch me the rest of the way up." Nic grabbed a chair and Cam claimed the adjacent one Nic pushed out for him. "He's Garrett Scott, yes? The GS on your back. Your almost stepmom's son?"

Nic's eyes narrowed. "You looked into it?"

Cam jutted a thumb at himself. "Professional investigator."

"Nosy, more like it."

"About you, yes." He took Nic's blush as a good sign. "I admit I've been looking for GS since April." Nic's brows snapped together, and Cam waved him quiet before he could object. "You can be mad at me about that later, but I didn't get anywhere. Until the pictures of Victoria. Once I had a name, Victoria Scott, I figured GS had to be connected. There were some trace records of her son, Garrett Scott—team pictures, high school ROTC—but then they both disappeared twenty-seven years ago. Right about the time of your graduation."

Nic nodded. "They moved across country, changed their names, hid from my father."

"Until Garrett approached him."

"Blackmailed him. Let's call it like it is."

Well, in that case, if they were calling things like they saw them . . . "You two were in love."

Nic stared at him head-on, a deer in the headlights, some emotion Cam couldn't pinpoint giving Nic's blues a panicked edge. "Cam, I—"

"Let's call it like it is," Cam returned softly. Because that explained the intimacy he'd witnessed between the two men when he'd walked in earlier. "His initials are on your back. If nothing else, judging by your other ink, he was important to you."

Nic pushed back from the table and stood, hand rubbing over his left hip.

Cam worried for a second but there was no limp or other sign of injury as Nic began to pace the length of the room. "Before you, he was the only other man I'd loved." Nic hung his head. "Fuck, I've never told anyone that, outside of Garrett and Victoria, and my father and Mary."

"You've got nothing to be ashamed of."

"It's not shame. More like fear. I was halfway around the world in the Navy, and I was still afraid a mention of them would somehow get back to my father and set him off. That he'd go looking for them if I dared to utter their names. And now with Vaughn . . ."

Cam rose, splaying a hand on Nic's lower back. They'd talk about how to deal with Vaughn, with that fear, in a minute. For right now, though, he wanted to know more about the past, and he sensed Nic needed that out too. "Tell me about him."

"He was everything I wasn't as a kid. I was quiet and reserved. The beanpole dork in the corner who didn't say anything." He flapped one arm and stretched out a long leg. "I hadn't grown into these, and I didn't want to draw attention to my severe lack of coordination."

"For fear of drawing your father's?"

"Every now and then he'd asked why I hadn't made this or that sports team. I never told him I didn't bother trying out. I'd shove my report card under his nose and that usually did the trick."

"Straight As?"

"Usually, except for French, which is why I wasn't vale-dictorian. Another disappointment on Dad's list." He rested against the table edge and Cam sank back into his chair, giving Nic space but also still close, letting Nic know he was there. "Victoria had Garrett when she was very young —his dad wasn't in the picture long—so it was just the two of them for a long time. They were more like best friends than mother and son. She loved him unconditionally and let him be who he was, which was a little wild, a lot flirta-tious, and supremely confident. He was popular, athletic, charming, but also kind and loyal. Open. And always moving, hyper-like."

"I bet they both drew your father's attention."

"Victoria did, the good kind at first. You can't help but be drawn to her. I'm not surprised Vaughn was in love with her. Hell, my fifteen-year-old self was half in love with her, and I'm gay."

"And you were in love with her son."

Nic shivered, like the thought had run up his back and out the branches of the cypress tree tattoo. "Garrett wasn't around the first few months, but then he started working with Victoria over the summer. I remember this party one night, a fundraiser Curtis hosted for the local conservation society, trying to impress Victoria. I wandered outside and found Garrett fucking one of the waiters in the gazebo." Nic's faraway eyes came back to the room, focusing on Cam. "I stood in the shadow of the cypress trees, watching, and I knew then. Accepted it. That I was gay, that I wanted him, and that he was the most gorgeous thing I'd ever seen."

Cam thanked all that was holy for his undercover training. He wasn't sure he'd have been able to keep his emotions off his face otherwise. He shouldn't be jealous; he'd had other lovers too. Nic's affair with Garrett had been three decades ago, and earlier Nic had made clear to Garrett that he and Cam were together. Cam's gut still burned, jealousy roiling with second guesses. Despite what Nic had said, would Cam ever live up to the memory of Garrett? Especially when the memory had come to life again?

Had he made the wrong call committing to San Francisco and Nic instead of returning to Boston? There were other reasons to be here, of course, but without the biggest one, the man he loved, would it be worth staying?

Christ, he thought they were past this, thought he was past this, but doubts resurfaced, loud and nagging. What did he have to offer? A broke FBI agent versus a decorated Marine major and the family he sensed Nic had always wanted.

The squeak of the chair as Nic sat next to him snapped Cam out of his spiral. "How'd it turn to the bad kind of attention from Curtis?"

"He was gone more and more with work, which suited the three of us and Mary fine. He'd proposed, and Victoria and Garrett had moved in. I had a happy life, a happy home for the first time since Mom died. But as Dad's staff grew to love Victoria, he started tearing her down. He couldn't have someone else be the center of attention."

"Physical abuse?"

"Emotional, at first. Snide remarks, cutdowns, controlling her life. Asking her to quit her business. Dictating when, where, and what she could do, most of which she ignored the second he left, but word got back to him and the physical abuse started. First with smaller exertions of power—grabbing her by the arm too hard, dragging her where he wanted her. He had to own her."

The way Nic spat the words, there was nothing small about it, at least in his mind. And so much of his work—fighting for victims' rights—made sense to Cam now.

"Garrett was worried," Nic carried on. "So were Mary and I, more and more so as the abusive behaviors escalated. Then a couple weeks before graduation, Curtis came home unexpectedly. He found me and Garrett together under the cypress trees—dancing, kissing, and half undressed already."

Cam forced down the resurgent sting of jealousy, focusing on his anger at Curtis. He was the reason Nic wouldn't dance with him; Curtis had ruined it for him, associating it with a bad memory in Nic's mind. "Curtis blamed Victoria?"

"He fucking blamed everyone because Lord knows Curtis Price couldn't have a gay son. He already thought me weak. Seeing another man lead me in a dance, kissing me, undressing me, that was the straw that broke the camel's back. She took a hit for me that day."

"And then graduation day happened . . ." Cam could only imagine the two-week spiral of hell that had preceded that final confrontation.

"You know the rest of the story from there. Looking back, she must have known she was pregnant. She wanted to protect her children."

Cam put a hand on his thigh. "Including you, by the sound of it."

Nic swallowed hard and threaded their fingers together, struggling with the memory of one of the worst days of his life. "I finally argued with him that day. Long and loud enough that I got a broken jaw for it. But at least Victoria and Garrett, and Lette it turns out, got away."

Cam squeezed his hand. "I just have one question."

A short bark of laughter escaped Nic's lips, and Cam bumped his knee, smiling. He lowered his other hand on top of Nic's, holding tight. "Why is any of this a regret, baby? Or a mess? That's what you told me the tattoo on your back was about, but I don't get it."

Nic held tighter, nearly cutting off the circulation in Cam's hand. "If I'd held myself back from Garrett, not fallen in love with him, hell, with them and the idea of a real family, or if I'd left sooner, or if I'd called the cops instead of angering Dad more, then maybe they could have stayed and Curtis would have been the one to leave. Maybe we could have made it work—Garrett playing football at San Jose State, me on an academic scholarship at Cal, Victoria getting her business back up and running. But I forced the situation. I forced them to flee. Garrett turned down a full ride to college, Victoria turned her back on her business and hometown, and now, knowing she was pregnant too . . . I forced them to leave the only place they'd ever known with nothing." Pain and regret tore across his face, tugging at the corners of his eyes and mouth, before he looked away.

Cam's heart wanted to beat out of his chest again. Wanted to wrap this man in all the love and kindness he deserved, shield him from taking on the blame he didn't deserve, and make him understand the love he had to offer was not a curse in any way, shape, or form. It was not something to be ashamed of or regret.

Heart trapped behind his ribs, he settled for reaching out and grasping Nic's chin, bringing his face back around. "No, Dominic, love is never a mistake, especially not yours. And be honest with yourself, your father was growing more abusive, even before he found out about you and Garrett. Would you have wanted them there without you? With only your father? And what would have happened to you if you'd stood up sooner? How many more punches would you have taken or Victoria or Garrett for you? What would the cops have done if you'd reported your father? A wealthy, well-connected local businessman. You've worked these cases; you know how limited the options are. And you know they're about the abuser, not the abused or the others in their life, though the abuser makes them think it is. Just like you're doing."

Nic jerked against his hold, the instinct to turn away and hide the truth in his eyes.

"Exactly." Letting Nic's chin go, Cam glided his hand up to his cheek. "You left behind your whole life too, baby. Don't discount that, the sacrifice you made. And in doing so, you saved them and yourself."

Nic nuzzled against his palm. "That's what Mary says."

"Because that woman is smarter than the both of us." He brushed his thumb over Nic's clean-shaven cheek. "Okay, now that we've dealt with the past, how do you want to deal with the present?"

"My top priority is keeping the Sares safe. We get Vaughn indicted and locked up, then I'll deal with the estate and my new insta-family."

"You have a sister."

"Not how I imagined this morning would go."

"I suspect not, but this is good news." At Nic's quirked brow, he chuckled a little, adding, "Present circumstances notwithstanding. Tell me about her."

Nic gave him the highlights of the conversation he'd shared with Lette, his features far more revealing than his words. The morning's tension faded from his frame as he described how his sister's resembled his own. His face lit with pride as he recounted her acceptance into art school. Hope melted the ice in his eyes as he revealed she carried his class ring with her, that she and her mother had tried to see him multiple times on base, that Lette wanted to know him better and was interviewing for jobs out here.

Cam's heart cheered for his lover. Family was important, he knew that better than anyone. But doubts continued to simmer in his belly. Low-level enough to ignore, but they were still there. What did this mean for their future? Was there room for him in Nic's new insta-family? Questions for another time. He needed to be here for Nic; they'd worry about family and the future later, when the possibility of both were secure.

When Nic was done, and Cam had assured him he was doing everything a brother should, he stole a quick kiss on his way to standing. "All right, let's go talk to Lauren. See what other evidence she's found, and if it's enough for indictments."

"It better be. I already called the grand jury for tomorrow morning."

Cam grinned. "Now there's the overly confident Dominic Price I know and love."

Eyes blazing, Nic grabbed his tie and yanked him closer, nose to nose. "There is one thing I stand corrected about. You, Cameron Patrick Byrne, are the most gorgeous thing I've ever seen."

The kiss Nic laid on him chased away Cam's doubts. For now.

FOURTEEN

Idling the truck at the freeway exit, Nic drummed his thumbs on the steering wheel, off rhythm from Pearl Jam on the radio and Cam's off-tune sing-along, but right on rhythm with tomorrow's opening statement running through his head.

Cam reached out, first turning down the music, then cuffing the back of Nic's neck and massaging. Nic closed his eyes, savoring the dig of strong fingers into tight, tired muscles. "You're ready for tomorrow," Cam said. "You've got it."

A horn blew behind them, and Nic opened his eyes, the light green in front of them. "And you?" he asked Cam, as he turned onto the surface street that led to Gravity.

"I'm ready, though I'm still not convinced it shouldn't be Aidan."

"You're not the only agent testifying. El will be up before you, Lauren after. And you're the agent running point on this operation. You've been present both times we questioned Vaughn."

"But I wasn't the first agent on scene at either your father's death or at Harris's."

"You are the agent with the most recent field experience, though."

"But—"

"No more buts."

He swung the truck into Gravity's parking lot, only Eddie's sand-crusted Wrangler left at this hour. He parked next to the main entrance, turned off the ignition, and shifted in his seat. He needed Cam to walk into that grand jury room tomorrow with no doubts about the case they were presenting or about his credibility to present it.

Bowers was right; they didn't have a smoking gun. No murder weapon with Vaughn's prints on it. What they did have was a growing mountain of evidence that pointed to a pattern of behavior, enough to make a case as long as the whole team sold it. Especially Cam. Because if Cam was at his best, Nic would be too. They fed off each other that way. As upside down as the rest of his world was right now, Nic was certain of two things—his place with Cam and his place in the courtroom—the both of them converging tomorrow.

"As well as I know Aidan," Nic said, "I know you better. I know how you're going to answer and I know you can follow me—my moves, my thought processes, any curveballs thrown at you—better than anyone. I have to think fast on my feet in a courtroom; you make that easier."

Cam averted his gaze, one corner of his mouth hitched up in a bashful smile. "Well, okay then."

For as cocky as Cam was ninety-five percent of the time, Nic lived for the other five percent when he could remind

Cam what an amazing man he was. "Don't be nervous. You'll be perfect."

"I'm not nervous. You're ready. I'm ready. So are Moore and Lauren." Cam picked at a shredding piece of vinyl on the truck seat. "I just don't want to compromise this case. I know what it means to you."

Stretching across the console, Nic covered Cam's restless hand, then his lips, saying with his kiss how much he appreciated the sentiment and how much he trusted Cam to live up to it.

Nic reluctantly pulled away as breath became necessary, just as the parking lot lights shifted into late-night safety mode. "We better go. I want to catch Eddie before he leaves for the city." He'd called his teammate earlier and filled him in on recent developments. Eddie was scheduled to relieve Mel on Sare guard duty at midnight. "I've gotta sign some checks too and you can grab a stout."

Cam stole another quick kiss. "You're too good to me."

At the front door, Nic punched in this week's entry code, and the keypad flipped from red to green. He opened the door and winced at Eddie's grunge music, the same that had been playing in the truck, turned way up. Cam picked up singing right where he'd left off while Nic wondered at what volume he'd blow out an eardrum. This was loud, even for Cam or Eddie.

They entered the tasting area and Nic suddenly understood why.

Behind the bar, Vaughn was pulling himself a pint of stout, and on the other side, his two goons sat sprawled at a table. Between them, Eddie wasn't nearly so comfortable, his bulging, muscular arms curved behind him, wrists handcuffed to his chair.

A/V remote in hand, one of the guards lowered the volume. Vaughn turned around, grin smug. "Late night, Dom?"

At his side, Cam drew his weapon, sight trained on Vaughn.

"Now, now, Agent Byrne, we're all friends here, aren't we?"

"Friends don't handcuff friends to chairs."

Nic put a cautious hand on Cam's firing arm, pushing it down. "Eddie's not in any danger."

Vaughn strolled around the bar, taking a long swallow of the beer. "See, Dom knows me well. Of course I wouldn't hurt his friend and business partner." The gangster's photogenic smile turned sharklike. "I'm just using him as leverage."

"Afraid you're wrong there," Nic said before giving Eddie a nod.

A blink later, Eddie was out of the handcuffs and standing, laughing with his arms spread wide. He made a *come-at-me* gesture to the guards, who foolishly did exactly that. Did these idiots never learn?

Toe under the seat, Eddie flipped the chair up into Goon One's face, sending him sprawling back, blood pouring from his nose all over his shiny suit. Eddie caught the chair on the rebound, swinging it against Goon Two's rising shooting arm. The pistol went skidding across the brewery's polished cement floor, and Eddie took a second swing with what was left of the chair, whacking the guy in the exposed ribs and sending him staggering back into his bleeding cohort. Eddie stood among the chaos, laughing, that little bit of crazy Nic had depended on when they were SEALs.

Eddie tossed the wooden leg at Vaughn's feet. "You owe me a chair, Blondie."

Vaughn's brown eyes flickered down and up. "Noted."

"Not a pair of handcuffs he can't get out of," Nic said as Eddie strode over. "Or a bar fight we ever lost." He held out a fist to Eddie.

Eddie bumped back. "They had Ang," he said, referring to their assistant manager. "Traded myself. Figured I'd keep them here for you."

"You figured right. Thanks for that."

"You good here?"

Nic nodded.

"Okay, then I'll go do that errand you asked about." The display he'd put on just now . . . that was why he was on rotating Sare guard duty with Mel. Only Nic's best, most loyal, most deadly people. Eddie clapped his shoulder with a "Hooyah," then disappeared down the hallway, the front door clicking shut after him.

Vaughn paid no mind to his ineffective muscle hobbling around, bloodying up the fucking bar towels. Instead, he walked right up to Nic and Cam, casually drinking his beer. "I like your friends, Dom. SEALs and FBI agents. Sexy."

"What are you here to threaten me with now?" Nic cut to the chase. It was late, and he had a big day of nailing this asshole to the wall tomorrow.

"How did it feel to find out you had a sister? Nicolette Sare, right? Or should I say Scott? Or worse yet, Price?"

Nic's blood ran cold, freezing him where he stood. Same as it had earlier when he'd first seen Victoria and Garrett again, when he'd finally put together who Nicolette Sare was, in Dennis's office.

Dennis.

Was that how Vaughn knew about Lette? Had Dennis betrayed him again and spilled everything?

While Nic was silent, mind whirring, Cam was practically growling. "You'd really threaten an innocent young woman?"

"Innocent," Vaughn scoffed. He set his empty pint on the table by Nic's hip. "She's been siphoning off my money for a decade now."

"Wouldn't you want Victoria's daughter taken care of?"

Vaughn's handsome face transformed into something truly ugly. "Victoria made her decision."

Nic had never seen Vaughn's face look like that before. It did the trick for startling him out of his panic. "You really are despicable."

"I may be." The shrug accompanying the words said *I don't give a fuck*. "I'm also first in line for a piece of your father's assets. I mean to get every penny I'm owed. If you keep delaying the disposition, I will remove the obstacles."

"Nicolette?" Nic bit out.

Vaughn smirked, retreating and wagging a finger at him. "Nuh-uh-uh, Dom. You want me to say that in front of your pet agent here so he can tell the grand jury tomorrow."

Nic suspected he got that news from Bowers. He'd made sure to leave the grand jury call request in view of his boss, testing his theory that Bowers was Vaughn's USAO mole.

"I simply meant I'd take the legal steps necessary to enforce my rights as your father's primary secured creditor."

"You couldn't call him to say that?" Cam said.

"Then I wouldn't be here to see your handsome faces in

person." He stepped forward again, and Cam moved slightly between them, shoulder blocking Nic from Vaughn's advance. Nic didn't object. He wanted Vaughn to understand how united a front he was facing.

Catching on, he raised his hands and backed off. "Let's go, guys," he called to his goons. As they staggered up behind him, Vaughn said to Nic, "The imperial is your best yet. Hope it's around long enough for everyone to enjoy."

A subtle threat but Nic heard it, loud and clear.

———

Cam banged on Jamie and Aidan's front door, careful to avoid the glass panes. If the doorbell worked, he'd use it—less likely to wake the neighbors this time of night—but the ringer had recently died from overuse and the frantic knocking was a much more accurate indicator of their current situation.

Beside him, Nic shined his phone's flashlight on their faces so they'd be visible on the security cameras. Wouldn't want the trained marksmen inside thinking a stranger was trying to break in.

At least that's why Cam assumed Nic was doing it. He couldn't ask, though. Someone was listening.

Lights inside and out flickered on, and Cam watched through the panes as Aidan trudged up the stairs from the ground floor primary. He opened the door, hand raking through his tousled red hair, dressed in a college tee that was two sizes too big and flannel pajamas that were six inches too long—both Jamie's obviously. Cam would have laughed at any other time. Instead, and before Aidan opened his mouth to no doubt complain about the late hour, Cam held up the legal pad on which he'd scribbled **WE'VE BEEN BUGGED.**

As soon as Vaughn had left the brewery, he and Nic had sprung into action, Nic contacting Dennis, him contacting Mel, trying to determine how Vaughn had found out about Nicolette. Mel had confirmed no one saw them come or go, and Dennis had had them listed under fake names in his calendar. Nic believed him, which left only one explanation. A listening device, on their person most likely, possibly their phones, because Vaughn had known bits and pieces of information from multiple locations. Good thing they knew someone who kept a bug sweeper on hand at all times.

Cam flipped over the top sheet, writing out the second objective with the marker he pulled from his pocket. **WE NEED JAMIE AND THE BUG SWEEPER.**

Nodding, Aidan opened the door wider for them to enter. They were gathered in the foyer of the split-level home, trying not to trip over Jamie's scattered detritus, when the man himself called from the bottom of the stairs, "What's going on?"

Aidan spun, finger to his lips, shushing him. Jamie was up the stairs the next instant, long legs eating them up three at a time, but it was too late. To anyone listening, they'd know where he and Nic were. They had to cover.

"This one decided he needed a late-night doughnut run," Nic said, likewise catching on. "And the place near us wasn't good enough. Only the all-night place down the street from you guys would do, so I decided to share the misery."

While Nic talked, Cam flipped pages and brought Jamie up to speed. His best friend's face morphed from concerned to doubly concerned to mission-critical in quick succession.

"Misery loves company," Jamie said. "But I'm not eating doughnuts without coffee, especially at this hour. I'll put it on." He led them up to the main level, but it was Aidan who went into the kitchen, grinding beans and waking up the coffeemaker, disguising the sounds of Jamie rooting around in the desk in the adjacent office area.

"You didn't tell me how Seattle was," Cam said, making conversation to further cover their activities. "I mean, I know you won the game, but otherwise." He dropped the legal pad and marker on the end of the kitchen island for anyone to write on.

"Sunny and beautiful, as usual. I don't understand what all the griping is about."

"Because that's not normal," Aidan said while he scribbled **VAUGHN?** on the legal pad. "Yet somehow every time you go there, the weather's perfect."

Nic nodded and took his turn with the pen and paper. **HE KNOWS ABOUT LETTE.**

Brown eyes widening, Aidan's pale, freckled face blanched even whiter. They'd filled him in this afternoon about the Sares, and if there was anyone who prioritized protecting family, it was Aidan. **MEL?**

EVASIVE MANEUVERS.

Cam had been mid-call with Mel when he'd realized what was going on. He'd told her to treat the family to In-N-Out, their secret code for evac and benign enough for anyone listening to think they were taking the tourists out for a late-night California snack.

"I must bring the sun with me." Jamie returned to their circle by the island, a small screwdriver in one hand, the bug sweeper in the other. He mouthed the word *Phones* and each of them tossed their devices on the white quartz countertop.

Cam affected a laugh. "Despite what a certain Irishman says, the world does not revolve around you, brother."

"Yes, but apparently I can blow sunshine out of my ass." He passed the sweeper over each device—only green lights.

"Earmuffs," Cam objected, both real and for effect, while Jamie made frighteningly fast work of opening and inspecting each phone.

Green.

"Any good recruits?" Nic asked as Jamie swept him up and down. Green.

"Yes, actually. I think I've swung us a point guard who was going to commit to Gonzaga."

He stepped over to Cam next, and Cam clapped his shoulder. "Now that's what best friends are for." The first pass over his front was clear.

"Figured you'd be—" The device vibrated at his collar.

Nic's eyes widened, the red lights from the sweeper reflected therein.

Aidan's grew just as wide, but he was also making a keep-talking gesture. "Figured you'd what?" Cam asked.

Jamie flipped up the collar of his suit coat. "Figured you'd be happy." And from under it, extracted a tiny listening device. None of them were making happy faces.

"One less chance for them to be a spoiler." Jamie held the bug pinched between his thumb and forefinger while Aidan retrieved a mason jar and lid out of a cabinet.

"Fuck, I hope so," Cam said, also hoping that was the last thing anyone heard.

Jamie dropped the bug into the jar, then Aidan screwed on the lid and shoved it into the freezer.

"How the fuck did that get there?" Aidan whipped back around. "And when?"

"Good thing you hate wearing your jacket," Nic said.

"See, my suit aversion pays off." A small silver lining, but Cam was grasping at straws.

"So when were you wearing that jacket?"

Cam leaned back against the island, mentally retracing his steps. "It was in the bag from the dry cleaner this morning, I put it on for the drive in, took it off in my office before going to the conference room, put it back on when I—"

"When you what?" Nic prompted.

"I was coming down to see you when Agent Cole stopped me outside the elevator. Clapped me on the shoulder like this." He brought a hand down on the top of Nic's shoulder, just like Cole had done him, and sure enough, his fingertips skirted Nic's collar.

"It could have been inserted at the dry cleaners," Jamie said.

To which all three of them replied, "It was Cole."

"He's our lead suspect for Vaughn's mole in the Bureau," Cam explained.

"How much does he know?" Aidan asked.

"I went down to Nic's office." He rotated on his hip toward Nic. "I had the coat on when we talked with Garrett."

"You weren't wearing it when I came back up from walking him out," Nic said.

"That's right. I ditched it in my office before we went into the conference room and discussed the actual details of the case."

"And on your way home? Or to here?" Aidan asked. "You came in here wearing it."

"We spoke generally about the case on the way to Gravity," Nic said. "But nothing specific."

"And we've been playing chalkboard"—Cam nudged the legal pad—"ever since we realized we were bugged."

"Good." Aidan rested against the opposite counter next to Jamie, who threw an arm over his shoulders. "It's as contained as it can be."

"Except for the fact Vaughn knows about my sister now."

A surge of guilt slammed into Cam. Vaughn knew about Nic's sister because he'd been wearing a bug. He hadn't thought to check after Cole stopped him. Honestly, and obviously, he hadn't given the double agent enough credit. "Nic, I'm so—"

"Not your fault, Boston. Aidan's right, it could have been worse. And we've got Vaughn on tape now, making threats, if veiled. We need to get hold of that audio."

"Do we need to get extra protection on your family?" Jamie asked.

"I don't think so," Nic said, eyes still on Cam, seeking confirmation, which he gave with a nod. "Mel and Eddie are both with them now. Garrett's MARSOC." Jamie's eyes went round as saucers. "And Lette's a black belt." Aidan's widened to match.

"Badass runs in the family," Cam summarized.

"We should still move them into a safe house," Aidan said.

"No, not if Cole—" Nic started.

"Mobile Command," Cam said, referring to Aidan's brother's former bachelor-pad yacht that Mel had converted into her own private command center. "It's secure, mobile, and stocked."

"It's the best option we've got," Aidan said.

"Do it," Nic agreed, and Aidan and Jamie went into motion, Jamie reassembling phones so Aidan could set up transports. Nic, however, didn't look all that reassured.

Cam scooted closer, laying a hand over his where it'd curled around the counter lip. "We've got this. We'll protect your family. You work your legal magic and get Vaughn locked up for good."

FIFTEEN

Nic sat behind the prosecutor's desk and spread his hands over the wood, soaking up the quiet calm before the storm. Not that there would be a full-blown storm here, not like in a normal courtroom. There wasn't a judge's bench or jury box, no other table for the defense, and no peanut gallery full of spectators. Hell, there wasn't even a lectern. In this renovated grand jury suite, there were display screens behind a folding faux-wood wall, an L-shaped box for the court reporter and bailiff near the entry door, the prosecutor's boxed desk on the opposite side of the room, and in the middle, at the front, a boxed desk where either he or his witness would sit when addressing the three elevated rows of federal grand jurors.

It was more like a classroom than a courtroom, and it reminded Nic of mock trials in law school or JAG court-martial proceedings. He appreciated the changeup but only on occasion. Grand jury proceedings were a double-edged sword. Less adversarial, the prosecutor worked with the grand jury—no judge, opposing counsel, or defendant were usually present. But the cases heard before the grand jury were not the sorts of high-stakes endeavors he'd want to regularly endure. So much more was on the line.

The click of the door's electronic lock jostled Nic out of his thoughts. Standing, he buttoned his gray suit coat and adjusted his blue tie as the bailiff ushered in the grand jurors. Nic greeted them cordially, saying *hellos* and *how are yous* to the faces that had become familiar over the past few months. They filed past with their case tablets in one hand and their beverage of choice—soda, water, tea, or coffee—in the other. They were due hospitality and appreciation, no matter how they ruled. They'd been accommodating with their time and attention, meeting on short notice when he needed them and handling the evidence in a professional and expeditious manner. Today was the culmination of their work, and Nic wanted to do right by them as much as he wanted to do right by all those he was protecting by prosecuting Vaughn.

Once the jurors were settled with their tablets plugged in and the court reporter signaled ready, Nic nodded for the bailiff to close the door and start the session. The bailiff called them to order, then handed the proceeding off to Nic.

"For the record, Dominic Price, Assistant US Attorney for the Northern District of California. I have called this federal grand jury to assess the merits of the case, the United States versus Duncan Vaughn and related entities." Nic strolled to the center of the room and rested back against the witness desk. "Now that that's done, thank you all for coming in on such short notice and for your continued service. We've seen a rapid mobilization of this matter in the last week, including two suspicious deaths.

Time is of the essence before more crimes are committed and more lives lost.

"With your help issuing warrants earlier in the week, we've made significant progress on the case. Today I intend to present evidence and testimony supporting the issuance of indictments based on the charge sheets you'll find on your tablets." He waited for the *tap-tap-tap* of nails and pens to quiet, the appropriate documents on everyone's screens. "The US government aims to indict Duncan Vaughn, his affiliate enterprises, and his associates identified on the charge sheets with racketeering, bank, loan, and wire fraud, witness tampering, assault and battery, conspiracy to commit murder, and murder."

"There's a charge sheet for your boss, US Attorney Bowers," the jury foreman said.

"And for an FBI agent," added another juror.

"Hence the reason I brought this case before you, the federal grand jury. We're avoiding a public hearing to one, make sure it's in the best interest of the people to bring this case, and two, because we're dealing with several high-profile individuals and very sensitive legal and financial matters.

"Duncan Vaughn is an influential local investor. Implicated in his operation are multiple federal, state, and municipal employees. Before charging these individuals, before uprooting their lives and their companies and agencies, we want to be sure the evidence meets the highest standards justice requires. You, the federal grand jury for Northern California, are charged with protecting the people of this district and the United States. This falls under your purview."

Realizing the true enormity of the case, some of the

jurors appeared understandably cautious and apprehensive, but an equal number sat up straighter, features determined. Nic was likewise determined to have them all looking that way when he was finished today.

"I'd like to start by calling Elton Moore, Assistant Director of the FBI for Northern California." The bailiff stood and opened the door to the holding room. Walking confidence in a tailored navy suit, El flashed his smile at the jurors, shook Nic's hand, and slid into the witness box like he owned it.

Which he did over the next ninety minutes, working with Nic to guide the jurors through the full case background—displaying timelines on the wall screens, laying out Vaughn's organization, and detailing the FBI's efforts up to last week. By the time he was done, Nic understood how El had scaled the FBI ladder so fast. He was concise, clear, and charming as hell.

He had the jury eating out of his palm, the background set up and the bases loaded for Cam and Lauren to knock it out of the park.

Cam's dark gaze was carefully neutral as he entered the room. A voice in the back of Nic's head had warned him that maybe this suit and tie—Cam's favorite—wasn't the best idea today. Too distracting, too on the nose. A louder voice, however, had shouted that it was exactly the confidence boost they needed to tackle this as a team. Together. The louder voice had been right. Cam took a seat in the witness box, their gazes briefly locked, and they were instantly on the same page. The both of them at their best.

Their back-and-forth was easy as they explained the past week's developments, walking the jurors through crime scene photos, toxicology results, biometric readings, and interrogation transcripts. Charming in a different way than Moore, Cam wasn't slick or polished. He was your next-door neighbor, your average everyday FBI agent—granted, an assistant special agent in charge, but he'd been the one putting in the work on the ground—at the crime scenes and at the interrogations. And his experience dealing with kidnap and rescue cases, with grieving families, translated amazingly well to the courtroom, giving him the patience and ability to speak in plain English that Nic would readily admit was often lost on lawyers and higher-ups.

The jurors asked questions about the evidence, about the interrogations and conversations Cam had overheard and relayed—because hearsay was not prohibited in this context—and about the inferences they drew. Nic gave Cam the floor. Tying A to B to C was more convincing from him—the investigator explaining the facts and helping the jurors make the connections. Not the attorney trying to manipulate the facts or sway the jury to his position. Sometimes Nic had to do that if a witness wasn't convincing or if the evidence wasn't strong enough, but in this case, while there was no smoking gun, the way Cam plainly put what they did have all together made it seem a near thing.

Lauren got them that much closer. Nic had contemplated putting her on the stand before Cam, but right after the lunch break, with the food coma and multiple hours of testimony taking their toll, Lauren was the shot of energy and humor he needed to keep the jurors engaged. She was a bit over the top at first, but Nic got her settled and got her explaining the financial and document trails that Duncan and Bowers had left behind. If a juror had a question, she had an analogy or pop culture reference that made the complicated soup of numbers and transactions relatable, the jurors nodding their heads along with her. She magically made the sea of bank statements and spreadsheets comprehensible.

When she finished, Nic offered the jurors a short break, but the foreman, after a quick survey of the jurors, declined. "We've just got a few follow-up questions for you, Attorney Price. I don't think a break is necessary. Time is of the essence. You made that clear in your opening, and it came across clear in the presentation as well." That sounded promising. It had not been something he'd mentioned directly after that first statement, but the fast-moving developments were impossible to miss. As was the need for action.

"I'm happy to answer any questions you have." Rather than sit behind the desk in the witness box, he swung the chair around and sat closer to the front row, emphasizing that this was a conversation.

"It's about US Attorney Bowers. Your boss."

Nic unbuttoned his coat and rested an ankle on his knee. He had to play this cool. Impartial. Not like the put-upon, frequently hamstrung subordinate who'd been under Bowers's dirty thumb for years.

"Indictments against Duncan Vaughn are one thing," a juror said. "Against a US Attorney are another."

"I completely agree," Nic said. "I don't introduce the prospect lightly. I know the oaths and obligations of attorneys practicing at the USAO—I made them and accepted them myself—and that's precisely why I've proposed indictments against Attorney Bowers. He's lost sight of those oaths and obligations. He's compromised."

"The evidence does seem to indicate that," the foreman

said. "If we assume he is, why do you think Bowers is working for Vaughn?"

"Speculation. I can't answer that." He could personally, but not professionally.

The foreman smiled, one hand raised in concession. "I had to try to ask." Nic chuckled, as did the other jurors. "Let me try it this way," the foreman persisted. "Why would you do something like that? What would you risk your career and freedom for?"

Not to climb the political ladder, was on the tip of Nic's tongue, but he bit it back. That would be as good an answer as any to the foreman's original question, and it would be speculation Bowers could later argue in a case against him. Nic had to answer for himself, truly, and let the jurors draw their inferences from there.

He grabbed his shin, stopping his foot from bouncing. "I'd like to think I wouldn't do it under any circumstances. This"—he gestured at the room around them—"is too valuable to me. As is my reputation as someone who upholds and protects the law. And so too is my other job, my home, and my family." He had jobs and a life he wouldn't want to compromise, but . . . "I think the only reasons I'd consider breaking my oaths would be to protect my family or someone I loved."

"Attorney Bowers could learn from you," one of the other jurors said. "About reputation and how to get it the right way."

Nic bowed his head, the compliment meaning more than he could say. At the same time, he didn't want to compromise the case. This wasn't about picking favorites; he didn't want it to seem that way. But it was rewarding as hell to have someone impartial commend him for doing his job, the thing Bowers was daily threatening and telling him he didn't know how to do. "I appreciate that," he said sincerely.

"So do we." The foreman closed his tablet and tucked the stylus in its elastic loop. "We'll get back to you quickly, Attorney Price."

"Thank you."

Nic stood as the bailiff led the jurors out, back into their holding room.

Then Nic exited and met up with the rest of his team in the lobby. "Good job, everyone."

"We should be telling you that," Moore said, hand outstretched. "Damn impressive, as always. You are by far the easiest AUSA to work with on the stand."

"He's right," Cam said. "You don't try and move us. You nudge maybe, one direction or the other as far as what part of the story to tell, but you let us tell it."

"You're all professionals. You know what you're doing."

"Well, I didn't," Lauren said, shrugging one shoulder. "But it was a lot less scary than I thought it would be."

"You did great," Nic said with a smile. "Though it won't always be that easy, especially when there's a cross-examination."

She flailed her arms dramatically. "Now you tell me."

"Moore was right," Cam said after the AD and Lauren left, headed back to the FBI's floor. "That was damn impressive." He stepped closer, a growl in his voice. "Seeing you in that suit in action makes me want to take you home and show you just how sexy you are."

"Do you have a suit porn fetish, Agent Byrne?"

"No, I have a *you* fetish, Attorney Price."

"Later, Boston. We have some work to do first."

"Sooner, Price," Cam argued, dark eyes swirling with intensity. "Much sooner if I have anything to say about it."

A commotion at the stairwell broke their heated stare-down. On the other side of the security guard, Nic spied a panicked Garrett with bruises and bandages on his face. What the fuck had he missed while locked in that courtroom?

"He's clear," Nic called to the guard. "He's with us." The guard stepped out of the way, and Garrett charged over. "What's happened?" Nic asked, dreading the answer.

His instincts weren't wrong. "Lette's gone."

SIXTEEN

Cam had never been in a louder silent room.

Aidan loomed at one end of the conference table, hands braced on the edge like he was about to roar into the speakerphone.

At the opposite end, Moore stood with his arms crossed, his huge body and presence filling the room.

Lauren fidgeted behind her computer, compulsively swiping at the bangs that kept falling into her eyes.

Garrett practically thrummed, holding up one corner of the walls, propped foot bouncing.

And Nic stalked the length of the room like a caged animal from Garrett's corner to the one where Cam stood, arms outstretched, letting Jamie sweep him for bugs.

Jamie had had the unenviable task of checking all of them, only the fact that he was as big as a giraffe keeping him safe from an outburst. He stepped back from Cam with a nod. "All clear."

Aidan slapped the Mute button on the speaker. "Unmute Mel."

The silent conference room was at once awash in noise, the organized chaos of a hospital on the other end echoing over the line. Loudspeakers called for doctors, wheels squeaked and doors banged, muffled conversations rose and fell, and in the middle of the cacophony, Mel's "I'm here."

Aidan, calming slightly, lowered into his chair. "What happened?"

Earlier, outside the grand jury room, Garrett had opened his mouth to tell them, but Cam had slashed a hand in front of his throat—*cut it*—and mouthed, *Wait*. Garrett was a new variable, as were all the people in the crowded courtroom lobby, any one of whom could have brushed up against them and deposited a bug.

"I was moving the Sares," Mel said. "From the hotel to the boat."

They'd agreed last night that daytime traffic in the city would provide more cover than being one of only a few cars out in the wee hours of the morning. Clearly it hadn't been cover enough.

"We were almost there," Mel continued. "And then we got T-boned south of Third and King."

"Injuries?" Cam claimed the seat next to Aidan.

"Yes, just some scratches for me and Eddie. Victoria took the worst of it."

Nic, practically vibrating, came to stand next to where Cam was seated. "Is she—"

Garrett shot out of his corner, moving to Nic's other side. "Would I be here if she weren't?"

Nic hung his head, hand raking over his jaw. "No, of course not."

Mel corroborated. "Victoria's got some bruised ribs and a broken wrist. They're setting it now."

Nic's blue eyes swam with worry. Cam had seen a version of that look before, last spring when he'd been anxious about their informant's safety. Now, however, the worry was amplified exponentially. "How'd they get Lette?"

The desperation in his voice matched the distress in his eyes. This wasn't Nic the federal prosecutor; this was Nic the brother. Cam reached out a hand under the table and cuffed Nic's calf, letting him know he was here for him.

Grounding him, like Nic had done for Cam time and again.

"I was pinned," Mel said. "I told her to stay put, but she was desperate to get to her mother in the front. The kidnapper held a gun on Victoria and snatched Lette from behind. I couldn't get a shot off without further compromising their safety."

"I was on the side that was hit," Garrett said. "I was knocked out for a few minutes while all this was happening. I wouldn't have let her . . ." Garrett cast aside his gaze, Adam's apple bobbing.

Drawing out of Cam's grasp, Nic inched closer to Garrett, eyes sweeping him up and down. "Are you okay?"

"Concussion."

Nic lifted a hand toward the bandage on his head. "You should be in the hospital."

Garrett batted the hand away. "You know as well as I do that worse shit happens in the field. I'm trained, I'm qualified, I can help find my sister. I can't sit in the hospital and do nothing."

"Fucking jarheads," Nic mumbled around a chuckle.

Garrett shoved him in the shoulder, likewise smiling. "Fucking frogs."

Meanwhile, Cam, having vanished from existence, couldn't help but dwell on what he and Nic didn't have in common versus what Nic and Garrett did. Their shared past, Victoria and Lette, military service. Being fucking hardheaded when it came to protecting those they loved.

But wasn't Cam the same in that last regard? Would their dissimilarities versus Nic and Garrett's similarities stop him from loving Nic? No. Nothing would stop him from doing everything he could to protect Nic and those Nic cared for. Especially when doing so was also his job— the one he did best.

Clearing his throat, Cam leaned toward the speaker. "Did you get the details on the car? The kidnapper?"

"I'm texting all that to Lauren now," Mel said. "Given that location, there should be footage from multiple sources." Across from him, Lauren was already focused on her computer. "I didn't recognize the guy who grabbed Lette. He wasn't one of Vaughn's usual men."

"Too recognizable at this point," Aidan said. "If they're smart, they've fled."

"They're not," Nic and Cam answered together.

Nic's smile and his hand on Cam's shoulder made him feel a bit less invisible. They shared things in common too, including a life they'd begun to build. A pretty damn good one. And if Cam wanted to keep Nic in it, not watch him spiral further into the regret and self-blame that had haunted him for almost thirty years, then Cam had to be there. Had to be the best at what he did.

"Lauren," he said, "we need the list of all of Vaughn's

properties, personal and commercial, and supplement it with any properties owned or leased by his associates. Same for Bowers."

"On it."

He turned to Jamie next. "Planes, trains, and automobiles. Any mode of transportation Vaughn might use to move Lette."

"Your warrant wide enough for that?" Moore asked Nic.

"Fuck it."

Cam bit down hard on the inside of his cheek, biting back the warning that wanted out.

Aidan, not so much. "Price."

"I'll make it work."

"We can't lose her, Nic." With all the escalating voices, Garrett's was hardly audible, and not what Cam expected out of the Marine, especially after the earlier back-and-forth. But of everyone in the room, he had the most at stake. "After everything we went through to keep her safe, we can't lose her now."

Nic drew him into a hug. "We'll get her back, G."

"I will do anything."

"We'll do everything." Nic's gaze locked with Cam's. "We've got the Bureau's best kidnap and rescue agent on the case."

Cam nodded, on board with the everything plan and willing to do anything for the man he loved.

———

Nic opened the door to Holding Room Two and the urge to strangle the man sitting relaxed on the other side of the table beside his attorney was damn near irresistible.

Since he couldn't do that, maybe a snarky remark instead? About how nice a good night's rest must be? Golden hair swept back, bespoke suit pressed, shoes shiny enough to reflect, Vaughn looked his normal, cocky self.

On first glance.

On second glance, however, the man's normally bright eyes were dull and bloodshot, his hands looked like someone had taken a chainsaw to the cuticles, and his foot was bouncing where it hung over his knee, and not in the bored kind of way. No, it hadn't been a restful night for Duncan Vaughn. Nic didn't intend to make it a restful day either.

Keeping it in neutral for now, Nic slid into one of the chairs on his side of the table. "Thank you for coming in on such short notice."

"Careful, Dom," Vaughn said with a put-upon smirk. "I'm starting to think you like me. Wouldn't want your boyfriend to get jealous."

Cam lowered into the chair next to Nic. "Oh, I'm not worried."

"Not even at Dom's first love being back in town?"

Nic cut off that line of distraction, because that was what Vaughn was trying to do. Not today, not while every second counted. "Speaking of first loves, I'm surprised you'd risk yours. Victoria could have been seriously injured in that accident. And now you're risking her daughter, all for this grudge of yours against my father."

"I have no idea what you're talking about."

"Or maybe it's because Nicolette is Curtis's daughter," Cam said, picking up the thread Nic had started. "Does that outweigh whatever love you had for her mother?"

"My client—" Patton started.

"Doesn't know anything. Right." Cam tossed a mugshot on the table. "Then why is this man who kidnapped Nicolette Sare on Mr. Vaughn's payroll?"

With witness statements, traffic cams, and surveillance footage from a nearby ATM, they'd been able to identify the hulking bald man who'd wrapped his arms around Lette's middle from behind and hauled her away from the transport and into another car. She'd been wobbly, still disoriented from the crash herself, which was probably the only reason Mr. Clean had managed to subdue her, given her martial arts training. That and the gun he'd held on Victoria.

Vaughn didn't bother to look at the picture. "Sure, it's possible he's on my payroll. I do hire private security from time to time."

Private security or muscle? The guy had the build for either—six-three, three-fifty, bulging arms and legs—and the rap sheet of the latter, numerous charges of assault and battery.

"Tell me," Nic said, "why does a legitimate businessman like yourself need so much muscle?"

"Debtors get desperate. I need private security professionals for my protection."

Nic scoffed. "Or your muscle makes them desperate like they did Harris."

"I keep telling you, Dom, I had nothing to do with Harris's unfortunate decision to take his own life. Why would I do that to my own niece?"

"Why does a gangster do anything?"

"Careful, Counselor," Patton warned. "You're getting awfully close to slander and defamation."

"To which truth is a defense."

"What evidence do you have of the truth?"

Cam pushed another sheet of paper across the table. "Scopolamine was found in Harris's system. A drug that in certain high doses can make a victim prone to suggestion. A drug one of your"—Cam curled his fingers in air quotes—"private security professionals used to date-rape a young woman last year."

Vaughn's eyes narrowed, like he was finally paying attention and hadn't liked what he'd heard one bit. "You have no evidence of that."

Cam leaned forward, the kill in his eyes. "You sure about that, Duncan?"

Some of the color drained from Vaughn's face, and Nic didn't bother to bite back his prideful smile. He'd never tire of Cam on the hunt, especially when he had his target dead to rights.

"Scopolamine is a prescription drug," Patton said. "Who's to say Harris didn't already have it? That he didn't accidentally or intentionally overdose?"

"No prescription on record," Cam replied. "He didn't already have it."

"But you already had that reconveyance, didn't you?" Nic said, speaking directly to Vaughn. "Drafted in advance before Harris's suicide."

"Basic planning for any real estate deal."

"Except you have no history of forgiving debts, even for family members."

Vaughn shifted in his chair, foot dropping all the way over his knee, legs crossed and spine straight. He picked at a cuticle, then, noticing both Nic's and Cam's attention drawn by the nervous gesture, he laced his fingers together in his lap and lifted his chin. "Did I say 'any'? This one —*Beth*—is special."

"Is this the evidence you presented to the grand jury?" Patton asked.

Nic forced himself not to react, not to rise to Patton's bait. He focused instead on what Patton's question had revealed. "Heard about that, did you?"

"I have my sources at the courthouse too."

"Maybe," Nic said. "But I think it's more likely you got that information from your client."

"Who had one of his lackeys bug me," Cam finished.

Vaughn shrugged. "I have no idea what you're talking about, Agent Byrne."

"You don't know a lot of things," Nic replied. "But I think you know where my sister is and you're going to tell us."

"Actually," Patton said, "what we know is that your grand jury presentation was compromised."

"How's that?"

"By having your lover be the agent who testified."

"Agent Byrne testified because he knows the case best."

"And you know him best," Vaughn said. "You knew how he'd answer and react if there were any curveballs."

Cam stiffened beside him, the tension rolling off him and filling the room. He'd been worried about testifying, not exactly for this reason, but Nic was sure it had crossed his mind. It had his. It was a risk he'd been willing to take. The reason they'd maintained their personal distance in professional contexts. Until Vaughn had bugged them, invaded their personal space, and was making it a professional issue. One that didn't exist—a fabricated straw to clutch at—and that pissed off Nic more than anything.

Patton made space among the papers on the table for a new one. "This letter has been sent to your boss and the Deputy AG. You are not an impartial party in this case, and neither are your witnesses. You're both conflicted. We're demanding this matter be stripped from you and the grand jury and either be dismissed or brought before the federal district court in a public preliminary hearing where I'm confident it will get dismissed. You have nothing, Attorney Price. That's why you're using the grand jury, testing out your case."

"Wrong." Nic put a hand on the paper and sent it flying off the table. "I'm using the grand jury because people are dying at the hand of your client."

"Who wants a trial so he can intimidate and tamper with witnesses," Cam added, then spoke directly to Vaughn. "You want to try this case in the court of public opinion. You do that, we'll air all your dirty laundry."

"Are you prepared to air your lover's dirty laundry too?" Vaughn replied. "An affair with his almost stepbrother. An abusive father who ran the family company into the ground. A sister he didn't know about for almost thirty years. Why'd they keep her away from you, Dom?"

"If you continue to keep her away from me, I swear I'll—"

Cam's hand on his knee stole the rest of the threat he was about to speak.

One he couldn't walk back.

"You'll what, Dom?" Vaughn's smirk killed the moment of calm clarity.

Nic slammed his palm on the table. "Where is she, you sack of shit?"

"Further evidence of impartiality." Patton looked as

smug as his client. "We'll add that to our complaint." He stood, gathering his papers.

"And we'll be sure to add kidnapping to the charge sheet," Cam said.

"You won't win this," Nic added.

Vaughn stood, buttoning his coat. "Oh, Dom, but I already have."

SEVENTEEN

Cam trailed a fuming Nic into the observation room, closing the door a split second before the prosecutor's long arm whipped out and cleared half the desk of everything, his calm, cool mask cracking to bits.

To her credit, Lauren, sitting at the other end of the desk behind her laptop and two screens, didn't flinch. "He's got her."

"No fucking shit he's got her," Nic bit off.

"His biometrics were all over the place. Didn't expect that from Mr. Cool."

Stepping past Nic, hand coasting across his back, Cam peered over Lauren's shoulder. "What's that spike early on?" He pointed at the uptick in the readout on the left-hand screen.

"Your dig about Victoria." She tapped her frosted nail at another spike later in the conversation. "And that's when Nic nailed him on Harris."

"How do those two things translate to that asshole having my sister?" Garrett asked from where he stood in the far corner, shifting on his feet. "I mean, I believe you that he does, but—"

"He didn't react when we put the picture of the kidnapper on the table," Cam said, straightening. "He's supremely confident in that regard. That's what we're used to seeing when he's guilty."

"Well then, let's go get her."

Nic halted in his pacing. "Where, Garrett?"

"I have some possibilities," Lauren said. A flurry of flying keystrokes later, a map popped up on the right-hand screen. Cam recognized San Francisco Bay in the middle, but the map's area as a whole was much larger, stretching north to Humboldt County, east to Tahoe, and south to Santa Barbara. And scattered all over the wide swath were little red dots. "These are all of Vaughn's northern and central California holdings. Assuming his thug didn't hop a plane with an injured hostage, which one, obvious, and two, I've got no record of that, including Vaughn's private plane, these are the possible locations he could have traveled by car since the incident."

Garrett whistled low while Cam said, "We need to narrow it down. We can't canvass that many locations."

Nic hustled to Cam's side, examining the map. "Remove the ones that are actively leased. Vaughn's not going to hold a hostage in one of those buildings." More than three quarters of the red dots disappeared.

Nic was right. Vaughn wouldn't have his goons take a hostage someplace full of people where his true illegal underbelly might be exposed by FBI and SWAT teams beating down the door. Along those same lines, Cam suggested, "Remove the ones actively under construction. Maybe those would work if he'd taken the hostage in the middle of the night but not during the day when there are workers around to see."

Nic nodded, Lauren entered the commands, and half the remaining dots came off the board. Better but still not great.

"Now, pull up GPS tracking," Cam said. "Have any of the cars Jamie tagged to Vaughn and his associates, including the one at the scene, been to any of these sites?"

Within a minute, during which the two military men paced circles behind them, one of the red dots began to blink.

"Bingo!" Lauren declared.

Nic reappeared at Cam's side. "Satellite map," he ordered. "What is that?"

Lauren flipped the map to street view, the pin dropping on what looked like an abandoned building south of San Jose in Morgan Hill. Zooming in, the old bowling alley looked the part—sign half gone, fenced in, deserted— but . . . "Why would Vaughn own that?" Cam asked.

"He bought it for the dirt," Nic said, and Lauren was speed typing again while he explained. "The Bay Area is expanding daily. Morgan Hill used to be the country, but now it's another burb, a stop on the Caltrain even. And it's affordable, relatively."

"Guessing that's why Vaughn has a change-of-use permit pending for a mixed-use complex of townhomes and retail on this property."

"All right, let's go, then." Garrett turned for the door.

Nic shot out a hand, grabbing him by the arm. "G, no. We have to handle this carefully if we want to be sure she doesn't get hurt."

"What's to say she's not already?"

Cam stepped beside Nic, addressing Garrett. "That's not in Vaughn's interest."

Garrett's brows climbed his forehead. "Not in his interest?"

"Vaughn may be an asshole, even a sociopath, but he's not psychotic." Cam had seen what happened to hostages and kidnap victims held by those.

He couldn't stop the mental reel of images from their case in Boston. Two different girls kidnapped by the same monster who'd also taken his sister. He might have stayed lost in those memories if not for Nic's hand on his back, returning the earlier gesture and bringing him back to the present.

He shook off the memories and focused on finding Nic's sister, hopefully in a relatively better situation. "In this case, the hostage is leverage to force Nic to do what Vaughn wants, which is pay him and make the case go away."

"So you're expecting a ransom demand?" Nic said.

Cam nodded. "The hostage—"

Garrett banged a fist against the observation glass, startling them all. "Lette. Her name is Lette."

Thank fuck for reinforced glass, and for Vaughn and Patton being long gone from the interrogation room. Nic crossed to Garrett, sliding the hand that'd been on Cam's back over Garrett's. Cam felt the sharp sting of jealousy, no denying it, but he also felt an overwhelming wave of sympathy. He knew exactly what these men were going through, what they were feeling with a sibling lost. Under the circumstances, he wouldn't deny them any sort of comfort. Or let jealousy compromise his efforts to find Nicolette.

"I'm sorry, Garrett," Cam said, one hand raised. "It's a

distancing mechanism we're taught, same as you probably were in the Marines. And I need it more than most."

Garrett lowered his fist, listening intently.

"I've been where you are, except my sister didn't come home. That's why I do this." Cam gestured around the room and out at the bullpen. "So don't think for one second I don't know how you feel. How badly you want to find Lette. I don't intend to let what happened to my sister happen to yours and Nic's."

Short of a promise to bring her home—he tried not to make those—but a promise to do everything he could to make that happen.

Garrett's tension eased a measure, somewhat reassured, and he let Nic guide him into the empty chair beside Lauren.

Nic knelt in front of him, a hand on his knee. "Lette's no good to Vaughn seriously injured or dead," he said softly, visibly swallowing hard around the last word. "He knows the stakes here too. That the whole force of the FBI and DOJ will be behind us."

Lauren bumped Garrett's shoulder with hers. "And he did love your mother. The spikes in his readout, his torn-to-shred cuticles, other cues . . ." Of course the trained analyst had been paying particular attention. "I think a part of him maybe still does. He won't hurt Lette."

Garrett took a deep breath and relaxed back in the chair. "Okay, so what next, then? Do we wait for the ransom demand?"

"No," Cam said, leaning against the wall next to the glass. "We do recon on this location in Morgan Hill. Confirm she's there. And if she is, we have a tactical game plan ready for extraction."

Garrett shot right back out of the chair. "I want in."

Nic was having none of it, stepping into Garrett's space, attempting to loom over the shorter man. "So you can become another hostage? Hell no."

Garrett was having none of Nic's answer or his attempts at intimidation. He might have been shorter, but he outweighed Nic by a good thirty pounds, if not more. "I'm a fucking major in the Marine Corps."

"Which is why you need to stay with Victoria."

"So all the hostages are in one place for him to take?"

Cam would have laughed if he wasn't so worried about the two shredding each other in a fight. And if Garrett didn't have a very good point. "He's right, Dominic."

Blue eyes glowered at him.

Cam shrugged. "A compromise. Garrett, you can join the recon team, but if they're there, and I make the call to go in, you stay back. That way all three hostages and the levers on you"—he gestured at Nic—"remain separated."

"I can live with that," Garrett said.

The door opened just as Nic asserted, "I'm going with you too."

"'Fraid not, Price." AD Moore's charming smile was absent, his face hard and severe. Not someone Cam would want to cross when he was this obviously angry. "Deputy AG is on the phone for you. We've got a problem."

———

Moore paused outside Aidan's office, hand on the doorknob. "Bowers is on the line too, making the case against you."

"I figured as much."

"He's also making the case that the entire Vaughn matter be dropped."

Nic stepped closer, then noticing they were drawing curious looks from the bullpen, led Moore into Cam's office and shut the door behind them.

Aidan's raised voice echoed from his office at the other end of the conference room between them. Nic needed to get in there, defend himself and the case to Bowers and the Deputy AG, but if he couldn't convince Moore first, he was in deeper shit than he realized.

"Of course Bowers wants the case dropped. You're up to speed. You know what he stands to lose if Vaughn goes down and he gets exposed."

"And you have just as much, if not more, to lose, Price, if you're making the wrong call. And the rest of us will lose too if you're gone from the US Attorney's Office when this is over."

Nic felt like he'd been slapped. "You think he'll convince Jack."

"I think I worked hard to build this case for longer than you've even known about it, sacrificed parts of my life for it, and I don't want to see all that go to waste."

Nic wondered if maybe it wasn't only the lack of seasons that had caused Moore's ex-wife to leave him for the East Coast. "El—"

"More than that," the AD talked over him, "I want that asshole Bowers gone. I know he's a climber. So am I. But he's also an insult to what we do every day. He's right, you're conflicted, but not like he is, and you are the best attorney to try this case. And I want it done, once and for all."

Yes, there was definitely more to that story, for another

time over a beer maybe. Hopefully when all this shit was decided in their favor, and everyone was safe and sound. "Jack's on our side, El," Nic said. "I'll get this done. Your work, your sacrifices, won't have been for nothing."

Moore still didn't seem one hundred percent convinced, but he was enough of the way there to open the door to the conference room. They crossed through to Aidan's office, and it was not a pretty sight when they got there. Aidan sat behind his desk, elbows propped on the blotter, hands doing a number on his auburn hair. His brown eyes were hot with anger as Bowers droned on from the other end of the line.

"This is an abuse of power, Jack. Price is conflicted as hell and all his little friends are in on this too."

Aidan dropped his arms, glaring at the phone like he could blow it up with his mind. "His little friends are sitting right here, Lou."

"And they're all blatantly insubordinate."

"I'm not your subordinate."

"Gentlemen," Moore interrupted as he and Nic claimed the guest chairs across from Aidan. "Jack, I've got Price with me."

"Deputy," Nic said.

"Did you have your boyfriend testify earlier today?" Jack asked.

Nic didn't second-guess or hesitate in answering, "I did."

"You don't think that's a conflict of interest?"

"My boyfriend happens to be the ASAC of the local field office. He would be the agent on this case regardless of whether I was involved."

"That's correct," Aidan chimed in.

"Not you, Talley?"

"I'm just a desk jockey now." Nic had to bite back his guffaw, which turned into an eye roll with Aidan's next words. "And I dated Price too so that argument's moot."

"That office—" Bowers started with some insult or another, which Moore shut down with indisputable facts.

"Talley's office has the highest close rate in the country."

"Respectfully," Nic said, interjecting before this got further out of hand with the testosterone jockeys. They were dealing with two attorneys on the other lines; that's how Nic needed to approach them. He had to win the argument. "Agent Byrne was the most qualified to testify. He's been with me each time I questioned Vaughn, has been the point person with the local morgue, and is fully up to speed on the case."

"What about this statement that you knew how he'd answer and react if there were any curveballs?"

"That statement was obtained illegally, through an unauthorized listening device planted on a federal agent and in the context of a private conversation."

"A conversation you wouldn't be having," Bowers said, "if you weren't fucking the lead detective on this case."

"I beg to differ. If I'm doing my job right, of course I'm supposed to know how my witness is going to testify, regardless of my relationship with them. And I wouldn't even be having that conversation or this one if Vaughn hadn't been allowed to proceed unchecked for this long."

"That sounds like an FBI problem," Bowers replied snidely.

"Or a no one wanted to prosecute him problem," Moore bit back.

"Until Nic's father became indebted to him," Bowers said. "And now he does all of a sudden. Another conflict."

"He's got a point, Price," the Deputy AG weighed in.

"And I've got a case." Nic stood, bracing his hands on the front edge of the desk. "One the FBI started building before I was involved. I just had enough motivation to bring it. I also have enough evidence to support it. I should be permitted to bring this case to a conclusion, and Vaughn and his associates to justice, which will be soon."

"You've got nothing," Bowers sneered.

"If we drop this now, we're going to lose Vaughn for good. He's funneling assets out of the country. It's only a matter of time. He gets his vengeance and he's gone."

"His vengeance?" Jack asked.

"My father stole the woman he loved decades ago. Now he's kidnapped my sister. Another reason why Agent Byrne, whose expertise in kidnap and rescue, is uniquely qualified for this case."

"And you're not conflicted?" Bowers scoffed.

"And you sound like a broken fucking record." Nic pushed off the desk and took up pacing in the area behind his chair.

"Jack," Moore said, "I agree with Price. Vaughn has gone unchecked for far too long. We've been building this case for over a year, and together with Byrne and Talley, we're closer than we ever have been to closing it. We're not gonna get another shot at him. Let 'em close the deal."

"Jack—"

"Enough, Lou." The Deputy AG generally had the patience of a saint, the fools on the Hill far more trying than this internal squabble, but even Nic could hear the weariness in his voice. This had gone on too long. "Price, the grand jury wants to hear from you tomorrow morning. Can you do that, given the situation with your sister?"

"Yes." He clutched the back of his chair, hoping it wasn't a lie. "Agent Byrne is pursuing a lead on her whereabouts. I trust him to handle that. I can handle the grand jury."

"I want to be there," Bowers said.

"Fine," Jack said. "Let them hear from both of you."

"That's not how the grand jury works," Nic objected.

"Would you rather air all this in a public prelim, Price?"

"I'd rather—"

Aidan's sharp glare shut up the foolishness that was about to escape from his lips.

"Fine," he said instead.

"Let me make this clear," Jack said, "to all of you. Duncan Vaughn is DOJ's top priority. Make a case, make it stick, and do not embarrass Justice doing it."

"Our department's reputation is what I'm trying to save here," Bowers replied smugly.

The earlier insult was on the tip of Nic's tongue, and Aidan narrowly avoided it this time by saying a hasty goodbye and slapping off the phone.

Nic let loose as soon as the display clicked off. "The only person's rep that little shit is trying to save is his own."

"And you"—Aidan jutted a finger at him—"need to worry more about saving your own."

Nic spread his arms out wide. "Really, Talley? Coming from you that's fucking rich."

"Hey!" Aidan pushed to his feet. "I'm not the enemy here. I'm your friend. I'm trying to make this case and protect you."

"I can take care of myself."

Moore stood and rested back against the desk, facing him. "I'm not sure you can, Price."

Two against one, then, and the person Nic needed most was absent, searching for his sister. "I'm done here. I've got a hearing to prep for."

"Nic—"

He waved Aidan off and left the office, heading for the elevators. Inside, he wanted to punch the button for the lobby, leave the Federal Building, and go search for his sister, but that was exactly what Bowers would use against him. No, he needed to prepare for the hearing like he said he would. He punched the button for the USAO's floor instead.

The doors had just opened again when his phone vibrated in his pocket. He pulled it out as he stepped into the lobby, expecting a text from Cam.

It wasn't that at all.

EIGHTEEN

Cam sat in the driver's seat of the surveillance van, surveying the run-down bowling alley through night vision binoculars. The car they'd tracked was parked out front, right where GPS said it would be, and there was a light on in the main structure, but there was no visible movement inside, no other lights flickered, and no other cars came or went. Cam was starting to think the kidnapper was gone from this site already, moving Lette elsewhere.

He wordlessly passed the binoculars to Garrett, as had been their routine for the past hour. This time, however, Garrett set the goggles on the dash and fell back in the passenger seat with a huff. "She's not in there."

"Agreed," Cam said. "But I want surveillance to confirm no heat signatures before we move in. I called in the drone. Should be flying over soon."

"Those things aren't foolproof. If there's a basement . . ."

"Oh, I know." Two months ago, he'd had a drone fly over a farmhouse outside of Boston, looking for a kidnap victim. The drone hadn't detected any bodies, and the house had been clear of the suspect, but they'd found the victim, thankfully alive, in the basement. "But the drone will give us some indication of what we're walking into."

Garrett shifted in his seat, reached for the goggles again, and peered through them. The flurry of movement was consistent with the past hour in the car and with the other instances Cam had been in the same room with him. "You're awfully fidgety for a Marine."

"I did my share of recon, then I got in the air. Never looked back. Plane or chopper, I'm always in motion. This sitting-still shit"—he waved a hand in the air, gesturing around the car—"is for the birds."

Cam chuckled. "One and only stakeout for you. Got it."

"How do you do it?"

"Sit still?"

"Wait."

Cam briefly took his eyes off the building to send a sympathetic glance Garrett's way. "It's your sister. You're more anxious than usual."

"How are you not? You said you understood."

"I do, better than you think." Cam's gaze was back on the bowling alley, but his mind was in a different time and place. "My sister was taken when I was a teenager. She was twelve. It almost tore our family apart. It's why I joined the FBI, to find her. And it's why I do what I do, to try and save other families from the loss my family suffered."

"Did you find her?"

"Twenty years later, thanks in no small part to Nic. And I will do everything I can to make sure he doesn't go through what I did, including being extra careful how we approach this." He pointed at the building. "In case she is in there. He's lost enough already."

Garrett raised the binoculars again, one more look, before handing them off to Cam. "So you guys make this work? Living and working together?"

Cam peered at the building through the green-tinted lenses. "We do."

"But what if it craters this case?"

"It won't." Still seeing no movement, he dropped the binoculars in his lap. "It hasn't. If anything, it's helped us in cases we work together. Predictability in a world of unpredictability is a gift. When my sister's cold case heated up again and I needed someone who could handle a delicate situation with Justice, Nic was the only person for the job, and not because I was fucking him. We closed fifteen cases that week, including my sister's. We can use that to our advantage to find yours."

Garrett propped an elbow on the car window, head in his hand. "This conversation is both reassuring and awkward."

"That it is." But it was also needed. To reassure Garrett they were doing everything they could and to reassure himself of his role in this at Nic's side. "But you need to know I'm invested too, like he was in my sister's case."

"That's good." Garrett's nod was cut off mid-motion, the soldier turning his ear to the window.

Cam heard it too—the drone passing overhead. "That's good too." He lifted the binoculars, tracking the drone as it flew a pattern around and over the building. After another couple passes, it rose into the clouds and disappeared. Cam's phone rang a minute later.

"What've we got?" he answered on speakerphone.

"All clear," Jamie said. "No heat signatures, at least in the part of the building the drone can read."

"And that's all of the building," Lauren cut in. "I managed to get the demo plans from a very irate city planner. No basement."

"All right, then," Cam said. "Stand by for entry."

"I want to go in with you," Garrett said as soon as Cam ended the call.

Cam hesitated and Garrett jumped all over it. "There's no one in there, but my sister may have left something behind. Will you be able to spot it? Know its significance? If it might be a clue? There's no time to waste here."

He was right and he was qualified. More than that, Cam didn't trust him to stay in the car. Better to have him in sight. "Fine, though just because there are no bodies doesn't mean the place hasn't been rigged. We go in slow."

"I know what explosives look like, Agent Byrne."

Yeah, he definitely wouldn't have stayed in the car. "All right, let's go then." He radioed for the tactical team stationed a block away, and five minutes later, they were through the fence and converging on the structure. With their flashlights, they checked each doorway and threshold for explosives before stepping through or over. All clear. But there was evidence someone had been here.

Tread marks across the dusty floor where someone had walked. Bigger swaths of dust cleared where someone had been dragged. The lingering hot metal smell of a neglected radiator heater recently cranked. The stale, pungent odor of convenience-store coffee.

As they neared one of the back rooms, Garrett froze, inhaling deep. "Lette's been here."

Cam breathed in and detected two things—the same citrusy soap he'd noticed earlier on Garrett, likely from the hotel, and blood. Garrett moved to rush forward, and Cam grabbed him by the arm, hauling him back. "We need to clear the area first."

The other agents crept past them, doing their checks. At the call of "Clear," Garrett wrenched himself free and darted into the room. Cam followed, stopping behind where he knelt in the far corner.

It wasn't as much blood as Cam had feared—God knows he'd seen worse—but it was still enough to be worrisome. Collected in one general area. Lette had an injury on her person somewhere.

Garrett, however, wasn't focused on the blood. He was staring down at an object in his hand. "She was definitely here." Still crouched, he rotated and lifted his hand, palm open. In it was a high school class ring on a chain. "It's Nic's."

The one Nic had told Cam about—the ring he'd given to Garrett, and Garrett had given to Lette. Cam folded Garrett's fingers around the ring and rested his other hand on Garrett's shoulder, as much to comfort himself as the major.

"We have to find her," Garrett croaked, and Cam nodded.

Once he could swallow around the lump in his throat, Cam took his phone out and rang Lauren. "They were here," he told her. "But they're gone now. We need to widen the search area. He's probably headed south, maybe west, away from us in any event. Pull up traffic cams, ATMs, any source of surveillance. Let's see if we can spot a car leaving this area with passengers meeting their description. Lette is likely injured."

"On it," Lauren replied.

"Cam," Aidan said, coming on the line. "We've got a bigger problem."

He squeezed Garrett's shoulder, then stepped away, not wanting to shake him up any more than he already was. "How the fuck can it be bigger?" he asked, voice lowered.

"I have alerts on Nic's bank accounts."

"You what? Why?"

"Moore's orders."

Fuck, had Nic been right not to trust the AD? "What the hell? Why's he keeping tabs on us?"

"Cam!" Aidan clipped, more boss tone than he'd ever used with him. And also with an undercurrent Cam had heard before when Jamie was in danger. "It doesn't matter right now. What does matter is that Nic withdrew a large sum of money an hour ago."

"How? It's way after hours."

"Not if you used to fuck the bank manager."

Cam gritted his teeth, trying and failing to block out the reminder of Nic's past conquests. Never mind that one of his other lovers was also in the room with Cam. One who was straightening up from his crouch, glancing Cam's way, and definitely cluing in to the fact that something else was amiss.

"How large?" Cam asked.

"Enough to pay off his father's debts."

"Fucking hell."

Ransom demand; it had to be. And after the pile-on Nic had had to endure this afternoon, Cam wasn't surprised he'd finally decided to take matters into his own hands, especially with his sister's life at stake. "Where's he headed with it?"

"Cam, are you sure you want to do this?"

"You're tracking his accounts for fuck's sake. Just check the GPS on his truck and keep me posted. I'm headed back now."

"He may not forgive you," Aidan warned.

"I won't forgive myself if I let him do this."

———

Gravel crunched under tires, headlights cut through the darkness, and Nic clicked off the safety on his Beretta, laying it behind the briefcase on the table. Out of sight but within easy reach.

He'd left the front door unlocked and a single light on in the kitchen.

Vaughn undoubtedly knew Curtis's house well enough. He could find his way through, and Nic, sitting on the back patio, would see him coming, and who else might be with him. Assess what he was up against.

But rather than Vaughn and his henchmen, a lone figure appeared in the shadows between the foyer and the kitchen. Judging by his size and shape, the man wasn't Vaughn. Nic reached for his Beretta, was halfway to standing, when the intruder stepped fully into the light, revealing his identity.

One sort of tension rolled out, another rolled in.

Nic clicked the Beretta's safety back on, set the weapon atop the briefcase, and stood at the far end of the table. Waiting. Crossing his arms and clutching his biceps, containing the urge to rail. Planting his feet shoulder width apart, fighting the instinct to run to him.

Movement drawing his attention, Cam emerged onto

the patio a moment later. "Just listen," he said, hands raised.

"What the fuck are you doing here?"

"Stopping you from doing something stupid. And if I can't stop you, being your backup."

No way, especially to the latter suggestion. "I can't let you do that."

"And I can't let you do something stupid." Hands still raised, he approached slowly. "Think, Nic. Vaughn's not going to give you Lette."

Nic pointed at the briefcase. "I have his money. All of it."

Cam grasped his wrist, squeezing between him and the table. "And you also have his balls in a vise with the grand jury. What do you think is more important to him? Millions, which he already has, or the future to earn more millions."

Nic diverted his gaze, cursing the truth. Cam was right. He also couldn't shake the image of Lette tied to a chair, bleeding from a head wound. "She's injured." He thrust his phone at Cam. "And Vaughn's getting desperate. I can't not do everything in my power to get her back."

Cam looked long and hard at the picture. Maybe he could see more in it than Nic had, worry having fogged his brain. "It's consistent with what we found in Morgan Hill," Cam said, handing the phone back. "This tells us it's a head wound. Could be superficial." He lifted a hand, tracing the small scar at Nic's hairline left over from their case in Boston. "You know as well as I do that they bleed more than others, even if it's just a scratch."

"Or it could be serious. Until we get her back, we won't know."

"The money won't make that happen. It'll only give

Vaughn more leverage. He won't give Lette back unless you drop the case, which you can't do."

"We might not win it." Nic drew back and collapsed into the chair, head tilted back, staring up at the night sky. "Bowers recommended against it."

The chair beside him creaked, Cam taking a seat. "Of course he did."

Nic righted his head, looking into Cam's dark eyes. They usually brought him comfort, but nothing was getting through the fog of panic that had gripped him since that text had come through. He needed to take action, more than what he was doing. "The Deputy AG wasn't convinced either."

"But he's letting you argue the case tomorrow, yes?"

Nic nodded. "With Bowers there."

"Good, prove the fucker wrong." Cam scooted closer and curled a hand over his thigh. "You, Moore, the rest of the FBI have put too much time into this case to let it go. Even if you don't win, the next person is going to think twice before taking a loan from Vaughn or going into business with him."

"But we're not trying this case in public."

"Word will get out. Everyone will learn he's been under investigation."

"But if someone's desperate enough . . ." Like his father had been. A few bad investments, the economic crash he'd never recovered from, debt and more debt.

"All the more reason to shut him down for good." Cam nudged the briefcase. "This won't."

"I know that." Nic hunched forward, the weight and pressure of the past week, of the past months, crashing down on him. Yes, he had Cam and the rest of his family helping him, but he had another family now he needed to protect. He tangled his fingers with Cam's, clutching them, desperate for the comfort he couldn't find. "I can't let them down again."

Fingers grasped his chin, Cam gently angling his face toward him. "And I can't let you down. I won't let you cut the rope. You made me promise, remember? Let me rescue your sister instead while you nail Vaughn."

Closing his eyes, Nic buried his face in Cam's big palm, wanting it to all work out that simply. There was no one he trusted more to find Lette than Cam nor anyone he trusted more to try Vaughn's case than himself. But so many of the other players on the board were wildcards. He ignored them for the moment, ignored reality, and drew what comfort he could.

It didn't last for long, Cam's vibrating phone interrupting the silence. Dropping his hand, Cam pulled it from his pocket, flashed him Lauren's face on-screen, and activated the speaker. "Hall, what's up?"

"Vaughn's not coming."

"Why not?"

"Cole tracked the sedan you checked out of the pool. He told Vaughn where you were headed."

"Fuck."

Nic shook his head. "Doesn't matter." Cam had made his argument convincingly. Paying off Vaughn wasn't the way to rescue Lette. At least now they knew for sure who the mole was inside the FBI. "How'd you confirm it was Cole?"

"I pretended to turn on you."

Cam lurched forward in his chair, matching Nic's

posture, bent over the phone on the end of the table. "You did what?"

"I know where they're holding Lette. One of Vaughn's properties down in Cambria."

"You did know he was the mole." Nic let every bit of admiration he had for her color his voice.

"Of course I knew. I was playing him the entire time. I told him I wanted in on some of his share of what Vaughn promised to pay him. Which was the bullshit song and dance he gave me, because we all know he's up to his eyeballs in hock to Vaughn, like everyone—"

"Lauren," Cam clipped, cutting off her ramble. "What happened tonight?"

"He wanted to win points with his boss. Told him I'd help divert you."

"Divert me?"

"From where they're taking Lette."

"Nice end around."

"Thank you," she said. "And I've already called in the tactical team."

"I'll be there in twenty." Cam ended the call and pushed to his feet.

Nic rose beside him. "I'm coming with you."

"No." Before he could object, Cam's hand flattened over his lips, pressing back the argument. "Cambria's four hours south. No way you'll make it there and back in time to present to the grand jury tomorrow morning."

He wrenched his face away and slammed a palm on the table. "She's my sister, goddammit."

Cam didn't back off. He crowded closer instead, backing him up against the table, both hands wrapped around his neck. Nic fought to get free but Cam held him steady. "I know, baby," he said, more gently than Nic deserved. The de-escalation worked, calming him a measure. "I know more than most what that means." Both thumbs scraped over his rough cheeks, the noise loud in the otherwise quiet night. "You brought my sister back to me. Let me bring yours home to you. I won't let this be another regret."

His lips brushed against Nic's, sealing a promise Nic knew Cam never liked making. The fact that he would, together with his kiss, wiped away the last of Nic's arguments.

"Okay," he breathed before drawing Cam into a deeper kiss, getting a last taste of that certainty, that confidence, to buoy him through the hearing tomorrow, through the hours he'd have to stand by doing nothing. Standing down was against all his training, but also right in line with it in this instance. No running to his death or his sister's. He had to trust Cam to do his job while he did his in the courtroom.

"I'll bring her home," Cam promised again.

Nic needed more than that. He rested his forehead against Cam's, holding tight while he still could. "Both of you come back to me."

NINETEEN

"Everyone knows their approach routes and positions?" Cam straightened from where he stood, huddled over the topographical map of Vaughn's seaside property. Each team leader around the table nodded. "Great, we move out at the top of the hour."

The agents scattered, debriefing their individual groups and checking their gear. With Danny's help, they'd secured an empty hangar at the municipal airport in Paso Robles about forty minutes east of Cambria. They could have set up base closer but vans full of FBI agents would have been too noticeable in the smaller seaside towns near Vaughn's fifteen-acre estate. Word would reach Vaughn before they did.

They were less likely to draw attention here in busier Paso Robles, and from this spot, they could execute his and Aidan's raid plan, approaching the property from multiple directions, not drawing too much notice in any one. Doubly important as they no longer had the cover of darkness. The sun was well on its way up, rising over the two-strip airfield and the surrounding vineyards, their leaves a spectacular splash of fall colors. Cam was used to seeing the reds, oranges, and yellows on trees, but this was just as pretty. A rolling spread of autumn. He'd like to visit here again with Nic.

He'd also like to call Nic, let him know all was handled on this end, but he'd be in front of the grand jury by now. Making his case and hopefully putting the final nails in Vaughn's coffin. Bowers's too. Cam didn't want to interrupt. He did have Garrett's number though, and unlike yesterday's recon, Garrett was there, not here. He'd appreciate an update, would relay the same to Nic when he got out of the hearing. Cam got as far as opening Garrett's contact card when the surveillance van doors banged open, Jamie flying out with a phone in hand.

"What—"

"We've got a problem." Jamie handed him the phone, Aidan's face on-screen. Raised voices blared through the speakerphone, an argument mid-progress.

Cam stepped to the side of the van and kicked down the volume before everyone in the hangar overheard.

"That's enough, Lou," Moore barked, followed by a *thump*, like someone being shoved against a wall.

"Your golden boy missed his hearing," Bowers shouted back. "He's done."

Cam punched off the Mute button. "Nic missed the grand jury hearing?" he asked, stomach sinking.

"He sent a junior AUSA in his place," Aidan answered. "To request a continuance, which he's within his rights to do."

"I'd throw him in contempt if I could," Bowers spat, as if he were judge and jury. "He's made a fool of my office."

"I think you've done that all by yourself," Cam said, sick and tired of Bowers badmouthing Nic. The US Attorney was an easy target for his frustration. Get angry or get sick with worry. Or worse, with betrayal.

"What the hell is that supposed to mean?" Bowers demanded.

"It means your days are numbered, Lou."

"Agent Byrne," Aidan warned.

"Was the case actually compromised?" Jamie asked.

"Delayed, but not compromised," Moore said. "The grand jury will continue to review the evidence. They work with the prosecutor, not against."

"Maybe Price needs some checks on him," Bowers said.

"That's what we do," Cam replied. "We make sure the evidence is there."

"For your boyfriend."

"You the one who fed that argument to Vaughn's attorney?" Aidan asked.

"It's a valid one," Bowers answered.

Part of Cam wanted to cheer. The asshole had sidestepped Aidan's question, not denying the truth of it. The other part of Cam wanted to reach through the phone and strangle Bowers because of that truth, because he was in a criminal's pocket and was destroying Nic's name on Vaughn's behalf.

"We were investigating Duncan Vaughn well before Nic's or Cam's involvement," Moore said. "You know that as well as I do. Why would you crater the case now when we're this close?"

"I'm not bringing a case that has no basis," Bowers countered.

"Neither are we," Cam said.

"Price better be back this afternoon or he's out of a job." A door slammed, Bowers leaving whatever conference room or office they were in.

"Is he gone?" Cam asked.

"Yes," Aidan gritted out.

"He better be gone for good by this afternoon."

"That only happens if you find Nic and get him back here," Moore said. "Otherwise, he's going to be the one out of a job."

Cam fell back against the side of the van. What the fuck was Nic thinking? "We talked about this last night. We were on the same page."

"Aside from us and Mary, he hasn't had a family in almost thirty years," Aidan said. "All of a sudden, he does again. He might not be thinking clearly."

Cam shook his head, not that Aidan could see him. Everything about Nic not thinking clearly was wrong. "Does that sound like Nic to you?"

"Not at all," Jamie answered. "But we don't know this Nic. The one he used to be."

Except Cam did, or at least he'd seen glimpses of another Nic. The SEAL who'd chafed at being sidelined in the van, who wouldn't let those he loved get hurt.

Fuck.

"He's gone after Lette himself."

Cam had made his point about the ransom—that would never work for getting Lette back—but had he driven Nic to take other action instead?

"Garrett went with him," Lauren said, entering the fray on the other end of the line. "He was lurking outside the room when I got the location out of Cole."

"Victoria?"

"Confirmed Garrett never returned to the hotel last night. She said she thought he was with us."

No, he was with Nic, if Cam had to bet. His stomach took another tumble. The Marine and the SEAL going after their sister. "Where's Nic's truck?"

"At Curtis's house still."

"Fuck!" Cam cursed loudly, drawing the attention of several agents. He lowered his voice back to normal and added, "We'll have to track him another way."

"Hold a second," Lauren said. "Nic used a credit card thirty minutes ago. A motel in San Simeon."

"One town up from Cambria," Jamie said. "Text us the address now."

Why would Nic do that? He had to know they'd trace it and find him. Was that what he wanted? The address came through along with a map.

"I'm on the way out the door now," Aidan said. "Jet's being fueled. It's an hour flight down. Jamie, get the teams ready to roll as soon as I land there. Cam, you head out now. Go get Nic. We'll be right behind you."

But how far behind Nic were they already?

———

"Why didn't we just go in there and get her?"

Nic closed the hotel room door behind a fuming Garrett. "Because it's a fucking fifteen-acre estate, G. We needed to do recon first. Assess entry and exit points and determine the best and safest approach."

Garrett spun in the middle of the room, looking every bit the keyed-up jarhead in his camo pants and service sweater. All that was missing was the olive piss hat, which would only make his hazel eyes burn brighter. "I'm tired of fucking recon." He ripped off the damp, sandy sweater and hurled it at the chair by the blazing corner fireplace.

For his part, Nic wanted to hurl himself on the bed in his room next door.

Garrett was tired of recon; well, Nic was just fucking tired. And just plain fucked. He was supposed to have met with the grand jury an hour ago. He hated to think how many voicemails were on the phone in his pocket. Save for the early morning call to his colleague about the continuance, he'd kept his phone off since Garrett had shown up at the house last night, five minutes after Cam had left.

Maybe he wouldn't be in this position if he'd tried harder to talk Garrett out of his plan. Or maybe both his sister and former lover would be hostages by now, given Garrett's bullheaded determination to go after Lette on his own. Maybe Nic didn't have much of a fucking choice.

Exhaustion seeping into his bones, Nic dragged himself across the room. Ignoring the tempting fireplace, he yanked back the gauzy balcony curtains instead and opened the sliding glass door to the chilly sea breeze. The brisk blast chased off the exhaustion nipping at his heels. He dropped into one of the patio chairs and removed his shoes, dumping out the sand over the rail.

He hated sand, having had more than enough of it for one lifetime. So of course Vaughn's Cambria property was oceanfront. And of course the best vantage point for recon was the sandy beach cliff. He and Garrett had climbed up over the edge to lie on their bellies in the tall beach grass, looking into the mansion through the tall floor-to-ceiling windows. Their sister had been gagged and bound to a living room chair, unconscious but breathing, her chest rising and falling regularly. Nic closed his eyes, prayed she stayed breathing, then banished the image so he could function.

A shadow fell over him, Garrett stepping out onto the patio. Leaving off his shoes, Nic slumped back in the Adirondack chair, staring up at Garrett resting against the rail, his biceps straining the sleeves of his drab undershirt. "You're a fucking USMC major. I know the Marines didn't teach you to act without a plan or without backup."

Which was why Nic was stalling like his life depended on it. He'd been stalling since he'd agreed to come with Garrett, who'd overheard Lauren and Cole discussing Lette's location. Between Garrett's single-mindedness and Victoria's imploring text last night to keep her kids safe, what was Nic supposed to do? Let Garrett go rogue alone? Not an option. Yes, he could have tried to subdue him before they'd left, but one, Nic wasn't sure he could win that face-off, and two, even if he had, he'd only be able to watch over Garrett for so long before he had to leave for the grand jury. As far as Nic could tell, the only reliable way to keep Garrett from doing something stupid—from putting their family in even more jeopardy—was to go with him. And stall. He hoped like hell Cam would get here in time and that he'd forgive him.

"You're stalling," Garrett said, as if reading his mind. "Waiting for the feds."

Nic didn't deny it. "Because I'm a SEAL. We don't run to our deaths, and me and you"—he waved a finger between them—"going into that house alone, that's what we'd be doing."

"Were you ever going to go in there with me?"

"Not if I could stop you."

Garrett pushed off the rail, pacing the tiny balcony in front of Nic. "Everything Mom and I have done since we left has been for her."

Guilt walloped Nic, crashing over him like the waves pounding the beach below. "I'm sorry you had to do that alone."

"I'm not."

The waves rolled him under, the riptide dragging him out to sea. It had always been his worst nightmare as a SEAL. Something his teammates couldn't save him from, the ocean bigger than all of them.

Just like his past, inescapable.

"Do I wish you'd been there?" Garrett carried on. "Yes. Do I know you couldn't be there? Yes. If Curtis would have known too soon . . ."

"He might have come for her." Air was hard to come by, a flood of regret filling his lungs. He braced his elbows on his knees, head held in his hands. "Since I didn't live up to his expectations."

"That is the most absurd thing you've ever said. Salutatorian, Navy SEAL, JAG Captain. Dude, you're a fucking legend, even in the Corps."

Nic dropped his arms, letting his hands hang between his knees, eyes drifting back out to sea. "I am not."

Shadow shifting, Garrett crouched in front of him, forcing his gaze. "Do you know how hard it was to keep my mouth shut when I heard the stories? To not tell them every bit of it was true? That I loved you."

Nic's heart leaped into his throat at the same time his stomach hit the floor. "Garrett, that's not—"

He laid a hand on his knee. "*Loved*, Nic. And a part of me always will, but I'm not the same boy I was, and you're a man in love with someone else. A good man." He squeezed his knee, then fell into the chair beside him. "We share a sister. You're family."

How many times had Nic heard that the past year? And just as he was starting to believe it, he felt like he was letting them down, at risk of losing them all with one wrong step. Had he already made it? Chasing after Garrett —trying to protect him and Lette—at the expense of the grand jury hearing? Not to mention all the wrong steps he'd taken in the past.

"I'm sorry I couldn't do more for you," Garrett said. "We had a life—a good one—because of you."

"But what about the life you gave up? Your football scholarship, Victoria's business, the only home you'd ever known. Maybe if I'd made different, better decisions and held myself back from loving you, you and Victoria wouldn't have had to start over."

Garrett reached out and grasped his wrist. "Then you wouldn't have loved us enough to let us go. To save us."

"I need you to know I never forgot you. That I'm this person who fights because of you." Shaking off his hold, Nic stood. "That I'm sorry even if you say I don't need to be."

Garrett stood, clasping his shoulder. "I know that."

Yes, but he needed Garrett to really understand it. To know Nic had lived with it every day. That he'd used the past to try and be a better man in the present. He needed to give Garrett what was his so they could all move into the future, hopefully as a family, assuming they survived the next twenty-four hours. Unzipping Cam's camo jacket that he'd grabbed from the truck last night, he tossed it on the balcony rail, then reached for the hem of his black Gravity tee.

Garrett shot out a hand, stopping him. "Nic, what—"

"Please," Nic said, voice hoarse. "There's something I need to show you."

Nic held his gaze until Garrett lowered his hand and stepped back. "Will you at least come inside where it's warm?"

No, he needed to do this out here in the cold bright light of day, and where, despite how much he hated the sand, the crashing waves could drown his guilt and regret and carry them out to sea. He tugged the shirt off over his head, and Garrett gasped at the tattoos on his front. Before he could ask about those, Nic turned, and Garrett's sharp inhale died on a choked half sob. Nic braced his hands on the balcony rail, inviting a closer look. "I never forgot, G."

Cold fingertips touched his back, at first tracing the GS, then fanning out over the cypress branches. Nic shuddered, not with desire but with such profound relief he had to clutch the rail to remain standing. It wasn't just the waves washing him clean. It was giving Garrett a part of what belonged to him. A part of Nic's past that he needed to give to its owner so he could move on. So he could answer the phantom tingling on his left hip that grew stronger every day.

Garrett's hands disappeared with a soft "Thank you," followed by an unexpected laugh.

Nic turned, tossed his T-shirt inside, and shrugged into Cam's jacket, zipping it up halfway. "What's funny?"

Garrett smiled, both sweet and sly, like Nic remembered so fondly from their childhood. "I do regret we never got that dance."

"I don't."

"You still telling that lie?" Garrett grabbed the ends of the jacket, drawing him closer. "I know Mom taught you how."

Taking Garrett's offered hand, Nic slid his other over Garrett's hip and they moved in a slow, jerky circle, the crashing waves for music. "I'm a bit rusty," Nic said.

Garrett shrugged. "So am I."

Nic raised a brow. "No special guy out there?"

He shook his head and then, suddenly shy, buried his face in Nic's shoulder. "We can't all find our own hunk of Boston gorgeous."

"He is, isn't he?" Smiling wide, thinking of Cam in this moment, was as cleansing as the dance, as the rest of his conversation with Garrett had been. He'd let a part of his old life go, getting more of his new life in return. His family, bigger and better than expected. He pulled Garrett closer, arm wrapping around his waist. "I missed you and V. Missed knowing Lette."

Garrett hugged him back. "You don't have to miss us anymore."

"Unless he's in jail for contempt of court."

Nic's gaze whipped up, finding Cam standing in the middle of the hotel room.

The chilly sea breeze gusting around Nic had nothing on the anger and betrayal swirling in his lover's cold, dark eyes.

TWENTY

Cam froze, forgetting how to move when his every thought was consumed by the scene in front of him.

By his world falling apart before his eyes.

Nic didn't dance.

Except with Garrett, apparently.

Making matters worse, his training had him cataloguing every other damning piece of evidence in the room.

Fire blazing. Gravity tee tossed over a chair. Nic in *his* camo jacket, half zipped, exposing the tattoos on his torso. His bare feet.

Like he was at home, right here in Garrett's room.

In Garrett's arms.

Had Nic been lying all those times he'd said or implied he no longer had feelings for Garrett? That his heart now belonged to Cam? Cam didn't think he'd lied, at least not intentionally, but maybe Nic's heart had needed a few days to warm back up to Garrett. To remind Nic of his first love. Of the family he once had and could have again if he just claimed it. Claimed Garrett, which it looked like he was on the way to doing.

Nic stepped out of Garrett's embrace, and self-preservation jump-started Cam's motor functions, propelling him back toward the door. "I'll be in your room next door," he said to Nic. "When you're ready to talk about the rescue and your case." Then to Garrett. "Stay here. The rescue teams are right behind me, fifteen minutes max." Getting Lette out of Vaughn's clutches and getting Nic back for his grand jury hearing had to come first. He'd deal with his aching heart later.

He hustled out the door, Nic's "Boston, wait!" echoing behind him.

Outside on the elevated walkway, he exchanged card keys, swiped the one for Nic's room over the automatic lock, and opened the door, just as the one next door opened again. Cam hurried inside, letting the door go, but Nic's bare foot stopped it from slamming shut.

"Fucking hell, Boston." Yanking back his foot, Nic pushed open the door and hobbled inside, collapsing on the end of the king-size bed.

Cam's first instinct was to go to him. He hated that his second instinct was to check his first, paralyzed again in the middle of the room. "I'm sorry."

Nic was examining his foot, propped on his knee. "It'll be fine."

"I meant for barging in. I didn't think you'd be in there. I was looking for clues as to where you and Garrett might have gone."

"Don't apologize. I meant for you to find us."

"Dancing?" The word was out before Cam could catch it or temper the spite that colored it.

Nic lowered his foot and flopped back on the bed, eyes slipping shut. "I owed him that one."

"Half naked?"

"I showed him the cypress tattoo. I owed him that much too."

"You don't owe him your career."

Nic opened his eyes, and the sun streaming through the sheer curtains turned his blue irises icy clear, stark against the bloodshot whites.

Captivated by the oddly beautiful and equally concerning sight, Cam almost missed Nic's reply, a heavily sighed, "I agree."

"You agree?" Cam stepped to the side of the bed and fisted his hand, resisting the urge to run his fingers through Nic's brown and silver strands. "Then why are you down here?"

"Because he was going after Lette no matter what you or I said." He squinted against the sun's rays, forehead creasing. "I had to stall him."

Cam's chest ached, the need to comfort the man he loved warring with his anger and confusion. The former won, Cam's fingers smoothing over the deep groove between Nic's brows. "Is he gonna bolt on us now?"

"No, he knows the jig is up." Nic lifted an arm and grasped his wrist, drawing his hand into his and winding their fingers together. "And that you're our best shot for getting Lette back."

"You couldn't convince him of that back home?"

He guided the back of Cam's hand to his forehead, pressing it there like a balm, like it was somehow soothing. "He showed up five minutes after you left, along with a text from Victoria begging me to keep him safe. He was going with or without me."

Cam shifted closer, blocking the sun's rays. "Why didn't you call or text me?"

"From in the car next to him?" Nic lowered their clasped hands to over his chest, holding them there. "I could have tried, but I also knew you were in the middle of planning the op. I didn't want to compromise Lette's rescue further. I knew you weren't far behind us. You'd find me. You always do."

"What if you couldn't have stalled him?"

"I at least had to try, for Lette's sake. I won't add her initials to my back too. I won't let her be a regret for some action I failed to take. Or some mess I made." He tugged Cam down, to the edge of the bed next to his hip. "The only way we're going to save Lette is to let you do your job, and I do mine, but I had to get Garrett to stand down first or at least get him out of the line of fire."

"You're wrong."

The crease between Nic's brows reappeared and Cam lifted his other hand, soothing it once more. "You didn't fail to take action the first time." He coasted his hand down, cupping Nic's rough cheek. "You didn't make a mess."

"Garrett said the same thing before I showed him the tattoo."

Cam wondered what else Garrett had said then or when they were dancing. Doubts resurfaced like a sledgehammer, smashing the quiet moment. "Nic, he's your first love, if you—"

Nic rocketed up, clasped hands between them, free hand snaking around the side of Cam's neck. "I'm not in love with him anymore. I'm in love with you."

Proving his point, Nic captured his lips in a hard kiss that was the opposite of last night's soft, sweet assurances. This was an argument, plain and simple, and the familiarity of the approach, the bedrock of their interactions, comforted Cam more than words. But not enough to snuff out every wisp of doubt.

"But your family . . ." he whispered against Nic's lips.

Drawing back, Nic slid his hand to the side of Cam's face. "Got bigger. But you, Cameron . . ." His thumb brushed over his cheek, then his lips, and Cam's eyes fluttered closed. "You're the center of my family. Of my world. The one I've chosen and built for myself."

God, they were all the words Cam needed to hear, evidenced by the rough sincerity in Nic's voice and his tender touch. Cam moved to lean into it, to chase after everything he wanted, and nearly fell over when Nic shifted farther back. Only Nic's hand still clasped in his kept Cam from face-planting into the mattress.

He scowled at a chuckling Nic, who untangled their hands in order to finish lifting his hip so he could pull his wallet out of his back pocket. Nic withdrew a folded piece of yellow legal paper and handed it to Cam. It had been carried around for some time judging by the worn creases.

Cam unfolded it to find a drawing, clearly in Nic's hand. Cam was familiar with it, having seen Nic's sketch of the FBI Stout label, which this drawing resembled. Except where the label had had Gravity's falling apricot logo for a cloverleaf, this one had a Red Sox styled B.

Boston.

For him.

Heart hammering, Cam traced over it with his thumb,

only looking up when Nic took hold of his other hand and placed it over his left hip.

"When this mess with Vaughn is over and everyone's safe, that design is going right here."

In the spot Cam had seen Nic frequently rub a hand over lately. He'd thought Nic had tweaked a muscle there or that the motion was random, a tic he'd developed. It hadn't been random at all. This—he looked down again at the tattoo design—was why.

"You make me a better prosecutor. A better friend. A better man. And you are the only man I want to spend my future with."

The page went blurry, and Cam looked up, blinking rapidly. "Nic, what are you saying?"

"I want to spend the rest of my life with you, Boston. You're it for me." Nic was making a place for him in his life and on his body, permanently.

Clearing his throat, Cam laid the tattoo design on the bedside table, safely out of the way, before grasping Nic's hand and scooting closer. "You're it for me too, baby."

Nic's smile was as bright as the sun, burning away the lines on his face and turning his eyes to liquid fire. "What happens when the cavalry arrives?"

"You're flying back on the Talley jet for your grand jury hearing while I rescue your sister."

"Sounds like a plan." Nic rested his forehead against Cam's. "So then can I spend the next ten minutes kissing my future husband?"

Hand around his neck again, there was no way Nic didn't feel the stutter of his pulse. Cam's heart liked the sound of "future husband" very much.

Tension receding, the instinct to argue, to tease, roared back. "I don't remember saying yes."

"You will."

"Awfully confident."

Nic got that courtroom-ready look about him, the one that made Cam's blood boil. "I will win this argument. My life, our future, depends on it."

"Do your best, Counselor."

By the time the cavalry arrived, he'd kissed Cam's lips numb and stolen his heart for good, winning the argument.

TWENTY-ONE

Hopped up on adrenaline and luxury jet coffee, Nic took the stairs three at a time, up from his office to the federal courtrooms. He slammed through the door, sprinted down the hallway, and rounded the corner, spotting Lauren outside the grand jury room. The sheer relief on her face when she saw him was almost comical, as was the swift shift to raging anger. "When you're done in there, we're gonna talk."

"Already had the talk with Cam." He jogged to a halt in front of her, adjusting the spare tie and suit he'd changed into on the plane. "Then I asked him to marry me."

Lauren's anger evaporated, giving way to an exaggerated whine. "Dude, that's so not fair. I can't be mad at you now." She shoved a bulging bucket file at him. "Make good use of these and all will be forgiven."

He riffled through each colored folder inside, thumbing through the stacks of paper. Smiling, he tucked the folder under his arm. "Thank you for this. Can you bring Cole up in twenty?"

"You laying it all out for them?"

He nodded. "Now or never."

"I'll bring him up in fifteen, just in case."

She bolted for the stairs, determined. Similarly resolved and imbued with energy and confidence by the folder under his arm and Cam's favorite tie around his neck, Nic knocked lightly at the grand jury room door. The bailiff opened the door and Nic entered, just as Bowers stood to address the jurors. "Ladies and gentlemen, I need to apologize on behalf of . . ." His words drifted off, noticing the jurors' wandering attention.

"No apologies necessary, sir," Nic said.

Bowers spun, black eyes boring into his, equal parts fury and fear. He had hoped Nic wouldn't show. Had thought Nic had played right into his hands. But the very thing Bowers had counted on to discredit Nic—his relationship with Cam—was the reason Nic was here now.

To discredit him instead.

If Nic smirked a little, it couldn't be helped.

Stepping fully into the room, he addressed the jurors. "Thank you for the extension of time." He gestured with the folder. "I think you'll find I've used it wisely."

Bowers straightened his spine, feigning confidence as he shifted into arrogant boss mode. "Attorney Price," he clipped. "We should go over what you have there before you present it to the jury."

"No need, sir." He crossed behind Bowers and dropped the file on the prosecutor's desk. "Though, if you'll stay, please." He held a hand out toward the desk at the front of the room. "I'll be calling you as a witness."

"Me?"

"Yes, Lou, you."

Bowers's beady eyes darted back and forth between him and the jurors, none of whom looked surprised. Nic had already primed them for the case against the US Attorney, a possibility Bowers's own ego prevented him from even considering.

"Pardon, Attorney Price," the foreman interrupted. "But we have some questions for you first."

Nic returned his attention to the jury. "Of course," he said amiably. His ego wasn't so big that he didn't expect to have to answer some questions too. He'd rather get that out of the way now before presenting his case. He had to win back the jury's trust if he wanted to convince them of his arguments.

Smug, Bowers made a show of claiming the prosecutor's desk all for himself, leaving the witness box for Nic. Fine by Nic. It was easier to speak directly to the jurors from there, and he often did so in these hearings.

"We received a letter from the target's counsel accusing you of conflicts of interest and prosecutorial misconduct."

"I've seen the letter," he said with a nod. "Though it requires an update. Agent Byrne is no longer my boyfriend."

"Curious time for a breakup," Bowers remarked.

"Not a breakup." Nic relaxed in the chair, hands folded in his lap, one leg crossed over the other, bouncing a little as he smiled. "He's my fiancé now."

Bowers had quite the opposite reaction, slamming his palm on the desk. "And that's not a conflict of interest?"

"Attorney Bowers," the foreman said. "This is Attorney Price's case. I believe you're here as a witness. Not to ask questions."

"It's no problem," Nic said. "I came prepared to

answer." He rotated his chair slightly toward Bowers. "The green folder, if you'd please," he said with a nod to the bucket file on the table. "I'm sorry these aren't loaded on your tablets yet," he told the jury. "We didn't have time." And they didn't want to give Bowers a heads-up as to their strategy either.

Bowers pulled out the designated folder, opened it, and flipped through the sheets of paper held together by a large binder clip. "These are letters from the other attorneys in our office."

"And behind the second tab?" Nic said.

Bowers flipped farther back. "Letters from agents in the FBI field office."

"Saying what?"

Bowers pressed his lips together, reluctant to answer.

"What do they say, Attorney Bowers?" the foreman pressed.

Bowers stood, shoved the papers back in the folder, and walked it over to the foreman. "That there's been no evidence of unprofessional conduct between Attorney Price and Agent Byrne."

Taking the folder, the foreman quickly reviewed the letters inside, before passing it down the row. "Those letters all say cases run more smoothly when Attorney Price and Agent Byrne work together."

Bowers didn't have a counterargument for the truth. Nic, however, needed to explain the truth further.

"The letter from Mr. Vaughn's counsel is true in part." He rested his forearms on his knees, having a conversation with the jury. Not testifying, not preaching, and certainly not raising his voice like Bowers was prone to do. "Compared to other FBI agents I work with, I do know better how Agent Byrne thinks. I can anticipate his answers and strategies. Hell, I can finish his sentences. But that doesn't disqualify him from being a witness in my cases. Nor does it disqualify me from this one. I just don't have to prep him as much as I would any other witness. He makes my—*our*—job easier. I also trust him to do his job because I trust him implicitly. Otherwise, I wouldn't have left him to rescue my sister while I'm here."

"What about the fact that this case involves your father?" Bowers said, standing once more. "You have a vendetta against Mr. Vaughn. A personal stake in putting him behind bars. If he's indicted and found guilty of the crimes on your charge sheet, the loans he made to your father would be fraudulent, would be wiped out, and your inheritance would be safe."

"One," Nic said, ticking off with his fingers, "there's nothing left for me to inherit, and I'm not seeking remuneration from Duncan Vaughn. Only justice. Two"—he withdrew a folded sheet from inside his coat pocket—"this is a copy of the letter I previously presented to Mr. Vaughn's attorney." Nic waited for the bailiff to hand it over to the foreman. "If I do inherit anything, the proceeds will be donated to several charities. Organizations that help the sort of people my father abused. I do not want a cent of his money."

Bowers sneered. "That's a nice sob story."

"I don't want your pity either, Lou," Nic sniped. Then said more politely to the jury, "Or yours, respectfully. I just want to keep my family safe, along with what's left of Harris Kincaid's family, and all the other families and individuals Duncan Vaughn has threatened over the years. He should be brought to justice, as should his associates who have abused the system in his name."

It took all Nic had not to glance at Bowers as he delivered that line. But it wasn't Bowers he needed to convince. Bowers knew the truth of what he'd done. Nic's job was to convince the jury, who, as they passed the various papers around, had begun to nod their heads.

"I'd like to proceed with my case," he said, "as it's time sensitive. But if you need to consider this matter further, we can take a recess."

The foreman swiveled in his chair, canvassing the other jurors on whether they were ready to proceed. They all answered "yes." The foreman rotated back around. "You've been nothing but by the book, Attorney Price. Please proceed. We're eager to hear what you've got for us."

"Thank you." Standing, he stepped out from behind the witness desk and addressed the bailiff. "Agent Hall should be outside with my first witness, Special Agent Francis Cole." While the bailiff retrieved Cole, Nic moved to stand behind the prosecutor's table.

Bowers squirmed beside him. "If you've got this under control, then I'll go."

Nic lowered his voice for their ears only. "You do that, and I'll make sure the bailiff blocks your exit." He turned a shark's grin on his boss. "Is your house in order as well as mine was, Lou? Or did I just take your house?"

Bowers blanched, sinking down into his chair while Nic remained standing, biting back his smile as the bailiff led in Agent Cole. A half hour later, Bowers was even paler and damn near sweating. Nic had systematically laid out the evidence against Cole—his presence on each compromised op, the mysterious injections of cash into his account, his intense interest in the case against Vaughn, and the calls Lauren had traced between Cole's FBI-issued phone and another government-issued phone. Another of Vaughn's moles.

"Who was on the other end of that line, Agent Cole?"

The young agent lowered his chin, eyes downcast, until they rose again and skipped past Nic to the other attorney at the prosecutor's table. "The calls were with Attorney Bowers."

Several jurors gasped. While Nic had prepared them for this possibility, it was another thing to have the reality confirmed, especially from someone outside Nic's circle.

Two someones in fact.

He withdrew the blue folder from the file. "I've got another affidavit here." He passed the folder to the bailiff for delivery to the foreman. "From Rebecca Wright, a cooperating witness in custody, confirming she was contracted through Attorney Bowers to steal evidence from Assistant Director Moore's private safe. Evidence that incriminated Duncan Vaughn."

He had Bowers dead to rights.

And the US Attorney knew it.

Bowers shot to his feet, and for a moment Nic thought he was going to make a run for it. The door to the grand jury room was opening, but Bowers would have a hard time getting past him and the bailiff. Once AD Moore and the Deputy AG stepped into the room, however, Bowers knew the game was up.

"I'd like to speak with Attorney Price," Bowers said to the foreman. "I believe I have information that will be useful to the case."

So he was going to play it that way, then. Nic wasn't

surprised. Of course Bowers would try to save his own neck.

"Attorney Price?" the foreman asked.

He contemplated refusing—daydreamed for a second of tearing Bowers apart on the stand—but then the image of his sister flashed across his mind. A sister he wanted to get to know better. He had to wrap this up, as soon as possible, so he could get to what was most important.

"If you'll please excuse us for a few minutes," he said to the foreman. The jurors filed out, back to their work area, while the bailiff handed Cole off to Lauren at the door.

Once it was only Nic, Jack, and Elton left in the room with him, Bowers lifted his chin, proclaiming, "I want a deal."

"That depends on what you've got," Jack said.

"Proof that Duncan Vaughn ordered the murder of Curtis Price. I gave him the drugs that killed Curtis Price."

Nic knew that already from the info and pictures Mel, Jamie, and Lauren had obtained, so the hot, bright flare of anger at hearing Bowers actually admit it—knowing he had a hand in his father's death—took Nic by surprise. Nic despised his father, but he hadn't wished him death, hadn't wished for his heart to be blown up, hadn't wished for the danger that his murder put him, Lette, and all their loved ones in. And this spiteful, hateful man before Nic, another he'd labored under for years, loved power so much, hated Nic so much, that it was worth compromising his professional and personal ethics to keep his superior position. Fuck him for almost tearing Nic's life and family apart. He white-knuckled the edge of the witness table behind him, holding himself back from lunging. Noticing, Moore moved half in front of him, and

Nic both chafed at and appreciated the protective maneuver.

"Who exactly did you give them to?" Jack asked.

"To one of his associates, at Vaughn's express request."

"I've got the video of him stealing it." Nic reached into his pocket and produced the flash drive, handing it to Jack. "And of witness tampering. He paid Vaughn off to influence a witness in one of his cases." Nic got more than a little thrill at seeing Bowers sweat some more. "He's had you ever since, hasn't he? Including requesting Rebecca Wright to steal those flash drives from El?"

Lips thin, eyes narrowed, Bowers nodded grudgingly.

"And you'll testify to this?" Jack asked.

"For a reduced sentence, to be served at a minimum-security prison. I can't go to gen pop, not with the same criminals I put away."

Nic growled from behind Moore. "You're no better than them. Between this and the file full of complaints Moore's got on you . . ."

Jack turned to El. "That's true?"

Moore nodded, but Jack deferred again to Nic. "This is your call, Price."

He could have charged Bowers with any number of crimes—aiding and abetting, conspiracy to commit murder, felony murder. He'd aided in killing his father, for fuck's sake. Still, it was his crimes against justice, against everything they worked daily to uphold, that rankled most. How many more lives besides his father's had been lost or jeopardized because Bowers had turned his back on his oaths? Those were the violations, the crimes Nic wanted Bowers charged for.

"Federal witness tampering, theft of evidence, and reckless endangerment," he said. "Twenty-five years, parole hearing at fifteen." If he even made it that long. "Minimum security."

Jack nodded, then turned back to Bowers. "That's the deal, Lou, take it or leave it. And obviously you're relieved of your position, effective immediately, and stripped of any commendations and benefits. I'm also reserving the right to review the complaints Moore's got on you and take additional action if necessary."

"Fine. Just keep me out of gen pop."

The click of handcuffs around Bowers's wrists was only slightly sweeter than Jack making Nic acting US Attorney right in front of Bowers, with a promise to see about making the appointment official.

But neither the cuffs nor the promotion were as sweet as the indictment for Duncan Vaughn the grand jury handed him an hour later, after Bowers's testimony.

The only thing sweeter was Moore's order to "Go get him."

TWENTY-TWO

There was no great way to raid a mansion full of windows on fifteen acres of seaside property, except maybe at night, and Cam didn't have that option. He wouldn't risk Nic's sister for another six hours. She'd already been gone too long in his book, the odds of return decreasing with each passing hour.

They knew where Lette was. They had a tactical plan, enhanced by Nic and Garrett's earlier recon and Jamie's drone. The K&R expert in him and the boyfriend in him demanded action now.

Cam's plan of attack had four teams simultaneously converging on the property from multiple directions. Beta and Charlie teams from the north and south cypress groves. A SWAT team on its way down the freeway, headed for the drive and front entrance. Alpha team from the beachfront cliff, the closest position to the house.

"Alpha, this is Comm," Jamie radioed. "Ten heat signatures inside."

"Outside?" Cam asked.

"Two, guarding the front of the house."

"On the entry gate?"

"None, only the security cameras." Keystrokes on the other end. "Which are now on a loop. SWAT team is two minutes out."

"Lette?" Garrett asked from beside Cam.

"In the kitchen, assuming I'm reading the heat signatures correctly."

Binoculars in hand, Garrett crept toward the edge of the cliff.

"Careful," Cam warned.

Garrett side-eyed him. "Marine major, remember?" He peeked over the edge, just enough to peer through the lenses. "It's her, and she's awake now. Tied to a stool looks like." Per his and Nic's recon, Lette had been passed out earlier; this was good news. "She'll be helpful."

"She's injured."

"And by now, super pissed." Garrett grinned. "This is gonna be fun."

Nic's voice echoed in Cam's head. *Fucking jarhead.*

"One minute," Jamie radioed. "Beta, Charlie, second position."

Vaughn's guards would have to be watching the perimeter with high-powered goggles to spot their movement, if they were looking that direction at all. As much as it chilled them, the sea breeze also helped, disguising the extra sway of the overgrown beach grass. Cam signaled his Alpha team, including Lorton, to line up beside him.

"Thirty seconds," Jamie counted down. "All teams, strike position."

The perimeter teams inched closer, and Cam's team slid

their hands over the cliff edge, ready to lever up as soon as they got the signal.

Which was going to be pretty damn hard to miss.

Cam braced.

The crunch of metal screeched over the comm in his ear, the ram-fitted SWAT van barreling through the property's metal entry gate.

"Hostiles drawn to the front," Jamie reported as gunfire erupted over the comm.

Perfect. Just as they'd planned.

"Go, go, go!" Cam hopped over the cliff with his team and ran flat out toward the house, Beta and Charlie teams in his periphery doing the same.

"Comms going white for pop," Jamie said. "In three, two, one . . ."

White noise crackled in Cam's ear, a protective buffer, as Jamie's drone dropped out of the sky, fought for a terrifying second with the wind, then emitted a high-pitched pulse, muffled by the white noise, that instantly shattered every window in the house.

It cleared their path and distracted the guards inside, who'd instinctively ducked and covered their heads and ears.

"Go for entry," Cam called, and all around the redwood deck that circled the mansion, FBI agents leaped the rails and crashed the rest of the way through the blown-out windows.

Gunfire escalated from either end of the house, Beta and Charlie teams drawing fire while Alpha team blitzed the living room, headed for the kitchen. But between them and Lette stood half a dozen guards, shaking off their disorientation and drawing their weapons.

Cam charged the nearest one, grabbed his partially raised firing arm, and slammed his wrist against his raised knee, knocking the pistol loose. Cam kicked it clear, then rammed his shoulder into the hostile's chest. Keeping his center of gravity low, he flipped the guard over, sending him to the ground with a thunderous boom.

Beside him, Garrett had another guard by the arm, twisted behind his back. He ripped the pistol from his hands, kicked the backs of the guard's knees, and forced him to the ground. He knocked him the rest of the way over with a roundhouse kick to the head. "Lette!" he hollered.

A crack of wood sounded behind them. "Do your job, bro!" she yelled, sounding both exhilarated and winded.

Cam moved to turn, to check on her condition, but was cut short by two more guards rushing toward them from the hallway. "Lorton, clothesline, now!" he shouted.

Standing by the hallway entrance, out of sight of the charging guard, Lorton threw out a stiff arm. The hostile rammed right into it and flailed backward. The trailing guard hopped the downed one, charging forward, but Cam was waiting. He swept out a leg just as the hostile's feet touched the ground again, not giving him a chance to catch his balance. He went down hard on his ass with a startled yelp.

"SWAT's cleared the front," Jamie radioed.

"Send 'em in!" Cam replied. "We can use the reinforce—"

A sharp sting sliced across Cam's calf, turning his words into a hiss. The guard on his ass had a knife in hand, swinging, trying to land a second cut. Cam swung his uninjured leg, just out of reach but tempting enough for the guard to lunge forward, giving Lorton a chance to wrap an arm around his neck. Lorton dragged him back while Cam intercepted his flailing elbow with his foot, dislodging the knife and kicking it clear with the guns.

Cam straightened, turning toward Lette, and saw a hostile, gun arm raised, coming through the window closest to where Garrett had just disarmed the last hostile between him and his sister. As important as saving Lette was, so was keeping Garrett alive. Nic would never forgive himself if something happened to Garrett either.

"Sare, drop!" Cam shouted, doing his best to mimic Nic's captain voice. Garrett responded immediately, hitting the floor.

Cam fired at the shooter, hitting him square in the shoulder. The impact drove the guard back a step, but then the next instant, he corrected and lurched forward, right at Cam. Cam lifted his gun to fire again, but the guard's forward momentum stuttered. He wasn't charging—he was falling—and making a last-ditch effort to take Cam with him.

Cam jerked to the side, out of the way, and the guard hit the floor, face-first, a knife protruding out of his back. Gaze whipping up, Cam followed the knife's trajectory, right to Lette. She stood tall in the kitchen, another knife in her hand and another guard unconscious at her feet. She was pale and winded, chest heaving as she gasped for breath, and blood trickled from a cut at her hairline, but she was also smiling. "Glad I practiced that with Mel."

Teams radioed in "Clear," Jamie's the last, and Cam finally loosed a grin himself. "There's someone else you need to meet," he said to Lette. "Y'all are going to be best friends."

Hopping bodies, Garrett made it the rest of the way to

his sister and hauled her into his arms while Cam surveyed the room, counting the unconscious bodies and looking for a blond head among them.

All guards. No blonds. No Vaughn.

"Anyone have a twenty on Duncan Vaughn?"

"Negative," all around.

"Lette, did Nic show you a picture of Duncan Vaughn? About six foot, blond, light brown eyes."

"Yeah," she said. "Mom's old friend. He's not here. He never was."

Because he'd been waiting back in San Francisco for the last leverage point to be left alone and unguarded.

Nic.

———

Cam was shouting, but Nic couldn't understand the words for all the background noise on the other end of the line—the crash of waves, the wail of emergency sirens, the *whoomp whoomp whoomp* of helicopter blades.

"I can't hear you!" Nic hollered back, absurdly loud in the cab of his truck, but he had no idea if Cam could hear him either.

"Hold a sec!"

Nic swung his truck into their driveway and threw it into Park, engine idling and heater still running. He cracked a window and checked the home security app on his phone as he waited. All clear, he deactivated it just as the racket on Cam's end quieted.

"That better?" Cam asked.

"Much. Is Lette safe?"

"Yeah, EMS is seeing to her now."

Relief was a much-needed breath of fresh air. "And you and Garrett?"

"Garrett's fine. I got sliced by a knife—"

His fresh air blew right out the cracked window. "You what?"

"Superficial," Cam rushed to clarify. "We're safe, Nic, but you're not. Vaughn's not here. I think he's coming after you."

Nic flipped off the ignition, grabbed his holstered Beretta out of the center console and his bag from behind the seats, then climbed out of the cab. "Not that I've seen." He clipped the holster to his belt as he headed for the front door. "Hell, I've been looking for him all evening. I've got an indictment and an arrest warrant for him, but he's nowhere to be found."

"That was my next question. Good deal. And Bowers?"

"Folded under the evidence. Turned cooperating witness."

"He's been relieved of his position?"

"By Jack Hayward himself, and I've been named interim US Attorney."

"Now that's what I'm talking about." He clapped and Nic could also hear the smile in his voice. "Stick a bottle of champagne in the fridge for when Vaughn is on his way to lockup too. Where all did you check?"

Nic ticked off locations as he fumbled in his bag for the house key, the sunset casting shadows across the front porch and making it difficult to see. "Home, office, airplane hangar, Curtis's house, Gravity, and I even swung by Mobile Command, but he hasn't come looking for me, or Victoria, there either."

"One of his other properties, then?"

"Lauren's on it." Key found, Nic inserted it into the lock and jiggled it until it turned. Half the battle won. "Or he could be in the wind already."

"We need to get someone else on you," Cam said. "Eddie or Mel."

"I'm at home, trying to get the damn door unlocked as we speak, and Eddie's on his way over." He wedged the phone between his shoulder and ear and wrenched the ancient doorknob with both hands. "I'll get inside, activate the security measures, and wait for Eddie."

"Nic—"

Finally, the doorknob gave, clicking free, and he pushed the door open, stepping inside. "I'm not sacrificing Victoria's safety for mine."

"You sure about that, Dom?"

The dining room lights flickered on, and all the moisture in Nic's mouth fled as heat prickled under his skin. Duncan Vaughn sat at his dining table, spinning a Zippo lighter over a glass of whiskey, Cam's bottle of Jameson off to the side. Behind Vaughn stood his usual two henchmen, still bruised from their run-in with Eddie the other night, and they'd brought another goon who was standing in the hallway door. Their bulk filled the space, making the house seem tinier than it already was, and they were way too close for Nic to draw his weapon and get four shots off before he risked getting shot himself.

"Nic!" Cam yelled, plenty loud now. Then, at someone else, Aidan likely, "Vaughn's there at the house!"

Moving slow and deliberate, Nic raised his hands, waited for Vaughn to nod, then lowered his bag to the floor and took the phone in hand once more. He forced moisture into his mouth, licking his lips. "Boston, listen to me."

"Baby!"

The vibrating fear in the shouted endearment almost drove Nic to his knees. Almost. But he couldn't show that weakness in front of Vaughn.

"I love you, Cameron. If this doesn't go my way, Aidan knows what to do." He'd made those arrangements when he and Cam had gone public with their relationship and moved in together. One such measure included doubling the insurance on this house, which, with the amount of firepower in here at the moment, literally and figuratively, Nic deemed downright prescient.

Maybe too was this one last call with Cam, with the man who'd brought love into his life again. Who'd given him what he never thought he'd have. "I wanted to marry you, more than anything. Thank you for giving me a family."

"Christ, baby." Misery choked Cam's words. "I love you too, Dominic. I need you to stall one more time today. Fight and stay alive for me. For us."

"I'll do my best." He swallowed around the lump in his throat and switched up their usual sign off. "Sooner, Boston," he said, getting a choked "Sooner, Price," in return.

"Touching farewell," Vaughn said once they'd hung up.

"Hope you took notes," Nic said with as much confidence as he could muster. "Since you're the one who's going to be saying farewell." He stepped forward and the extra muscle converged, blocking his path.

"Check him for weapons," Vaughn said. "Then let him through."

"How'd you get in here?" Nic asked as one of the goons divested him of the Beretta and gave him a full pat down.

"You're not the only one with hacker contacts."

Satisfied there were no other weapons on him, the goon stepped back, and Nic approached the table. He withdrew the folded indictment from his jacket pocket and slid it across the table to Vaughn.

"Duncan Vaughn, you've been indicted by the grand jury on charges of racketeering, bank and loan fraud, witness tampering, assault and battery, conspiracy to commit murder, murder, and kidnapping. A warrant for your arrest has been issued. Your request for bail has already been denied. You will be tried, will lose, and will spend the rest of your life in jail."

Vaughn picked up the paper, skimmed it once, then refolded it. "You know as well as I do that I have no intention of doing any of that."

"Then what are you doing here?"

"Making an example out of you before I leave for parts unknown."

Nic didn't duck fast enough, or rather he didn't anticipate the baton in hallway thug's hand, extending his reach and clipping Nic across the back of his head. Nic went sprawling across the floor, barely catching himself before his face whacked the hardwood.

Feet approached, a shadow falling over him.

He grabbed the leg of the closest chair, the one that had been glued back together half a dozen times, and swung it forward. The leg cracked at the breakpoint, the bulk of the flying chair hurtling at the guy in front of Nic, sending him reeling back into the kitchen. Nic flipped to his back, clutching what remained of the broken chair leg, and jammed the pointy end into the shoulder of the other goon coming down on him. The attacker crumpled, bent in half, clutching his shoulder. Using his momentum, Nic flipped back over and scurried low, on hands and knees, into the kitchen, fleeing from the other goon who was fast advancing, weapon drawn.

"No shots!" Vaughn demanded. "He's mine."

Well, if bullets were off the table, Nic felt a lot better about his prospects. At least in the short term. Until the same broken chair came hurtling back at him. Too high, though, the thug anticipating he'd stand. He stayed low instead, letting the chair fly overhead and slow the attackers behind him.

"Dead end in there, Dom," Vaughn taunted.

Technically not—he could flee through the garage door if he had to—but that was a last resort if he couldn't make use of all the other weapons the kitchen had to offer. To help him stay alive and to help him get Vaughn.

He rocketed to his feet and swung the top oven door down, then did the same on the lower oven, creating more obstacles for the trailing attackers. That done, he spun and grabbed the cast iron skillet off the stovetop. "You really hated my father this much?" he said to Vaughn.

"He took everything," Vaughn said, as conversationally as could be, never mind Nic was fighting for his life. "I'm returning the favor."

"He's dead. How will my death make the bastard any more miserable?"

"I want all trace of his legacy gone."

Skillet in hand, Nic charged the goon blocking the knives he needed. He missed on the first swing, the guy dodging, then catching Nic in the side with one punch, in the chin with the next. The skillet, however, worked as a counterweight, keeping him from tipping backward. And when the goon aimed a right hook at Nic's cheek, Nic blocked the hit with the skillet.

Knuckles crashed into the cast iron and the pan went flying out of Nic's hand, smashing first into the cabinet doors, then to the travertine floor, the crack of wood and stone unmistakable. The crack of bones in the goon's hand had been louder, though, and with him bent over cradling it, Nic rammed his elbow to the back of his head, knocking him out cold. He landed hard, the spiderweb of cracks in the floor spreading.

"I am not part of Curtis's legacy," Nic shouted over his shoulder at Vaughn before darting past the fallen body, arm extended for the knife block.

He managed a swipe at it, tipping it on its side, sending knives flying, but then one of the attackers caught up to him, intercepting Nic's outstretched arm while the other goon grabbed his trailing one. Nic stumbled forward, chin first, into the granite counter, before falling the rest of the way to the floor, taking it on the chin again from the hard stone floor. He tasted blood and swore he could even taste the stars bursting behind his eyes.

Next thing he knew, Nic was on his back, arms pinned under him, guards holding him down by the shoulders and legs, as Vaughn loomed over him. "Your eyes don't lie, Dom. They're the same eyes that stole the only person I ever loved. Every time I look into yours, I see Curtis." All trace of the attractive, charming investor was gone—an angry, bitter man in his place.

Nic spat in his face, distracting from his hand closing around one of the knives under him. "And you were going to fuck me?"

"No," Vaughn said, pressing a knee into his chest. "I

would have gotten you right here, under me." He shoved off his goon's hand, ramming his own into Nic's shoulder. "I would have killed you before it got to the fucking." Vaughn's knee in his chest, Nic struggled for air. "Just like I'm going to kill your sister too."

"I don't think so." Nic twisted, enough to jostle Vaughn and stab the right-hand goon's foot.

Vaughn jumped back, and the other thug swung for Nic's face. Nic rolled into the first who was standing on one leg, his injured foot lifted. Feet taken out from under him, he toppled forward into the goon gunning for Nic, and they went down in a heap.

Nic seized another knife and lunged after Vaughn. "Not so fast, asshole." He grabbed him by the ankle, wrestling him to the floor just shy of the dining room hardwood. Nic vaguely registered someone banging at the front door, calling his name, but his primary objective was eliminating the immediate threat, the one to his family. Nic wrestled Vaughn to his back, pinning him down. "You're never going to stop coming at us, are you?"

Grin wicked, Vaughn didn't let an ounce of fear show in his light brown eyes. "Of course I'm not, Dom." Vaughn still thought he was running this game, even as his breaths grew short and Nic's knife hovered above him.

It would be so easy to plunge the knife into his carotid and eliminate the threat, once and for all. To never have to look over his shoulder again. To make sure his loved ones were safe. To protect at any and all cost. What was one more number added to the kill count inked on his skin?

Nic gripped the knife tighter, then startled as the timer light in the office to his left clicked on. In the lamp's halo sat Bird, green eyes big, orange tail swishing across the windowsill, threatening to tip the framed pictures Cam had lined up there.

A photo from Aidan and Jamie's wedding that Cam had scoured for after Nic had mentioned he regretted not being in the other wedding party ones. Nic was standing next to Aidan, the affection between friends apparent.

Another from Gravity, Nic and Eddie behind the tasting bar together, clinking pint glass rims in a toast.

One of Nic with Cam's family in Boston, taken after the memorial for Cam's sister.

A candid Lauren had taken of all of them at her agent swearing-in.

His family. The one Nic had chosen, the ones who'd chosen him.

He'd want to add one of the Sares too—Victoria, Garrett, and Lette—another family he'd just found. A family he wanted to get to know, maybe even be a part of, which wouldn't happen if he was behind bars.

A picture of Cam's face when he revealed the tattoo he was going to get on his left hip.

And a big family picture with everyone, maybe taken at his and Cam's wedding.

A happy ending he'd never get if he took Duncan Vaughn's life, which if he was being honest, wouldn't be nearly as satisfying as watching him suffer. And Nic would make sure of that. He'd make sure Vaughn never touched or threatened his family again, but he'd do that—protect them—without also sacrificing his future too.

He wouldn't cut through the rope.

He flipped the knife, smiling at the fear that flashed in Vaughn's eyes, the other man misreading his intent. "I think I'd rather watch you lose everything. And for the last fucking time, the name's Nic."

He brought the butt of the knife down—short of a deadly blow—but enough to knock Vaughn out.

Sitting back on his haunches, he took a giant breath and tossed the knife aside, just as Eddie, weapon drawn, came barreling around the corner. His dark eyes quickly scanned the area, counting bodies, before landing on him and Vaughn. "Is he dead?"

Nic shook his head. "Incapacitated. Death would be too easy."

Eddie holstered his pistol and held out a hand, helping him up. Once he stood, a phone was shoved under his nose. "Someone wants to talk to you."

Before taking Eddie's, Nic drew out his own phone and opened Moore's contact info. "Call the AD," he said, swapping phones. "Tell him to get a team down here stat."

Eddie nodded, turning to the living room with Nic's phone, and Nic brought Eddie's to his ear, the screen telling him who was on the other end.

"Boston."

"Oh, thank God." Cam's relief was as palpable as his earlier misery had been. "Baby, are you okay?"

Nic looked around at the destruction he'd wrought and smiled. He was better than okay. "We're going to have to remodel a bit."

Cam's watery laughter was the best thing he'd heard all day.

TWENTY-THREE

Cam swung the FBI sedan into the driveway beside Nic's truck and glanced at the dash clock. He'd seen two in the morning way too many times this week. The neighbors couldn't be loving it either. Porch and interior lights blazing, their home glowed like a beacon on the otherwise dark street. At least the police cruisers and emergency vehicles were gone by now, only Eddie's Wrangler left parked at the curb. Aside from their obnoxiously bright house, all was quiet and normal on their street. No indication that they'd closed a major case, that a local gangster was behind bars, that the corrupt US Attorney was ousted, and that Nicolette Sare was safe and sound with her family.

No indication that Cam had almost lost everything—his family, his future—in the process.

After the I'm-still-alive call from Nic—*thank fuck*—they'd both had shitstorms to deal with on their respective ends, making further calls impossible. He'd checked in periodically by text, but it had taken hours to get home. From Cambria, he'd gone to San Francisco General with the

Sares, then from the hospital to local lockup for booking, and from there to the office to debrief with Aidan and Moore. When he'd finally escaped the Federal Building, he'd decided against calling ahead in case Nic had managed to fall asleep. Nic would be keyed up, no doubt, same as Cam.

After days without sleep, he and Cam were both skating the same adrenaline-rush-exhausted edge. Cam was looking forward to his pillow almost as much as he was looking forward to fucking his boyfriend.

Correction. His fiancé.

Mind lingering in the clouds over that development, Cam couldn't care less about the busted-up front door lock. They'd needed to fix it for a while. Nor did he care about finding his traitorous cat perched on Nic's lap, happily getting scratches behind his ears, while Eddie and Nic shared a couple of beers at the dining table.

Cam closed the door and dropped his bag on the couch. "Is it sooner?"

Nic lowered his bottle and turned his bruised and bandaged face toward him. One look and Cam came crashing back to earth, wincing in sympathy.

Nic's lips tipped up in a tired, amused smile. "Much later, I'm afraid."

Bird jumped off his lap, bushy tail shaking high in greeting as he trotted across the living room and flopped on his side at Cam's feet. Kneeling, Cam gave him a belly scratch and surreptitiously checked out the room, assessing the damage besides that done to Nic.

Not too bad, considering. The dining table chair with the bum leg was missing—not a surprise—and the living room rug had been rolled back toward the A/V system, probably to protect it from foot traffic. If there'd been any actual damage to it in the course of the takedown, the rug would have been removed as evidence. Even the living room lamps, ottoman, and side tables were intact and accounted for. What remodel was Nic talking about?

"You got one of those stouts for me?" he asked, straightening.

Nic tilted his head toward the kitchen.

Bird raced ahead, hopping back into Nic's lap, while Cam followed, crossing the living room, skirting the edge of the dining area—a hand coasting over Nic's shoulder—before he turned the corner to the kitchen.

And ground to a screeching halt. "Holy fuck!"

"Watch your step," Nic belatedly warned.

"Watch your step?" Cam scoffed. "Where the fuck am I supposed to step?"

Eddie chuckled. "You should have seen some of the messes he made as a SEAL. That's amateur hour by comparison."

Bottles clanked behind Cam, who was busy cataloguing the damage.

Both oven doors gone, several cabinet doors removed, travertine floor tiles cracked and dented, granite countertops chipped at either end, the knife block on its side, and the knives missing altogether.

And where the fuck was the cast iron skillet he always left out on the stove? The only pan he used in the whole damn kitchen. They'd have to ask for a new one on the wedding registry. Silly thought, but Cam needed silly ones to chase away the much darker thoughts racing through his head. Like how the hell had Nic fought his way out of this? Which of those dents and cracks had he caused? How close had he come to not making it out at all?

He steadied himself with a hand to the bar, and Nic's touch ghosted over his lower back, reminding Cam he was still here. Banged up a bit, but he'd fought his way out. Survived. They still had their home and future together.

Cam breathed in deep, fighting back the panic that had threatened. "What can I touch?" he asked once it had receded. "Where can I walk?"

"CSU already processed," Nic answered. "They took the doors and such as evidence. Just be careful for your own sake."

He tiptoed around the cracks and dents, made it to the fridge, and grabbed a bottle of stout, popping the cap with the opener out on the chipped counter. Carefully making his way back to the table, he passed behind Nic's chair and ran a hand through his ruffled hair, desperately needing to touch him, to reassure himself again that Nic was here, to silence the worst-case scenarios running through his mind as to the gauntlet Nic had had to run.

Nic jerked away with a hiss, and Cam yanked back his hand. Nic caught it, fingers wrapped around his wrist. "It's not you," he said, looking up. "Took a baton to the back of the head."

More than he'd reported on the phone or over text and more than the bruises and butterfly bandages let on. "Medics check you out?"

Nic nodded, entwining their fingers, as Cam claimed the chair next to him. "And your cut?"

Cam lifted his pant leg, showing off the bandage around his calf. "All good. And so are Lette and Garrett," he said, anticipating Nic's next question. "They're keeping Lette in observation overnight." Worry sharpened Nic's features, and Cam squeezed his fingers. "She's a bit dehydrated, and the ER doc was concerned about a possible concussion. Probably nothing. She's pretty tough, like Mel and Lauren-level scary, so I'm sure she'll be fine."

"Should we go up?"

He shook his head, untangled his hand, and slumped back in his chair, taking a long swallow of his favorite brew. "Garrett and Victoria are there. We'll go up in the morning."

"Which is going to be here sooner than any of us want," Eddie said. "And I'm wheels up at oh-nine-hundred." He drained the rest of his beer as he stood.

Nic held his fist out for a bump. "Thank you. For everything."

"Always." Eddie next held out his fist to Cam. "You take care of him."

Cam bumped back, chest warming at being included in Nic's SEAL and Gravity family too. "I mean to." His gaze strayed to Nic, constantly checking that he was here, that he'd survived, that this case was behind them and this was their new reality. Fiery blue eyes burned back at him.

"Aww, fuck." Eddie waved a hand at both of them. "You're not even married yet, and you've already got honeymoon googly eyes going on."

Cam pretended to be offended at Nic. "You told him?"

"And Lauren." Nic shrugged, then said to Eddie, "After the week we've had, Cam and I deserve a honeymoon." He shot a sexy leer at Cam. "A good long one."

Eddie bolted for the door. "Never been so glad to have a morning call time."

"One day, Vasquez, you'll meet your match."

Wrenching open the door, Eddie grinned over his shoulder. "Nev-ah. No one can handle this." He shook his admittedly fine ass, then disappeared out the door, laughing.

Nic was laughing too as he nudged Bird off his lap and tipped Cam's direction, nuzzling his cheek. "Welcome home, to what's left of it."

"You're here. That's all that matters." Cam teased the corner of Nic's mouth, just short of a kiss, before he sat back and took another swig of his beer. He talked over Nic's throaty rumble of frustration. "It feels like we've been gone forever."

"Joe thinks so. Left us a surprise in your shoes."

"In mine?"

"'Cause he likes me better."

Traitor indeed, the both of them. "You stole my cat."

"I showed your cat a better way."

"No, you bribed him with extra food and treats. But I don't want to argue about that right now. Got something else in mind." He finished his beer, set the empty on the table next to Eddie's, and stood. Nic moved to stand too, but Cam kept him seated, a hand on his shoulder and a leg thrown over his lap. "This okay?"

Nic rolled his hips, bringing their groins in grinding contact. "More than," he said, voice rumbly for a different reason now. "This part of my body doesn't hurt, at least not in the bad way. But I do wonder about the chair. This is how we broke the other one, if you recall."

Cam waggled his brows. "How about we try to break all the chairs?"

"How about I get a kiss first?" Nic lifted his legs and bumped Cam forward.

Hands splayed on Nic's chest, Cam kept himself from careening into him, but Nic, despite his injuries, seemed to want it rough, seemed to crave it as much as Cam did. Driving one hand down his back and the other into his hair, Nic dragged him close, smashing their lips together. Drinking with each long, slow swipe of his tongue, he drew a moan from deep within Cam, from that spot where his love for him grew more and more each day.

"Still my favorite taste," Nic mumbled as they broke apart for air.

"You know . . ." Cam trailed a path of kisses along his jaw, softly pecking over the bruises. "Bird wasn't the only one you taught a better way."

"Even if I argue you to an early grave?"

Cam righted his head and gently took Nic's face in his hands. "No talking of graves. And no arguing tonight." He closed the distance again, wanting more closeness, more tastes of their future. "Just kissing. And celebrating this victory."

"And fucking," Nic growled. "Definitely part of this celebration."

Cam grinned. "No objection, Counselor."

The next second Nic was up, taking Cam with him, and swiping the bottles off the table. They hit the floor just as Cam's ass hit the table. "There you go," he tsked. "Destroying the place again."

The glint in Nic's eyes was pure fire. Hotter than hell. "One other thing I intended to destroy tonight." He ran a rough hand over the bulge behind Cam's zipper, and Cam was nearly destroyed right then. Back arched, hips lifting off the table, he thrust into Nic's grip. Nic stroked once, twice, down his hardening length, before setting about a more methodical destruction.

Ripping Cam's shirt off over his head, kissing a path

down his neck and along his collarbone, before torturing his nipples with tongue and teeth until he was boneless in Nic's hands, a writhing mess spread out on their dining table.

Tearing his pants and boxers down, then nipping, licking, and sucking everywhere, except where Cam needed him most. His ankle, the underside of each knee, the crease where thigh met pelvis, his taint and balls. Until Cam begged, loud and strangled enough, needing the hot heat of Nic's mouth around him, that Nic finally, finally, swallowed him down. Hands spread over his hips, Nic held him trapped as he sucked and teased him right to the edge.

But as ready to jump over it as Cam was, he wanted Nic there to jump with him, celebrating this battle won, partaking in the good kind of destruction versus the other sort they'd so narrowly avoided. Levering up, he clawed at Nic's shoulders, pushing him off his dick and yanking him up. Cam wove his fingers through his hair, bringing Nic's ear to his lips, whispering, "I need to feel all of you."

Groaning, Nic didn't hesitate, reaching for the hem of his shirt and tugging it up and off. Cam took a few precious moments to admire the tattoos on Nic's front, never one to pass up the opportunity, then, hands sliding down the toned and inked torso, he went to work ridding Nic of his pants, the *thunk* of his belt buckle hitting the floor another small victory.

As was the lube sachet Nic held aloft. So that's what he'd been digging out of his pants pocket before Cam had forced them down. Cam laughed, then groaned as, hand to the center of his chest, Nic forced him back down to the table. Spreading him out, Nic kissed his lips, the hollow of his throat, each shoulder, then his chest, right over his heart.

Cam felt the curve of Nic's lips on his skin, no doubt smiling at the thudding heart underneath.

The heart that wanted every part of this for every day of the rest of Cam's life. The words tumbled out.

"Love you, baby."

An even wider smile and a "Love you too," before Nic lifted off him. The rip of foil and a hand on his inner thigh were the only warnings Cam got before cool liquid dripped down his taint and over his hole. Cam's hips shot off the table, another "love you" choked off in a keening growl.

"Easy, Boston," Nic coaxed, slick fingers spreading the lube around his entrance, then inside, as he began to stretch and spread him.

Destroying him further. "Now, baby," Cam moaned.

Giving him what he wanted, giving him everything he needed, Nic hauled his ass to the edge of the table and a second later, he was pressing his cock against his rim, gentle but persistent pressure that forced his muscles to give, a pinch of pain before they greedily clamped down around Nic's cock, pushing in to fill him full.

Stretching out over him, Nic braced a hand by his head and stared down, blue eyes burning bright, full of everything Cam also felt. "I'm yours, forever."

Cam pulled him down for another kiss, hips rocking to meet Nic's thrusts, hands clutching at his back. At the branches he no longer feared.

They didn't spell disaster for their future. They didn't even represent a past or future mess, as Nic had once thought. The cypress and the initials carved into its trunk were a celebration too, of a heroic act by the hero right here in Cam's arms. A sacrifice—body and heart—Nic had made for those he loved. To save the family he'd chosen, the family he didn't even know he had, the family he'd reclaimed and saved again today.

Nic's family once more. Cam's now too.

"And I'm yours," Cam gasped as Nic pushed him the rest of the way over the edge, the two of them coming together.

Thoroughly destroyed and thoroughly in love.

TWENTY-FOUR

Nic was surprised at how many people were in attendance at the scattering of Curtis's ashes, though he suspected the crowd was there more to support him and Lette than to grieve Curtis's passing. Standing at the edge of the pond on the Hillsborough property, he and Lette tossed Curtis's ashes into the lightly rippling water while Garrett and Victoria, together with Cam, Mary, and Eddie, and Aidan, Jamie, Mel, Danny, Lauren, and Elton, stood below the cypress trees, a silent vigil on their behalf.

Everyone who had helped them survive. Who'd become their family.

Four months later, they closed the house for the final time, turning the keys over to the realtor who'd sold the property. He and Lette, whom he talked to or texted almost daily now, would deliver a check to RAINN. His sister hadn't wanted another cent of Curtis's money either.

Past behind them, the next day was all about the future. With Cam's brothers and Nic's retired JAG admiral in tow, they fought the St. Patrick's Day traffic in San Francisco to make it to the Federal Courthouse for Nic's swearing-in—as US Attorney for the Northern District of California. The appointment had been confirmed on the recommendations of Deputy AG Hayward, AD Moore, SAC Talley, the SFPD Chief of Police, and all of the other AUSAs in San Francisco. Even the AUSAs from San Diego, where he'd subbed in last summer, had sent in letters to the Senate committee overseeing his confirmation.

Thankfully, there'd been very little interruption to the USAO's work, which hadn't miraculously stopped with Vaughn's indictment. Nic had inherited a deskful from the now discredited and incarcerated Bowers, but with attorneys reenergized and willing to work *with him*—not *for him*, he'd emphasized—and with their FBI cooperation better than ever, they'd already made a dent in the backlog. And they'd officially closed Vaughn's case, striking a deal that would keep him in jail for life and divest him of all his holdings, legal and otherwise.

A year ago, Nic was unsure if he had a future at the USAO, debating whether to retire and work full time at Gravity. Now he held the reins, driving an agenda he was proud of and working with attorneys he respected, protecting victims and justice. And with a team of prosecutors he trusted, who wanted to work with him, balancing his day job with his other gig at Gravity became easier than ever. He had the best of both worlds officially now.

Nic could have been sworn in in DC after his confirmation hearing last week, but he wanted to do that here in his home courthouse, with his family, friends, and colleagues who'd helped get him here. He also wanted to be wearing his dress blues at his swearing-in, as a testament to that part of his life and career, many of his JAG colleagues and SEAL teammates also in attendance.

And because at the celebration afterward, Cam's heated stare from across Gravity's packed event space was molten, the twinkling overhead lights reflecting like flames in his swirling dark eyes. The uniform always did it for him. Except those dark eyes hadn't strayed once to the other uniformed servicepeople in the room. It was the same reason Nic's gaze kept roving back to Cam whenever he was between conversations.

Someone clapped him on the shoulder, and Nic turned to find Aidan, grinning like a tipsy leprechaun. About what Nic expected from the Irishman on St. Patrick's Day and on his and Jamie's anniversary.

"How many boilermakers have you had?" Nic asked.

Jamie slung an arm over his husband's shoulders. "Don't ask that question."

"Shut it, Whiskey." Aidan rolled his eyes, then withdrew a folded piece of paper from his jacket pocket and handed it to Nic. "I don't think this is necessary anymore."

Nic unfolded the sheet, eyes scanning down the increased insurance certificate he'd given Aidan when he'd moved in with Cam. Another piece of paper appeared over top of it. "Unless, of course, you want to carry that much extra insurance on your own house."

Nic gasped, staring wide-eyed at the deed in his and Cam's names. "Talley, are you sure?"

"Am I sure I want to sell—because you are gonna pay market value—my first home to one of my best friends?"

"And to my best friend," Jamie added, likewise grinning.

"Yes, Dominic, I'm sure." Stepping out from under

Jamie's arm, Aidan pulled him into a hug. "After all, it's staying in the family."

Nic didn't have the words, so he held on tighter, looking again at the deed over Aidan's shoulder.

To his and Cam's home.

They'd made it that already over the past year and now it truly would be. "Thank you," he said, drawing back. He folded the papers and tucked them inside his jacket, next to his heart. "We'll take good care of it."

Aidan cozied back up to Jamie's side, slinging an arm around his waist. "I'm sure you will, though maybe don't kill the kitchen again."

"It's his kitchen now, Irish," Jamie said with a wink over Aidan's grumbled objections. Until Danny shouted for another round at the bar and Aidan enthusiastically heeded the call, dragging the big man behind him.

Laughing, Nic turned, seeking out Cam and coming face-to-face instead with the troublemaking foursome that had become fast, extremely talkative friends, frequently blowing up Nic's phone with group texts. Eddie's and Garrett's uniforms did nothing to hide the servicemen's devious expressions. Nor did Lauren's and Lette's party dresses and matching clover tiaras make the arm-locked duo any less suspicious.

"Keg's tapped," Eddie said, giving him a thumbs-up.

"And that"—Lauren tossed a dark velvet pouch at Nic —"should be sized right."

"How'd you manage?" he asked.

"Pretended it was a piece of evidence. Told him his hands were close to the same size as our suspect's."

"You pulled a fucking OJ on him?"

She waved her hand in the air, fingers dancing. "Except

the glove fit." He hadn't intended for Cam to see it but if he hadn't known what it was, maybe Nic could still pull off the surprise he had planned.

"Can I steal you for five minutes first?" Lette said, interrupting his thoughts.

He held out his elbow, Lette transferred from Lauren's arm to his, and they walked together around the edge of the crowd. The overhead lights caught the ruby of his class ring around her neck, and he couldn't help teasing about another childhood relic. "You and Lauren exchange BFF necklaces yet?" Not that he minded. The more he got to know his sister, the more he liked her, and he already thought the world of Lauren.

"Do keys count?" She drew a shiny new one out of her pocket, brandishing it between them. "I can't wait to be her roommate."

Nic's step faltered. "Her roommate?"

"I wanted to surprise you. A gift on your big day." She smiled, big and bright, just like her mother. "You remember that job I was out here interviewing for?"

"You got it?"

"Damn right I did." Every bit as cocky as both her brothers too and that was just fine with Nic. Better than, and he couldn't wait to have her in the Bay Area full time.

"Congrats, Lette." He clasped both her shoulders, squeezing, and she barreled into his arms, hugging him tight. "Aww, look who's gettin' all sappy."

She reared back, playfully slapping his biceps. "And to make even more trouble for you, Garrett's put in for a transfer out of the Marines to the Coast Guard unit here. You can thank your boy Eddie for that one."

His reconnected family here, with him, but it wouldn't be complete without . . . "Victoria?"

"Will come too, of course."

This time he scooped his sister up in his arms, Lette yelping with surprise, and Garrett's and Eddie's combined "Coasties!" from across the room had him laughing out loud. Better than the tears that were threatening at the corners of his eyes. From no family to more than Nic knew what to do with. It was a problem he was happy to have—an argument he was thrilled to lose, especially now that the threats had been eliminated—and there was one person responsible for making his life whole again, who'd brought him into the fold with their friends, with his family, and then helped save Nic's too.

He found the cluster of dark heads across the room and caught Keith's eye. He tilted his head toward the bar, then started making his way there himself, trusting Keith, Quinn, and Bobby to herd their brother that direction too.

Sneaking behind the bar, Nic pulled two pints of stout from their newest tap and held one glass out of sight, below the bar top. He fished the special delivery from Lauren out of his pocket and dropped it in, waiting for it to hit the bottom with a *plunk*. Assured it was settled and relatively hidden in the dark beer, he set the glass next to the other on the bar top, circled back around to the front, and tapped a metal thief against a tap, the pinging noise echoing through the cavernous event center as the music lowered.

"If I can interrupt for a minute," he said. "I'd like to say a few words."

Danny started a chant of "Speech! Speech!" that lasted long enough for the Byrne brothers to deposit their charge at the front before moving off to stand with Aidan and Jamie.

Eyes dancing, Cam sidled up to Nic, coasting a hand across Nic's lower back and resting it on his opposite hip. Nic found it there on his left hip a lot these days, Cam touching the new tattoo every chance he got. He'd never forget the look in Cam's eyes the night he'd revealed the finished design. Wonder and appreciation, lust and love, swirled together in deep pools of molten heat. He'd wanted to live there, in that moment, in Cam's warm dark eyes, for the rest of his life. Until he'd remembered how much he'd wanted this one and all the others to follow.

"What are you up to?" Cam asked.

"Thanking our guests."

And more.

He gave Cam's runaway brow a quick peck before turning back to their gathered friends, family, and colleagues. "I wanted to thank you all for coming out today to the swearing-in and for joining us here to celebrate. When Cam and I first got together—"

"Without telling any of us," Mel quipped from where she stood next to Danny.

Nic laughed with the crowd. "Says the woman who knew all along."

She blew him a kiss.

He shot her the middle finger, smiling. "Okay, what was I say—"

"When you two started to bone," Eddie shouted.

More laughter. More than Nic had ever heard here at Gravity, which only made the moment more special.

"Right," he said. "When Cam and I first got together, he

made me see we don't celebrate the victories enough. I'm not exaggerating when I say it's been the wildest year of my life. Nor am I exaggerating when I say it's been the best. So I wanted you all here to celebrate with us, and I wanted you all here for the official unveiling of Gravity's newest brew, Fighting Boston Irish Stout, a special imperial brewed and named for the man without whom none of this year's victories would be possible."

Cam's face turned bright red, not expecting to be the center of attention, but it was split by the biggest grin Nic had ever seen on his handsome face. Handing Cam his pint glass, Nic picked up the other and clinked their rims together. "For you, Boston."

Cam's arm tightened around his waist. "I like how you celebrate." He raised the glass and took a sip. His eyes fluttered closed and his features went slack with bliss, a look Nic was more accustomed to seeing from him in bed.

He lowered the glass after another sip, opening his hooded eyes and teasing Nic with a flick of his tongue across his lips. "Baby, it's wonderful." Then he gave Nic a taste of the flavor he craved the most—his beer on Cam's lips—in a searing kiss that lasted until Eddie and the rest of the soldiers assembled began shouting "Chug, chug, chug."

As Nic had told them to do.

"Drink up," he encouraged Cam, and struggled not to appear too eager as Cam tilted his pint back for more. Nor too knowingly excited when Cam startled at the object inside the glass bumping his lips.

Brow furrowed, Cam lowered the glass and tipped it over. Into his palm fell a black titanium ring with an electric blue band around the middle. The same color highlights from Cam's hair on that undercover gig last April, the one during which Nic had fallen in love with him.

Cam gasped out a "Dominic."

Nic snagged the ring from his palm, then went down on one knee to thunderous shouts and applause. He was asking, officially, in front of all their friends and family.

"Boston, will you marry me?"

Cam's dark eyes were a mix of fire and water, heated to burning and on the brink of tears. "I thought we already went over this."

Nic smirked. "I don't remember you saying—"

"Yes!"

Nic shot to his feet, slid the ring on Cam's finger, and hauled his fiancé, officially, into a back-bending kiss.

When they righted themselves, coming up for air, Cam rested his forehead against Nic's. "Just one question," he said.

"You already said yes, Boston."

"Will you dance with me at our wedding?"

"I'll dance with you every day for the rest of our lives."

Cam kissed him again, hard, and Nic relished the love on his lips and in his arms, the promise of home in his jacket pocket, and the support of his friends and family all around them.

A future—a happily ever after—Nic never thought he'd get.

Victory was his.

Theirs.

Case closed.

———

Reviews are an invaluable tool when it comes to spreading the word about great reads. Please consider leaving an honest review for *Noble Hops* on your favorite review site.

Thank you for reading!

ALSO BY LAYLA REYNE

For the most up-to-date list of titles and a helpful reading order, please visit www.laylareyne.com.

Agents Irish and Whiskey:

Single Malt

Cask Strength

Barrel Proof

Tequila Sunrise

Blended Whiskey

Angel's Share

Trouble Brewing:

Imperial Stout

Craft Brew

Noble Hops

Final Gravity

Fog City:

Prince of Killers

King Slayer

A New Empire

Queen's Ransom

Silent Knight

What We May Be

Perfect Play:

Dead Draw

Bad Bishop

King Hunt

Best Play

Redemption Inc:

The Accidental

The Bounty

The Martyr

The Boss

Guard Duty:

High Winds

Rough Waters

Wild Type:

Variable Onset

Affinity Drift

Matched Pair

Soul to Find:

Icarus and the Devil

Jason and the Storm

Paris and the Reaper

Atlas and the Traitor

Table for Two:

The Last Drop

Dine With Me

Blue Plate Special

Over a Barrel

The Sweet Spot

Sigh of Relief

Changing Lanes:

Relay

Medley

Freestyle

Three Sticks:

Barn Burner

Dirty Dangle

ABOUT THE AUTHOR

Layla Reyne is the author of *What We May Be* and the *Agents Irish and Whiskey, Fog City,* and *Perfect Play* series. She writes sexy, intense LGBTQIA+ romance featuring competent adults in kitchens, sports arenas, car chases, and other high-stakes situations. Whether it's adrenaline-fueled suspense, rival athletes, vampires and shifters, or love mixed with mouth-watering foodie goodness, queer folks finding happily-ever-afters is guaranteed.

You can find Layla online at laylareyne.com and at the following sites:

BB bookbub.com/authors/layla-reyne

facebook.com/laylareyne

instagram.com/laylareyne

tiktok.com/@laylareyne

bsky.app/profile/laylareyne

www.ingramcontent.com/pod-product-compliance
Lightning Source LLC
Chambersburg PA
CBHW070521310726

48976CB00002BA/504

9 781962 010559